THE LAW OF BEASTS

Book 1 – Act 1

KHOVAHSH

Introducing Alicia Chay

"The Law of Beasts

Book 1 – Act 1:

Khovahsh

Introducing Alicia Chay

-

WRITTEN FROM JUNE OF 1998 – AUGUST OF 1998 AT AGE TWENTY-ONE in Salem, Oregon.
COPYRIGHT © June 1998 - March 2023 by Larry Wilson Jr. (DAPHAROAH69).
ISBN: 979-8869724038
Registered with the U.S. Copyright Office.
Book interior design by Brady Moller, (South Africa) and Dapharoah69.
Font on book cover by Rose M. (India).

THE LAW OF BEASTS

Book 1 — Act 1

KHOVAHSH

Introducing Alicia Chay

A Black Vampire, Romance, Action, Mystery, Horror, Paranormal Saga

DAPHAROAH69
——— Writing As ———
JA'BREEL LE'DIAMOND

Let it be put on record that this is not a true story. The characters do not exist outside of this publication. This is a work of fiction written for expression and entertainment. All names, characters, places, and incidents are products of the author's imagination or employed from actual events and used fictitiously. Any resemblance to actual persons, living or dead, events, or locales is entirely coincidental. All Rights belong to the author.

Most importantly, this is for my Heavenly Father, in Yashua's name. Thank you for this most precious gift.

CONTENTS

Acknowledgments xiii

Foreword xv

Prologue
Black Tar and Gold xix

Disclaimer xxi

Prelude
Curtains xxiii

One
Bloody Hands 1

Two
Bed Of Roses 9

Three
In Cadence 17

Four
Scraps 23

Five
Betrayed 31

Six
Anniversary 38

Seven
Docile Creatures 52

Eight
Daybreak 60

Nine
On Fire 66

Ten
Alicia Chay's Coronation 70

Eleven
How I Took The Throne 78

Twelve
Mega Church 91

Thirteen
Flashback 101

Fourteen
Genocide 107

Fifteen
Soulless Eyes 115

Sixteen
Alicia Chay 124

Seventeen
Combustible Sparks 126

Eighteen
Under Orders 130

Nineteen
Money and Promises 134

Twenty
Secret Meetings 141

Twenty-one
Hair Becomes Thornes 149

Twenty-Two
Body Hosting 153

Twenty-Three
Buffet of Terror 157

Twenty-Four
Abandoned 163

Twenty-Five
Building's Ablaze 167

Twenty-Six
Every Heart I Ate 174

Twenty-Seven
Council Meeting 180

Twenty-Eight
I Heard of 186

Twenty-Nine
Brenda 196

Thirty
Alleged Homebois 201

Thirty-One
Candid Words 208

Thirty-Two
Encountered 212

Thirty-Three
Sleeping Chambers 218

Thirty-Four
Birds Of Prey 225

Thirty-Five
Marble 229

Epilogue
FIVE OF THEM 231

About The Author 235

For my spouse, my soulmate. My biggest fan. Thank
you for sharing this journey with me
for nearly sixteen years.
I love you eternally, John Wilson.
For Carter and Camille Wilson, my nephew and
niece, my best-friends. Seeing the world
through your eyes taught me the definition of
family and love.

In loving memory of my brother
<u>*Lonnie T. Wilson*</u>
March 10, 1981 – April 11, 2021

In loving memory of my best-friend/brother
<u>*Chadrick Daquan Render*</u>
October 23, 1976 – July 27, 1997

In loving memory of my cousin
<u>*Nikita Rolle*</u>
January 4, 1970 - May 4, 2023

ACKNOWLEDGMENTS

For Kamilaih, my niece. Thank you for stopping me from throwing this series in the trash. For Kai and Zuri Brown. For my nieces and nephews on both sides. For my mother, Barbara and my mother-in-law, Jacqueline Wilson. For my siblings and in-laws. For Martez "Tez The Great" Mosley. For Leroy and Tekeidra James. For Waikiki, Jayii, Lawanna, Victor, Terry, Tshai, Tyrone, and Andrew. For Ana Rodriguez, my best-friend. For Ed Smith, my boi. For my cousin Quinton Harvey. Rest in paradise.

For my grandfather retired Air-force Master. Sgt. Luther L. McCray. Thank you for introducing me to reading and writing when I was a kid and laying the foundation for what I became. For my siblings and in-laws.

For Janet Jackson's "Control," "Rhythm Nation 1814," "Janet.," and "The Velvet Rope" being the soundtracks of my life, the blueprint. Thank you.

For "The Black Vampyre: Legend of St. Domingo 1819" features America's first vampire, who was black. For the vampire-role-playing legends and icons that paved the way: William Marshal and Vonetta McGhee (Blacula), Duane Gunn and Marlene Clark (Gunja and Hess). Grace Jones (Vamp), Eddie Murphy, Kadeem Hardison, and Angela Bassett (Vampire in Brooklyn), Sannaa Lathan and Wesley Snipes (Blade), and Aaliyah (Queen of the Damned). They opened the door for my artistic vision.

For aspiring authors. For the homeless. For the culture.

FOREWORD

BY: CYRUS WEBB

For years, DaPharoah69 has written books that engage, fascinate, and inspire readers and authors alike. His newest offering under the name **JA'BREEL LE'DIAMOND** is no different. THE LAW OF BEASTS takes you into a world of love, power, betrayal and layers of revenge: things that readers can easily relate to and be entranced page by page.

Having read many works by this author for nearly two decades, I can say that he has once again given us a glimpse into his ability to write whatever he desires, defying genres and boxes that can confine so many in this industry.

With THE LAW OF BEASTS, he will not just give his readers around the world another book to sink their teeth into, but he is sure to have new ones join him in the world he's created. Get ready for something that will have you talking and solidify DaPharoah69 as a storyteller you will soon not forget.

Cyrus Webb

For God so loved the world, that he gave his only Begotten Son, that whosoever believeth in Him shall not perish, but have everlasting life.

—John 3:16

I am the way, the truth, and the life. No one comes to the Father except through me.

—John 14: 6

PROLOGUE
BLACK TAR AND GOLD

As cool air blew over me, I opened my eyes amidst a random congregation to witness Pastor Danny Dacra's knack for sensationalized worship for profit. I blended in with sanctified humans, nursing a thousand untold secrets. Pastor Danny Dacra's image protruded on two wide projection screens.

"We are nearing the end of our privacy and one hundred percent human thought...."

I rose to my feet, clapping and whistling. I adjusted my reading glasses. He roamed the aisles. "Humanity has lost its soul! Introduce machines into the workplace, integrate them into regular society, I should say, to make it all plausible...."

I didn't know what came over me, but I sneezed, and every framed religious photo throughout the Super-dome fell from the walls and shattered on the floor. Everyone was silent. Before I could react, Pastor Dacra's mouth vanished, causing confusion.

Abruptly, a centuries-old vampire landed behind him, shoving his fist into the pastor's back. He donned black tar and gold. Traces of brimstone circulated around his pupils.

Thousands of frantic people ran for the exits.
I remained where I stood.

"Khovahsh…"

His voice shattered every mortal eardrum throughout the mega church. Screams and shrieks of undue torture made my skin crawl.

"How do you know my identity?" I asked him.

The vampire's face swirled into the Pastor's with devastating accuracy.

"That's not important. I have a message for you. Either destroy Alicia Chay and her animal treaty, or I will."

Dragon wings exploded from either side of my shoulders.

"You will not…" My mouth vanished from my face, erasing the rest of my words.

He grunted, amused. "Pardon my manners. My name is the same as your missing lips—Muzzle."

He burst into glittering particles that left the Pastor's mega church, filled with thousands of worshippers, burning to the ground...

DISCLAIMER

The opinions and views of my characters in vampire form throughout this story were done to enlighten myself and question all that I have been taught in the iron grasp of the church and the philosophies surrounding it, both by force and by my own free will. "THE LAW OF BEASTS: Book I – Act 1: KHOVAHSH" is a fictional story, but my faith in Yahshua is eternal. I still have questions about the very things taught to me in church and the deception within. Where do I continue?

Oh, okay! I know.

In fact, that's the perfect place to continue...!

PRELUDE
CURTAINS

ALICIA CHAY

Dr. Henry Ford looked outside his fifty-six-story window, overlooking downtown Dallas, Texas. In a building directly across from him was a man in a black suit. He had black granite skin. His eyes were black pearls, clear and cut. Shaken, Pastor Ford backed away from the window, drawing the blinds just as a masked man stepped out from behind the grandfather clock in his office and tried to grab him.

"No!" shouted Pastor Ford, near panic. "The Devil will not win! Not today! I rebuke thee in the name of Jesu…."

Unexpectedly, a cell phone rang, interrupting him.

For a few beats, they stared at each other. Impulsively, the Perpetrator knocked Pastor Ford across the head. In grave pain, he slumped his knees.

Reluctantly, the Perpetrator answered the cell phone. "Put the phone to the pastor's ear," said the disgruntled handler.

The Perpetrator obeyed.

"Your time's expired," said the demonic voice. The Perpetrator pulled a gun from the elastic of his waist, and planted the start of the barrel on the pastor's temple.

The pastor cried to God above, the one he didn't believe in.

Yet none of that mattered. He cried out to God to save him with everything in his being.

"Goodbye, pastor! You're worth more dead than you are alive!"

Instantly, he pulled the trigger. The pastor cringed as my granite hand covered the barrel of the weapon. The force of the bullet ricocheted off my porcelain fingers.

The pastor screamed in terror.

Masked CIA men thundered up the emergency stairwell towards the pastor's Penthouse to take me out.

I rammed my nails into the Perpetrator's heart and ripped it out.

I devoured it like a bum did an orange. I hissed at the living mortal.

Pastor Ford reverted to Christianity, turning his back on years of dedicated atheist service for a chance at eternal life through God when he thought that his life was over.

Frightened, he ran outside the front door.

Five CIA men hollered when I leaped at them. They opened fire.

I sprinted to one of the men and slashed his neck. I transitioned into invisibility.

Windows exploded. I ran along eighteen flights of stairs to the roof. I was there in five seconds. I spun in place, catching every bullet.

A supernatural being glared down into my eyes.

"Who are you?" I asked, knowing that he broke the laws of the Dershakney. No vampire or supernatural being was to inhabit a human host without the authorization of my government.

He glared at me with contempt. "I am Khovahsh Burgoos!"

ONE
BLOODY HANDS

ALICIA CHAY

Sometime in the 3,200 Millennium BC...

I told myself that if I was ever able to tell my story...
The story of a dark-skinned girl....

forced into a life as a rebellious vagabond...
against my free will...
I would do it in unconventional order.
Tell it as I remembered it...

I must admit that I didn't know much about being a vampire. As a creature of the night, I slaughtered and killed humans for decades, hoping it would erase the memories of my human life. Sadly, that never worked, not that I expected it to. Emotion wasn't a part of my vocabulary, nor did I mourn anything. I didn't wear my heart on my sleeve. I was always naked. The only attire I wore was a coat of blood. I fed on random humans all over the world at my leisure, without regard to who may miss them.

JA'BREEL LE'DIAMOND

I hunted humans for sport. It was a passion of mine. I studied them in the shadows. I loathed civilization, more so humanity. Inevitably, I'd found calm, peace, and discipline in loving animals because they were true to nature. I made a vow to protect them. Sigh, how naive and foolish I was.

Before I let you into my world, I must warn you that I wasn't friendly. I didn't need friends. I was a passionate lover. I hadn't time for impropriety when it came to self-preservation. In the realm of survival the fittest wasn't safe.

Cuneiform writing was just developed in Sumer, an ancient civilization of southern Mesopotamia and Egypt, hence the origin of my recorded history. I documented my beginning on Kish tablets to get a better picture of my reality. I did this until Ptahhotep, a city administrator (and vizier to Pharaoh Djedkare in the Fifth Dynasty) developed literary writing. This account would not have existed otherwise.

I didn't do this for attention. I didn't care about mortals and their opinions. With bloody hands, I chiseled my experiences on the limestone of this Kish tablet with hieroglyphics. It wasn't done for praise.

I remember pieces of my human life. I transitioned into a carnal fiend. I thrived in the shadows when the sun rose and lurked in the wilderness when it was time to hunt. I was in the beginning phase of my supernatural existence.

One day, the world would read about the system of betrayal that turned my heart cold, but for right now, that wasn't a priority. My heartbreaking story began in 2 B.C., Asia. I was covered with the blood of random humans I drained dry in Chad, Africa shortly after my painful transition.

I experienced a rebirth into a cold ball of death. Seeing life through human eyes was one thing, but seeing it as a vampire was frightening. I was on my own. I didn't have a home. I was hungry and tired. There was no need for rose-colored fantasy when a world that ran parallel to life as I once knew it lurked before my eyes as they turned black.

I refused to turn around and look at my once-human life with those eyes. Black shaded everything in its indefinite hue, so thoughts of my mortal life came to a halt. I'd turn to salt if I looked over my shoulder and the darkness cast its filter on my memories and experiences.

To my immediate right was a small pond. A few lilies floated peacefully on the serene water. Deeply overwhelmed, I fell to my knees. The moist grass cushioned them, but not the emptiness in my heart. I drank from the pond, but I spat it out. It was disgusting. I closed my eyes. I loomed over the water. Images of my past raked my brain.

I had on a linen dress. I was making love to someone. His face was cloudy. I was hugging a girl, laughing. I became ill, too weak to crawl.

My head snapped backward. I opened my black eyes. I stared at my reflection in the water, and she stared back. My face was reconstructed and more refined. I was alluring, seductive, elegant, and powerful, with a hint of danger.

My breasts, hips and thighs were fuller. Startled, I jumped sixty feet backward. I slammed into a rocky totem pole, cracking it down the center. My body ached from the blow. Asian faces were carved into the stone.

The dawn of my supernatural existence began, standing under a Waxing Gibbous moon. I felt alone, like I didn't belong. In front of me was the unknown, fear and opportunity. Behind me was a path of destruction. The boost in adrenaline caused me to lose my bearings. Before I knew it, I fainted.

I didn't know how long I was unconscious, but I was awakened by a strange man. I slowly opened my eyes. His calloused hands groped my forehead. I sighed with relief. His fingertips trailed the length of my legs, down to my toes. His dreadlocks were decades old.

He handled me with tenderness. Good energy radiated from his body wrought with the sands of time. Only one man touched me in this manner. I was choked up with emotion thinking about him. *Don't look back!* I really wanted to, but I couldn't.

This was harder than I thought. I didn't know who I was anymore. My wants and needs differed from anything human. What I used to crave I no longer desired, and what I never desired, I now craved.

I fell asleep once more. With a jolt, *I was running through the scary woods in fear for my life. Heat beat at my chest. Bile rose along my parched throat. I reached a clearing. I dashed along a winding path like a pack of deadly wolves were chasing me. A foreign sound betrayed the quiet of the belly of the forest.*

Wildly, I looked around, trying to find my way out.

There!

A few feet ahead was another clearing nearly hidden by overlapping branches. Frightened, I ran again. I was near the exit.

Suddenly, I saw the Village in the distance.

I laughed with joy, relieved that I was safe. I learned how to navigate through my environment.

A flash. I had my first orgasm.

I was weak in the knees. I ran back into the forest.

There was a dead gator by a creek. A snake sunk his fangs into the gator's tail and threw it in the air.

It rose like a King Cobra as the gator fell into its mouth. I was petrified.

Oh my! I shouldn't have stopped running!

Was I naive and blind?

I awakened from the dream.

The strange man grunted. I hadn't been this relaxed since I was human.

Nervously, he washed my feet with aloe and water. I was at peace.

No one had ever washed my feet before.

KHOVAHSH

I wasn't bound or gagged. There were no locks and chains. He was worried about me, even though we didn't know one another. His upper face was shaded. I couldn't see what he looked like. There wasn't much light. Flames burned on wooden staffs along the rocky walls. The air was stuffy and stale.

My eyes were half closed. I didn't want him to know that I was awake, but he knew; he didn't seem to mind. He didn't have company in ages. He was a loner. I was lonely by choice. I fell back asleep.

I was taunted with more images from my past. *I was in Africa as a little girl. I didn't think that I was special. I wasn't worthy of the gifts waiting to unfold as I grew older. My body went through major changes. My family's secrets hindered me. They unfolded before my veil-covered eyes. The lace was snatched away the day I fell in love and gave my body to a man that was a seducer of other women. Yes, I fell in love with him.*

Of course, I was naïve. I had a false sense of security. I didn't know that he slept with those women, women like me. He chose them in secret and with discretion.

The women Like Me were enchanting, sworn to secrecy. Amongst each other they discussed how good he was and how deep he could go. Twenty women, all Like Me!

From all over the Mother Land!

They hosted a "congregation" deep in the forest, down by a glimmering lake filled with fish. Gorgeous flowers spread as far as the eyes could see!

There was a secret garden outside of my Village we were prohibited from seeking. No one in the Village had broken those laws, except me and those twenty women.

One night I awakened with a start. I saw my friend's mother, Larshaw, creeping from her hut. There wasn't a light source in sight.

5

JA'BREEL LE'DIAMOND

The moon's glow failed to reach the Village. Any other night the glow was bright enough to cast a light that guided me in the remote darkness. My Village was a great distance from Town and the Upper Market Place. Larshaw and I never spoke to one another. I was a teenager, and she was an adult. It was forbidden to engage in chit-chatter with an adult that wasn't your parent, brother, sister or Elder.

Elders could speak to whomever. Unfortunately, they were the biggest concubines in all the land. I loved my Village, but the politics overwhelmed me.

Along dirt paths garnished with trees, random women were yanked into the brush and disapprovingly assaulted along with their self-esteem and environmental teachings by tribesmen from other territories. Because of that, I could hardly do a thing by myself. When I went to the Upper Marketplace, a man from the Village had to escort me.

Little murmurs broke my thoughts. I followed the gentle sounds that reminded me of ecstasy and pleasure.

I proceeded, one foot over the other. Along the way, I picked up a huge stick just in case I needed to defend myself. My heart pounded. My breathing came in short gasps. I reached another break in the forest.

The winding path made of soft mulch relaxed me.

I paused before a cliff, nearly tumbling over. I was two hundred feet above a rocky turf. Behind me lay the horror of a darkened forest. Something sinister lurked. It danced on my dirty skin.

To my immediate right was a large bridge. It took my breath away. I heard another voice.

"Proceed, my Curious Child. Cross the Bridge of Understanding!"

Across the bridge I ran!

Something appeared over the horizon.

The bridge led to an open portico made of flowers, leaves and branches.

KHOVAHSH

Spanish moss was everywhere. I slowed down and covered my mouth. It was beautiful. Amazing. Resilient! I was caught off guard by twenty women from my Village loving each other.

I awakened with a start, pushing away the memories. Before I knew it, I burst into tears. The stranger held me tightly to his warm body.

"It's okay to cry, young lady. I don't know what you've been through, but you're safe here. You are welcome to stay as long as you like."

His words didn't register in my brain. I wept. I let go. My body trembled, remembering who I used to be.

I hesitantly moved forward in the darkness.

The further I ventured, the darker it became. I didn't know how to deal with it.

How did I go on living if I was dead? I was an oxymoron with fangs.

I loved my friends; I loved my family. I had to love them enough to let them go.

I craved blood. It was a taste I had to get used to.

Taking me by surprise, the stranger kissed my lips. I welcomed it.

I melted in his arms.

TWO
BED OF ROSES

ALICIA CHAY

His lips were eager and cautious. Hesitantly, he pulled away from me. He tucked my hair behind my earlobes. Unexpectedly, he pushed me down and jumped backward over a pit of gators. He landed on a cliff a hundred feet above me. I was confused.

It was then I understood why his face was shaded.

"Why is your face covered in blood?" he asked, breathless.

"What are you talking about?"

"My garments are stained with blood. I don't know if I can wash away your purity. I hate the smell of blood."

I stared at him. "You don't have a nose. How is that possible? You don't have a forehead; your hair has an unpleasant stench. Who are you to judge? You resemble the totem pole that cracked open when my body made an impact. Faceless beings carved in stone."

"How do you remember that if you were unconscious?"

"I remember bits and pieces."

"You set me free with that act, thank you. I've been sealed in this cave for years. Once the seal was broken, the rush of fresh air rejuvenated my loins in unnatural ways."

I was deep within a cave. That was true. A cool breeze danced across my body. Lanterns gave off a soft glow. I hadn't noticed them before. I gasped at the simplicity. He smiled when I sat up on a comfortable bed of roses.

Looking around, I rose to my feet. The smell of his blood entered my nose. Something wild grabbed a hold of me. I looked at him with crazed eyes. He smiled inwardly.

I didn't care about him taking me to a safe place. The girl I used to be would have thanked him, but I knew that girl no longer.

She was lost within my subconscious until she vanished. I was a savage beast that craved blood.

I hissed at the strange man, startling him. I leaped over three rocky breaks. A few gators jumped up in the air with supernatural agility, trying to pull me down into the pit, but I dodged them.

I didn't know what he did to me when I was out of it. What if he put a spell on me, or did something indecent. I was unconscious. The smell of his blood was enticing, like a sweet treat. When I landed in front of him, I scratched him across the neck and began to drink.

I saw his life in quick spurts. *He approached me after I fainted. He picked me up and walked along the stream.* If he was locked inside the cave, how did he get out?

Then I remembered the crack in the stone totem pole. *He waved his hands. The divided stones magically opened. When he entered, leaving one pair of footprints in the sand, they closed. I saw all the other humans he had done this for. He treated them with respect.* I looked at him differently, knowing that he could be trusted. And then an image entered my head through the taste of his blood as I continued to drink. In the vision, *he circled my nipples with confidence in his touch; he traced his fingertips down to the pubic hair of my vulva.*

Everything changed. Out of all the people he helped, I was the one he did this to. I knew that smile couldn't be trusted. I should have escaped when I saw that he didn't have a face.

I was laying on a bed of roses looking up at a man that did unforgivable things to me when I was in a deep sleep.

He was never sealed in the cave. He could come out at will. He cared for hundreds of women and men. He clothed them with fresh linen, but I remained in the nude.

And in that was the deception. Why did he keep me naked?

A bigger red flag was why he lied to me altogether.

I saw his family. He had a son that was born a few decades ago. After his son's birth, he was attacked by vultures that were drawn to the dying baby.

I continued to drink.

I didn't realize that the gators and snakes of the pit rushed into his body at once and turned him into something that threw me forty feet back.

After a deafening roar, he sprinted towards me. Pulling enchanted blades from fleshy liaisons in his arms, he chopped off my hair, missing my scalp by a few inches. He tried to kill me. I was prepared to fight.

In an instant, my hair grew back, down past my buttocks.

We went through a series of punches, but neither one connected.

He tried to kick me in the face. I caught his foot and threw him over the cliff. As he fell, he dug nine inch nails into the rock. Kicking off the ledge, he flipped in the air and landed in front of me. He was extremely powerful.

He threw a bunch of jabs and uppercuts, but I deflected them.

He vanished and appeared above me.

He tried to drop down on top of my head.

His feet crashed into the ground. I was relieved that it wasn't my skull. I was just as skilled as he was. It took him by surprise that I matched his strength, but my energy was depleting.

The narcissist thought I was going to let him get away with taking advantage of me. Yes, I was foolish for thinking that he had my best interest at heart. I knew not to be that ignorant moving forward.

Another thing occurred to me. There was glass everywhere. Different types. Was he a glass-maker?

The more I thought about it, the more I realized he wasn't nursing me back to health.

He wasn't making sure that I was okay. I was not safe.

He violated me on top of the flowers. I was an exhibition. He wanted a keepsake. Was he going to knock me unconscious and hang me on the walls of the cave?

Was he trying to possess my beauty, giving him something to look at for the rest of his life?

I wasn't going to stay long enough to find out. Once I started drinking his blood, I saw him doing unspeakable things to me.

I had to get out of there and fast. He slammed me on the turf, splitting it in multiple directions. I didn't have time for this. I didn't know who or what he was, or why he brought me here. I flew out of the cave and a portal formed, sucking me in. I crash landed in Africa.

My eyes were no longer black. My heart began to beat backward, sending my blood flow counterclockwise. Still, a path of destruction I refused to look at ever again beckoned me.

I didn't want to remember that an hour before I arrived in Asia, I was a dark-skinned girl that had just turned eighteen in the mother land.

I had a happy life, yet watching two of my loved ones betray me made my transition easier to embrace when a vampire bat attacked me after they made love under the moonlight.

KHOVAHSH

I regretted it.

I wanted my life back, especially after encountering the faceless ghoul I just fought. I went on a killing spree, led by emotion. I drained humans and fled, bloody and naked. I flew through a sea of thick branches that parted for my exit. I roared like a savage beast set free after a century of restraint.

I still didn't look back.

The first two hundred years of my life were filled with deceit, chaos, and control. As I tried to find my place in a mysterious world, I was a homeless murderer, always on the hunt for blood without a coach or a teacher.

I tried to make it out of thirty feet deep water in absolute darkness when I couldn't float or swim. I needed a home. I been around the world! I saw a lot of edifices that captivated me.

With thirty thousand slaves, I built The House of the Hounds. I hypnotized them and gave grave instructions. Within a few years, my palace was built beyond my wildest dreams. It became a gritty place full of murder, games, and blood. I captured humans and forced them into bloody battles.

I was in control, a small-time Queen in search of herself. I became the Queen of the Hounds. I was one of the most feared beings in the world. I ruled alone, until I started yearning for a relationship outside of my own greed.

My consciousness was a series of blanks. I was filled with rage. I was angry for what I was, with memories of my human life taunting me.

I was thrust into dread and misery, forced to survive in the monstrous jungle of the unknown, the life of the condemned and the damned. Like my conception and my birth, I had no say in the matter.

Even though it was my life, my death didn't make a difference.

Being alone was good for the soul, but what good was a soul when I was dead?

Being alone for the first century of my supernatural life was hell. It drove me insane. I nearly lost my mind, with no one to confide in. As a result, I raided a family of brothers with skin as dark as the midnight sky. While they slept naked in an open field surrounded by trees and brush, I turned them into vampires against their will. Ki'Wah, Tresyon, Qu'stah, Zyath, Crusha and Dominyshus were their names.

Over a short period of time, we became a family of savage-ridden killers. We terrorized people around the world. There was infighting between the men for my devotion and affection, yet they were as thick as thieves. They were known as the Slaughtergus. They became urban legends overnight.

I didn't care about life, beauty, or emotion. The only thing I loved, the only source of life I craved, was blood. It became an addiction.

We visited Europe, Greece, and every island in between for food. When we arrived in Alexandria, Egypt, we stumbled upon a secret cult while scouring across a sandy desert on our quest for blood.

While we feasted on royal members of the cult, a funnel of thunderous smoke appeared in the room of high columns and pillars.

With supernatural speed, nine enormous mountain lions burst from the smoke and attacked us. They had manes of fire. Poisonous metal spikes extended from their body armor. We were no match for them.

We managed to escape, but one of the lions bit my right ankle before we jumped in the air and flew east. I looked back and smiled as my family flew behind me.

I sought a safer way to hunt without acting on impulse alone. Impulsive attacks came with consequences. Part of me felt guilty about turning my vampire family into savages, but it was too late for regrets.

With that in mind, I was hungry. I wanted blood. My stomach burned without it.

I hadn't seen The Slaughtergus in a very long time.

KHOVAHSH

I was sure they could manage without me. They were adults.

Pushing them to the back of my mind, I watched my prey like night and day. A tall, burly man with a complexion darker than my own searched for a place to rest. He seemed lost in the wilderness.

As his feet scampered across the wet grass, he tripped over a wrought log. He fell on a huge rock, piercing the skin of his upper arm.

I lost it.

I ran at him and tore through his flesh like I hadn't eaten in a decade. After I fled, I wound up behind a hidden castle in Europe. I was surrounded by towering trees and brush.

I was a freak of nature.

I could taste the end of summer and the birth of autumn.

A glowing moon beamed down on my exhausted body.

I was covered in blood.

I was wrought with temporary amnesia.

I floated along a beautiful rose garden leading to the entrance of an infrastructure built by slaves.

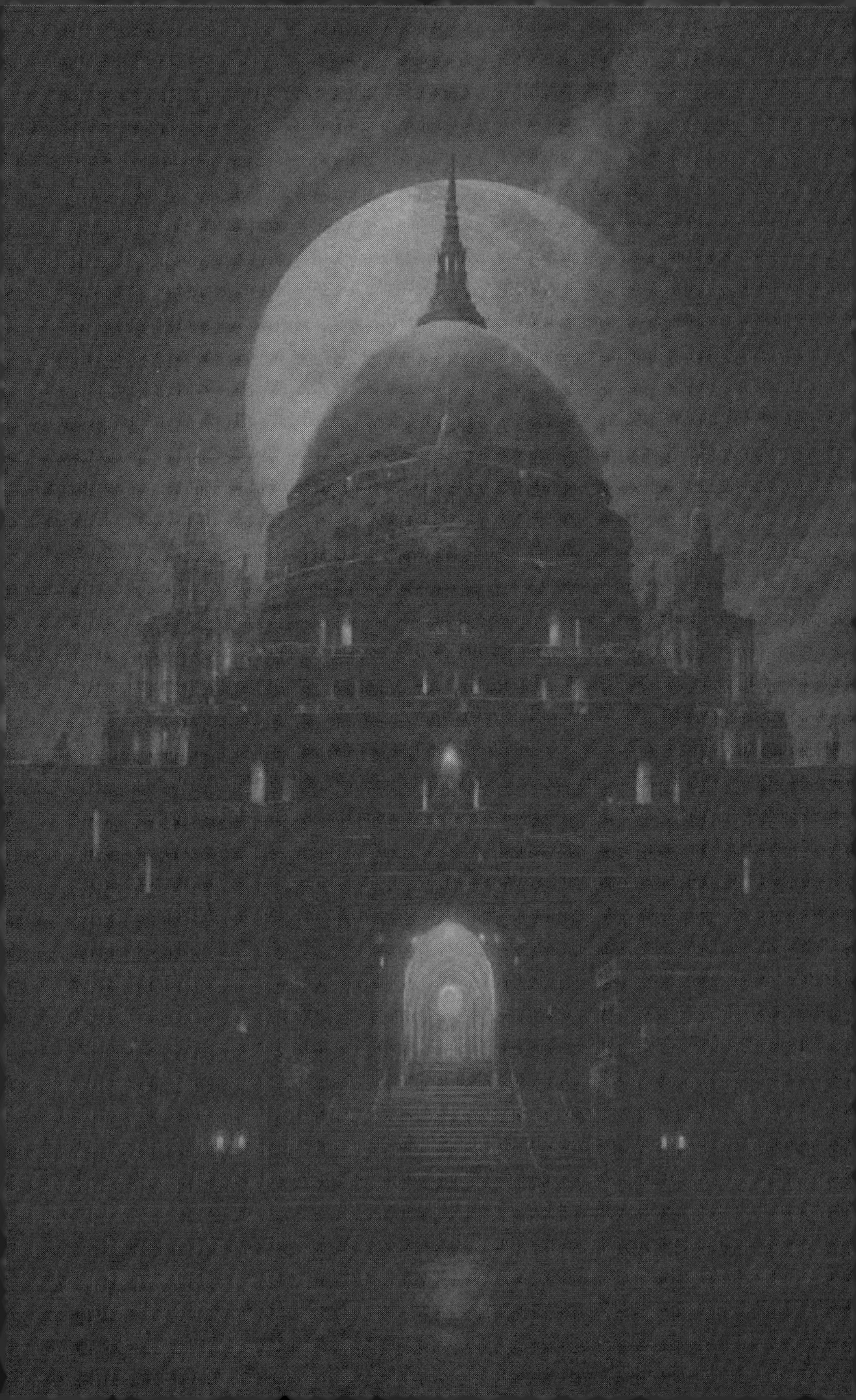

THREE
IN CADENCE

ALICIA CHAY

Settling on the threshold of the elite castle, I saw a tyrant named Queen Gree Lufu. Infatuated with her beauty, she lovingly stared at her reflection in a tinkling glass mirror on the wall of her bedroom. I inhaled her scent to learn her history, the origin of her being, and to better understand her. Behind me was an immaculate court yard filled with statues and flowers.

She came from a long line of royal figures. She was responsible for thousands of deaths in Egypt on her mission for power and control.

She inherited the throne after her Queen mother and King father was poisoned by an unknown perpetrator in the royal family. She was thirteen years old. Bearing a resilient blood diamond crown, she ruled for three decades with an iron thumb and a cold heart against her male contemporaries in neighboring countries. She poisoned her parents and took the throne. That act alone would influence me in the years to come.

Inwardly, I smiled. Queen Gree admired the shape of her breasts. I hated the bend of her frail hips and her flat romp. She was addicted to her incorrigible lovers, power and control.

I studied her breathing pattern. Her energy did nothing for me. I wanted to taste her royal blood. There were two entrances to her bathhouse. One for her, and one for the slaves. After four dark-skinned male serfs bathed her, a dark-skinned woman dressed in rations washed the Queen's hair. Fear and loss danced in her bright hazel eyes.

Queen Gree frowned when a few slaves told her good night. After bowing at her feet, they kissed her diamond pendant. Once the slaves left the bathhouse (connected to her bedroom) Queen Gree and the slave woman with mountainous thick hair noticed a falling star off in the distance.

Queen Gree wished she could live forever. Closing her eyes, the slave made another wish, one that befell my ears like someone screamed it at me. The instant the star lost its shine and faded into the glittery darkness, my heart pounded in cadence with hers. Could it be that when I looked at her, I saw a part of my past human self that happened to be her?

For a moment, the silence was deafening. Queen Gree groaned, dissatisfied with the performance of her slaves. She bathed twice a week. She burned incense to mask the musk under her hairy arm pits.

She should whip those serfs back into shape. They were her property. Property didn't have basic human rights, nor did they get treated with decency. With disquieting hate, Queen Gree gazed at the poor woman.

"I didn't like how you styled my hair for my last event, Coffey. I shouldn't have trusted you!" The dark-skinned woman refused to meet her critical eyes.

"Coffey, are you deaf? Do you need a beating?"

Coffey began to tremble.

Queen Gree hopped up to her feet in the alabaster wash basin and slapped her across the face.

A trolley horse captivated her right thigh, briefly crippling her.

"Ow! Ow!" Water splashed onto the mosaic tiled floor depicting the slaves carrying her on a golden chariot through the mountains.

"I'm speaking to you, imbecile! I didn't like the way you made me look with that hideous wig! My contemporaries tarnished my good name because of it!"

Coffey kept quiet. As long as she remained silent, Queen Gree would move on to more pressing matters in her privileged life.

Angrily, Queen Gree pulled Coffey by her hair, taking her off guard. "How dare you ignore me, you ungrateful girl!"

Queen Gree picked up a blade and cut patches of Coffey's hair from her head.

She stepped out of soiled bath water. "Wintertime is present. I need a new wool gown. I hate linen, don't you agree? I could use your hair for amazing things!"

Pushing Coffey onto the wooden floor, Queen Gree leaned over and scooped up Coffey's hair with trembling hands, gazing at her naked body in the mirror. "What's so special about this trash?"

Queen Gree pulled out black string from a wooden basket by a row of hanging ballroom gowns. They were handmade by the elder serfs. They also wiped her backside after every bowel movement. The pale-faced Queen wanted to be that beautiful dark-skinned woman. Closely, I studied Coffey. We had the same type of hair. She was a shade darker than me.

The last slave that protested Queen Gree's instructions was beheaded.

Once Gree was done tying patches of thick hair together, she held it atop her head. She wasn't as beautiful as the slave woman. Envious, she burned with jealousy

"Why doesn't my hair have this type of volume?" Coffey looked in the mirror, weakened by huge patches in her head. She refused to cry.

Queen Gree wore Coffey's hair as a wig. Satisfied, she took a few steps back from the tinkling glass mirror. Gravely, she looked herself over.

"You see, Coffey. I'm just as pretty as you." Queen Gree looked to the left, then the right. "What do you think, girl? Yes, no...?"

Coffey remained quiet. Tears rolled down her cheekbones.

"I'm prettier because I'm your owner. Never forget that. You work for me! I am your Lord! In fact, bow to me!"

Coffey refused. Queen Gree smacked her with her own hair.

"Bow to me!" she demanded.

Reluctantly, Coffey looked away. Queen Gree picked up a rawhide and whipped her until she fell to her knees in pain and surrender.

"Who is your Lord?"

Coffey remained quiet. She stared at the floor, brooding with anger.

If she acted on that anger, Queen Gree would have her slaughtered, and her husband would be slain as well. She refused to give Gree Lufu the satisfaction. Coffey never had the chance to mourn being taken from her homeland in Africa, along with her husband. She could still feel the linen cloth that was thrown over her face.

It smelled like expired resin. She remembered the conversation that filtered into her ears from her captors as she, her husband, and others from her tribe were put on yokes and whipped as they walked with clumsy footing toward the awaiting ships on the shoreline.

Her heart quickened. Strong gusts of wind caused the massive sails to dance with ear-splitting sound, like bats escaping the fires of hell in search of a colder climate.

She still felt the chains around her wrists and ankles. The rust broke her out in hives.

The air smelled of urine and feces.

She heard cries of pain once they were subdued and chained on the lowest level of the ship.

The screams of the disabled slaves that were thrown off the ships to the sharks made her skin crawl. They were too damaged to be taken to America. Her only brother, father, mother, and grandmother were tossed to the sharks as well.

All she could do was mourn the loss of her family in the dark with the other slaves. She cursed her captors for destroying her life.

She was helpless. There was nothing she could do. She was not strong enough to break the chains of bondage.

She couldn't save herself, let alone her family.

Some of her people decided that death was better than bondage, so they jumped to the sharks on their own merit.

Despite adversity, Coffey had a fighting spirit. She never gave up. She never grieved the loss of her family.

She made the most of her situation. She had to survive.

Presently, she lived for two people, her two sons she birthed behind Queen Gree's back.

She hid her pregnancy, twice. She promised to keep them safe for as long as she lived. There were seventy-five slave women on Queen Gree's plantation. They banned together, helping Coffey keep her secret.

Over time, the slave women threatened to tell her secret because they had eyes for her husband, Spike. He stood six feet, eleven inches tall. Spike was Queen Gree's personal assistant. He was at her beck and call. He chopped wood for Queen Gree during the winter, and defended her when she was taken by horseback into the hills.

The slave women informed Coffey that her husband was having sexual relations with the woman that kept them in bondage.

They hoped that Coffey left him so they could take her place.

At first, Coffey didn't know how to react. She remained obedient and quiet. On a cool night during the summer, Coffey confronted her husband, Spike. He didn't lie about it. He owned up to it. And he told her why.

He assured her that he slept with Queen Gree so their children could survive.

Coffey folded and did what her husband asked. She did anything to keep her kids safe. She was willing to kill if she had to. One by one, Coffey murdered whoever threatened to tell Queen Gree of her children's existence.

Over a two month period, fifty slave women mysteriously vanished. Coffey's kids were fourteen and seventeen years old. The only home her kids have ever known was a dungeon buried deep under a barn of horses.

Every day and night, she took care of her kids when Queen Gree retired to her quarters in a drunken stupor, bedding Spike all night. She heard their cries of ecstasy when she bathed her children, and fed them.

After she kissed her sons, she locked them in the dungeon, sometimes up to four hours a day. Spike cared for them while she cleaned the plantation.

Coffey assured her kids that one day they would be free. She apologized for giving birth to them into a system of slavery.

She couldn't control the outcome, but she could protect her children.

Spike promised to keep them safe.

FOUR
SCRAPS

ALICIA CHAY

As quiet as it was kept, Coffey wanted to snap her master's neck. She was angry that Queen Gree killed her immediate family, and put her in bondage. Her life wasn't her own anymore. However, she kept her silence, like she always did when Queen Gree loved her husband.

There wasn't a thing Coffey could do about it. If she was real with herself, she'd acknowledge that she didn't have a husband.

She married Spike, the strongest warrior among her people, before they were savagely taken from their native land. Queen Gree forced them to work at other plantations when they were short of slaves. Coffey and the slave women were sent back to Queen Gree's plantation exhausted and overworked.

Coffey worked as much as thirteen hours a day, with little sleep because of the welfare of her kids.

She was their lifeline and protector.

JA'BREEL LE'DIAMOND

Whenever Coffey cooked dinner for Queen Gree, she was disrespected. The Queen pleasured Spike on the table while they ate. Coffey was forced to watch. She fought back tears and the urge to stab her with a blade.

Last summer, Coffey catered one of Queen Gree's engagements. Twenty guests were in attendance.

Two red-faced men followed her into the back pantry and defiled her. After they were done beating her, she entertained Queen Gree's invited guests with two black eyes and a swollen lip. Queen Gree found it amusing, and so did her wealthy friends. There was a round of applause.

"Get up on the table, Coffey," said Queen Gree. "I'm thinking about putting you up for sale. You're washed up."

Coffey glared at her house nigger husband. He looked deep into her eyes. Queen Gree rode his loins four times a day. The other slave women poked fun at her behind her back. Coffey lowered her head in shame. Spike was dressed in expensive satin, velvet, and suede. His ruffled shirt brought out his pretty brown eyes. He looked better than any European man in the room.

Queen Gree goo-goo eyed him, making her guests uncomfortable. She lied about him being her right-hand slave. She said that she employed him only for sexual labor. To please her in every way. To love him more than he loved his wife. He didn't have a choice. If he said "no," she threatened to kill him and Coffey.

When she refused to obey, Spike and the two red-faced men picked her up and threw her on the table.

It was her husband that demeaned her. He spat in her face and struck her with the back of his hand.

"Why are you doing this to me?" she yelled at him.

"Don't you understand, Coffey, that I love her and not you?" Spike said, breaking Coffey's heart.

"Die a thousand times!" Coffey said. Spike treated her like a dog.

"Hold your head high!" He demanded. Coffey held her head high.

"Take off your clothes!" Coffey took off her clothes.

"Hold your breasts and turn to the left so these potential buyers can check out your assets."

The tears stung her swollen eyes. She saw him through blurs and floating colors that she couldn't grasp.

All the guests passed on her.

With a battered face, she was damaged inventory.

After the engagement ended, the guests raked all the uneaten food onto one dish and forced Coffey to eat it while they filed out of the room.

Queen Gree stripped Spike naked and made love to him in the middle of the table like a wild animal.

If Spike protested, she would kill him. Over the years, she killed fourteen dark men and chopped off their penises when they did not sleep with her, without batting an eyelash.

Coffey's husband feared death, so he pleasured Queen Gree in every way she saw fit. Once she was addicted, he remained the only male on the plantation. Spike also made love to Coffey in a way he would never make love to Queen Gree. Then they crept to the barn and slept with their kids in the dungeon.

"We have to obey to survive, my love."

"This can't be our life," said Coffey. "And I'm not your love."

"Mom, will me and my brother ever leave this dungeon?"

"In due time, sons."

"Coffey, snap out of it!" Gree yelled, bringing her back to earth.

"Huh?"

"What were you thinking about? I've been talking to you and you're standing there like you're in a trance. Have you gone insane? Are you crazy?

If you're thinking about doing something to me, change your mind before I kill you. I don't know what it is, but you need to do what I'm asking you to do, which is follow my directions."

Coffey remained mum.

"Coffey!"

"Ma'am, I apologize for my undue insolence," Coffey said, covering her face.

"Do you remember your punishment for disobeying me? Let me remind you! I will kill Spike!"

Only then did Coffey look up? "Ma'am! Please, he's my husband!"

"Is that a fact?"

"Yes!"

"But you're my property, so is he, correct?"

"Yes..."

"He's my laborer and my lover, and so are you. Either you do the job, or I'll make him do it right in front of you, like the night before."

Coffey gently pat-dried Queen Gree's body with cotton.

When Coffey's eyes locked onto mine through the mirror, I momentarily possessed her. Queen Gree gazed at Coffey with awe as the slave slowly rose to her feet, wide-eyed.

Coffey tempted her with a smile, then seduced her with a wink. Once Queen Gree led her to the balcony, she offered Coffey herbal resin tea in a porcelain cup adorned with glittering spectacle.

With huge black eyes, Coffey accepted the drink.

Spike was stripped naked, with chains around his neck.

The two red-faced men that assaulted her stood behind him, taking off their belts and loosening their trousers.

"I know you're wondering why I have your husband chained, Coffey. I'm sorry that it has come to this. My two brothers here, they're not my guests or my friends, by the way, informed me of you and Spike's deceit. They said that they heard Spike telling you that being with me was all an act. That he made love to you in a way he never made love to me."

Coffey looked at Spike. He didn't recognize her. He immediately knew something was off about his wife. He was helpless.

"I also hear your oldest son is about to be eighteen."

Spike growled. "What are you talking about?"

Gree whistled, and one of her brothers brought out his two sons. I had to give it to the boys. They were strong and well-mannered in the face of doom.

They didn't fold. Coffey was a fascinating woman. The pain of Spike's betrayal resonated with me. I understood her. We had a lot of things in common. I had no desire to feed on her. We were both forced into a life in the darkness, against our free will.

I couldn't imagine my captors throwing my immediate family to the sharks.

Coffey instilled so much fight in her sons over the years. They were prepared for anything if it happened. She taught them how to move if they were ever caught. Spike was too busy sleeping with Queen Gree, convincing his wife that he still loved her as well.

Queen Gree was pleased with the ability to outsmart anyone. She didn't become the Queen by being ignorant. She had always been intelligent, ever since she was a little girl.

Her extremely wealthy mother and father instilled in her all the education that wealth could buy.

She was always one step ahead of her younger brothers. She rarely spent time with them when they were kids.

Her parents didn't care about them.

They were well taken care of, but Queen Gree's father knew that one day she would run an empire they built with their bare hands by selling slaves.

"My, they definitely favor their mother," said Gree. "I knew about them for years. You think you're the only one capable of keeping a secret?"

Spike lowered his head.

Queen Gree continued, "I remember when your oldest child was ten months old. I was breastfeeding him."

Something died inside Coffey.

"As a matter of fact, I was breastfeeding both of your sons after I made love to your husband. Your sons used to lay with Spike and I while you cooked and cleaned my castle for the past ten years."

"I won't be fooled by your wild imagination!"

"Your sons kept it a secret. I showed them a world outside of my dungeon! I am always one step ahead."

Queen Gree glared at Spike. "When you made love to me, it was an act of defiance to keep your family safe." She kicked him in the face until she saw blood, getting me excited. I wanted to drink, but the entertainment gave me greater pleasure. "You said I felt better than your wife!" She turned away from her dark-skinned, well-endowed lover. "You were loyal to her behind my back, and in my home? A place where you have no rights, a place where you are property? A place where your sons will die!"

Queen Gree looked at her brothers.

"You can have him. I'm sure you can turn him out in ways I obviously can't. Make his sons watch. Afterwards, throw them to the gators like I did Coffey's disabled mother, father, brother and grandmother."

She handed Coffey the porcelain cup. "Drink this. It'll put you at ease," she said seductively. Coffey stared at her with a disquieting smile.

As Queen Gree's brothers prepped Spike for their perverted pleasure, she lounged on a marble bench, spreading her legs. Obediently, Coffey dropped to her knees while her husband was being beaten and assaulted.

Her boys were in shambles, closing their eyes.

"You're very good with your lips. I'm still inviting your husband to my quarters in the wee hours of the dawn to love me until I'm soft as a fawn."

Brutally, Coffey grabbed her by the neck. She was terrified. "What are you...? Why are your eyes black?"

"You discovered my children, how? Was it the slave women? I will kill every one of them right now. Who was it? Tell me which one of the women didn't hold water in the cup of secrecy."

Queen Gree was horrified.

Coffey squeezed her neck. Her pale skin started shedding from her face. Coffey's two sons cheered her on.

"I killed a lot of harlot slaves that threatened me, and it still got out. So, tell me who told you, now, before I rip out your heart and drain you dry!"

"I will take the secret to my..."

Repeatedly, Coffey slapped her in the face, until Queen Gree sank to her knees, begging her to stop. *Whack! Whack! Whack!*

"You abducted me from my homeland, threw my family to the sharks, breastfed both of my children, and repeatedly loved my husband."

"He doesn't love you," Queen Gree shouted bitterly. "He loves me! He told me of your son's birth moments before you delivered him."

The color left Coffey's face. She stopped slapping her. "You're lying! I don't believe you!"

"Both times you gave birth I was present, Coffey! You were in my dungeon. You thought I never visited my barn? I always talk to my horses. I just don't let the slaves know, so you monkeys can't plan things behind my back, like give birth to two sons and think I don't know about it."

"You destroyed my life, wrench! You will no longer abuse me."

"I own you, Spike and your sons!"

Wickedly, Coffey smiled.

FIVE
BETRAYED

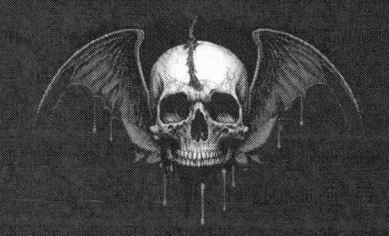

COFFEY

She raised her hand, cut off one of Gree's breasts with poisonous claws and threw the mound of flesh at Spike. She fed on Gree until she burped.

"Spike now is the time to deny her claims if she's being dishonest."

Reluctantly, he looked into her eyes. The words bubbled in the pit of his larynx, but they failed him, lost their function, their meanings. His credibility became bird droppings. Queen Gree wailed in pain.

Blood covered Coffey's mouth and hands. "Spike? Say something."

He looked away in shame. He refused to meet Coffey's demanding gaze. He'd have better luck staring at the sun.

"Why are you quiet? When you're deep inside Queen Gree and the slave women you secretly loved, you have a whole lot to say. I hear you through the walls. I heard everything you ever said to Queen Gree!"

"Once her loud cries subside," Coffey continued, "you sleep with me and your sons smelling like wet dogs trampled through the place. You say I'm the one you will ever desire, but through the walls, your words contradict your actions and your intent. So, again, is she telling the truth?"

It took a moment for him to say anything. He created this monster. The monster was so hideous he couldn't face it. He wasn't ready to acknowledge or accept what he'd done.

He was not man enough for that responsibility. He was not strong enough to handle the burden. It was too much for him to bear. It crushed him beyond understanding.

In the beginning, he slept with Queen Gree to keep his family safe, but he was sleeping with her before Coffey was pregnant the first time.

He was loving the slave women as well.

After she gave birth to her second child, he was sleeping with every woman on the plantation.

When she held her children in her arms, he was nowhere around.

"Spike..." He lowered his head. "Talk to me with the same intensity you had when you forced me to hold my head high with a swollen face!"

Still, nothing. "Forget it, fool! There's no need to explain. You were only her prize. She showed you off to her seedy friends. She was in lust with you, not love."

"You don't know that, Coffey!"

"Oh, now you speak! You found your voice! How fitting."

"She loves me and I love her! That is my truth! She promised to let my family live if I remained the object of her desire."

"You're in denial, Spike. I can't do this any longer. You're light-skinned. You can be white or black. I'm dark-skinned. Our children are dark-skinned. They can't switch complexions to fit in with those who feel they are above normal people. Now that the truth is out, what can you say?"

"Have mercy."

"You're pitiful. You're on your hands and knees, being the submissive one instead of your harlots."

"I'm sorry, Coffey. Somewhere along the line, I fell in love with Queen Gree. She's pregnant with my child right as we speak."

Coffey had a psychotic break. It was something she couldn't control. She wanted blood, vengeance, and retribution. Betrayed, she sank her fangs into Queen Gree's neck. Queen Gree shrieked with fear. Once Coffey sucked the life out of her, she tossed the sunken body over her shoulder. Glaring at her perpetrators, she rammed two hot pokers up their rear-ends. At that moment, I released the control I had over Coffey. Back to her human self, she walked over to Spike and spat on him.

"You betrayed me for the very woman that paid to have us taken from our homeland."

"Coffey, please!"

"We weren't auctioned; we weren't sold. We were brought to hell because of who her family was."

"What can we do about it, Coffey? We are a part of something out of our control."

"She poisoned her own mother and father to become a queen. She abducted our people and forced them to go into the mines and bring back diamonds, minerals, and sapphires, you name it. My immediate family was thrown to the sharks. You turned on me for her? You betrayed our children?"

"I don't know what to say."

Spike was truly remorseful, but the damage was too great to bear or ignore.

"I truly apologize," he continued. "I became addicted to her lovemaking, and her attention."

"This breaks my heart. Every time you made love to me, you thought about her. You told me to trust you. You told me to put all of my faith in your hands, that you would live up to your promises."

"You're too difficult to deal with."

Coffey laughed aloud. "Too difficult? And the one that tells you when to shit, bathe and lay is the beacon of light? Are you trying to be insulting, or are you purposely trying to hurt me more than you already have?"

"You must admit that I kept you safe in this whole ordeal. I helped keep our kids protected. Only death will free us from the binds of this plantation."

"You really believe that, don't you?"

"Queen Gree planted that in my head every time she rode me like a bucking bull. She promised she could love me more than you every time I exploded deep inside her."

"And that was keeping us safe?"

"She's uninhibited. She's easy to talk to. She never made me feel less than the peasants she owned."

"Yet she used you as a sex slave in order to be with you so her rich friends didn't burn her at the stake. You're a dirty man with an even dirtier member."

He scoffed. "You always benefit from its..."

"Just because I'm a woman doesn't mean that I'm a fool."

Spike sat cross-legged. "What can I do about it now? How can I make this up to you? Queen Gree can go to hell. I care nothing for her. I choose you. It will always be you and our sons."

"No matter what, you continue to lie in my face!"

"I'm going to be a man, no matter what kind of promises I make. A man is always going to do what he ought to do, and sometimes that ain't always the right thing. I have a right to make mistakes. We aren't perfect, Coffey. You have your struggles. I have mine."

The temperature began to drop.

"We're property. We don't have rights."

"I'm a slave. I'm not considered a human being. Are you? You don't talk about that. You live in a bubble."

"Excuse me?"

"You think we're happy and we're not. We're forced to pick cotton and beans, harvesting Queen Gree's field. We have no say in the matter. We do it for free. There is no reward. Our bodies are weather-beaten."

Coffey slapped him. "We are no more."

He averted his face. "I accept that. Can you forgive me?"

"I forgive you but I forget you. You will never have a place in our children's lives. We are finally free! You are on your own. You can have your new family. Oh, your queen and your unborn child is dead. My condolences."

Spike let out a scream that made Coffey smile.

I set the surviving slaves free after I erased their memories out of deep guilt for taking five humans and turning them into vicious vampires that lacked common sense and emotion, their true nature. Vampires that run **THE HOUSE OF THE HOUNDS** in my indefinite absence. I erased Coffey's trauma. She'd been through quite an ordeal. My heart went out to her. The slaves Queen Gree slaughtered were buried without acknowledgment. I couldn't imagine, but then again, I could feel Coffey's pain.

I could relate.

Shortly before I was turned into a vampire, my best friend and my love interest made love under the moonlight in a Hut. I watched from the back-curtained window. Yes, I could understand. It was the worst feeling in the world.

I didn't want to explore that part of my life. I forced myself not to think about it.

I would see that over and over, playing in my mind. My best friend and a man I loved with all my heart and soul. Unfortunately, he was not worthy of any kind of recognition. As for Spike, I left him chained and broken. I kept his painful memories intact. He was going to starve to death in a castle Queen Gree poisoned her parents to use for her own sick pleasures.

Just because I was a slave to the darkness didn't mean that others should suffer. I gave Coffey the life she deserved.

Coffey wished to return to her homeland with her sons. In that, I learned empathy. Even though I acquired the emotion shortly after the unlock new character feature via Coffey's human eyes, "empathy" was a trait that humbled me.

I wiped away my bloody tears as I stared at my reflection in the tinkling glass-encased on a wall in the bedroom of the dead Queen once the slaves were given her wealth and freedom.

After a moment, I turned away from my true essence, my reflection in all its splendor. I couldn't face her. My sadistic side I left imprisoned in the mirror forever. A great weight was lifted from my shoulders.

My reflection pounded on the tinkling glass with rage and anger. As her hair burned with flames, her face twisted into scorn.

She felt betrayed. "You can never escape me, who you are, and who you will always be!"

I wanted no more to do with the sadistic part of me. The hideous part that loved feeding on humans, hunting them, killing them like one mindlessly stomped a cockroach has ended. If this was my evolution, then I must trust the process. Who was I, truly? A killer?

Even though I murdered the Queen with the slave's hands, her blood was still on mine. As a result, I decided to feed on those who harmed precious animals. Innocent people didn't deserve to perish because of my thirst, even though my body count was astronomical.

Just as quickly as I thought about it, the quicker I let it go. I was Queen of *THE HOUSE OF THE HOUNDS*. Sparing humans wouldn't sit well with my contenders or the vicious vampires that helped maintain my empire.

I was deeply depressed about being a slave to the darkness. There wasn't a shred of joy in my bones.

"Alicia! You can't turn on me! Too much is given. Much is required! I will always be there with you, wherever you may be!"

I turned around and started to walk away, leaving the sick part of me behind.

"As long as this mirror exists, I will still be with you!"

I spun on my heel and screamed at the glass.

The mirror shattered into a million pieces that engulfed me...

Violently burning into my skin.

SIX
ANNIVERSARY

ALICIA CHAY

As I sat on Gree's bed, I thought to myself. I had a temporary home outside of THE HOUSE OF THÈ HOUNDS, if I chose to stay there. Gree wouldn't need the castle any longer, but it would be Spike's grave.

I took it as my own. A secret only I knew about. I was safe for the first time since I became a vampire. My heart was empty. Inside it, I built my sacred place and shielded it with cinder-blocks.

I was an éminence grise within my isolation, disorder, and thirst for blood, even though I didn't ask for the life of the lonely and the damned.

Somberly, I walked to the balcony and jumped in the air. I burst into flight with no destination in mind, leaving Spike and the castle behind.

Tonight was the two hundredth anniversary of THÈ HÔUSE ÖF THÈ HÔUNDS, come to think of it. Why didn't I remember?

Maybe because I had a lot going on in my life. Maybe because of everything I just went through. I was still trying to figure things out. I missed being alive.

KHOVAHSH

It was one thing to enjoy the roses, but it was another thing to never smell them again once I took my last breath, and started breathing as something sinister in the dark.

How could I not remember that today was the 200th year anniversary?

I treated myself to a delicious meal in Eastern Europe. Of all places to dine outdoors, Europe was an easy choice.

He was a random man dressed in rags and sandals, sleeping in an undiscovered part of the terrain.

I spotted him while I sprinted through the untamed forest cluttered with redwoods jutting into the sky. I had no destination in mind. Feeding on him was all I could think about. So much for curbing my appetite for humans.

Under a crescent moon, I sat and watched him sleep. He was totally at peace. To escape the problems of my life, I gently placed my hands on the top of his forehead.

Normally I would attack, drink, drain and run off to the next kill, but I was in a different mind frame since I encountered Coffey.

I studied my prey before I drank.

I saw his birth, his upbringing and the foods he enjoyed. He was on the run from his family.

He was charged with treason.

He tried to hire assassins to murder his mother. She governed a huge portion of Europe from behind the scenes, while her husband ran a continent.

It was uncommon for Czars, sovereigns, monarchs, and powerful men that ran entities and countries to take dictation, or orders from a species that had breasts.

I embraced the tranquility and the serenity of quietness.

At least now, I could think.

It felt good spending quality time with myself, especially when I didn't have anything to live for or look forward to.

When I was alive, I used to love laying in the middle of purple lilies. Yes, there were purple lilies growing on an open field in Chad, Africa. The petals were lavender.

The unusual color was the result of the sun shining its radiance on my skin and the field. I enjoyed being alive, but those I loved the most in the world betrayed me.

I didn't see it coming. So, when I was turned into a vampire, part of me embraced it, but the other part of me didn't.

Why was it so difficult to look back? If I wanted to be a pillar of salt, I would have been created in that form without my say-so, the way my birth was.

When I first built THÈ HÔUSE ÖF THÈ HÔUNDS, I wanted peace. Safety from the unknown dangers of breathing on the other side of a parallel universe. The Hound House was to be my home. I refused to sleep in a coffin. Unlike my family, I detested it.

There was a story behind it, and since I had nothing but time to watch the mortal have wet dreams, I ignored his enormous erection as much as I wanted to taste the decadent chocolate. I couldn't say that I saw a Black European before, yet I was looking at one in the flesh.

Even if I was a vampire, I did not like humans.

I hated them. I loathed them. I detested them.

They were spoiled. They were whiny creatures when they didn't get what they wanted.

The world was a cold place. Powerful men took control of countries because they didn't have the smarts or intelligence to conquer it on their own without thousands in an army seizing and taking advantage. If I ever took anyone's throne, I wouldn't need an army; if I took over a government, I wouldn't need warriors.

I wouldn't throw darts, I didn't need a bow and arrow, and I didn't didn't need a canon.

I would use what I knew to my advantage. I thought about my Savage family. Savage was the only word I could use to describe them.

I missed the way they smiled, the way their fangs glistened under the moonlight.

I missed the way they fed. I used to observe their faces as they drank. I had very strict rules that the Slaughtergus brothers were starting to rebel against, but in my mind, I thought they were acting out.

I didn't hold it against them.

Who was I to take their life because someone took mine?

I was supposed to be better, but then again, vampires weren't designed to be better creatures or better lovers.

As for the human, I attacked him the instant he awakened to relieve himself inside a hole he dug in the ground. Wide-eyed, he fought me, but I grabbed his lower arm, held it behind him and sank my fangs into the right side of his neck. It wasn't such a great idea.

After satisfying my hunger, I frowned. I was covered in his waste. The smell was horrifying. Deeply enraged, I held him close and jumped a few hundred feet in the air. I stuffed his lifeless body in a massive hive looming above a rocky slope.

To my dismay, I was stung by a sea of wasps. I couldn't ward them off. A nausea spell hit me, making me weak. Badly blistered, I flew thousands of miles away in a flash. Momentarily stunned, I accelerated in speed. My heart pounded; my pulse beat hummingbird quickly. It took a moment to realize that a heavily forested area was below me.

A bit exhausted, I paused midair and studied the land from a bird's eye view. I felt safe. I swiftly disengaged from the glittering sky a few thousand feet. The painful wasp stings healed while I was in flight.

I took in the ghostly beauty of the full orange moon, ensconced by purplish silver clouds in the midnight hour. Before I knew it, I was on the shoreline. The damp black sand beneath my feet was soothing.

Eagerly, I glanced around a deserted beach with an ocean a few feet ahead of me. The breathtaking mountains were silhouettes, surrounding the outer parameters with uncanny precision.

I closed my eyes.

I took in the rustling leaves. A cool breeze danced across my glistening skin of alabaster and mahogany brown sugar.

I was safe here.

I faced an uncharted forest to my immediate left. My heart was calm in pulse and rhythm. It took a while for me to settle down, considering everything I'd been through.

I didn't see any inhabitants, but then again, I just arrived.

How could I find the hidden mysteries of the forest if I never ventured into it?

I didn't see any clear or present danger.

It was quiet and serene.

I felt guilty for disturbing the peace. I decided to explore the woods.

As I headed towards the forest, the beauty of the water attracted me to its brilliance. I stared at it, taking a deep breath. I briefly thought about Coffey and the slaves I freed.

I should be flying, scouting, and traveling, eradicating cold-hearted mortals, but not tonight. I didn't feel like doing much of anything.

I wanted to stay here forever, but that was impossible. I wanted more out of life, but I didn't know where to start.

The gentle sound of crickets made me smile. I stared at the still waters of the ocean. I walked onto it, pausing twenty feet out. The water began to glow in cadence with the moon.

KHOVAHSH

A sea of flying bugs with glowing green eyes provided a barrier around me. I took in the beauty of silence. I sank into the warmth of the water. A few seconds later, my naked body rose above the ocean and floated back to shore, clean and refreshed.

The glow bugs were gone. Unexpectedly, a strange noise caught my attention. Instantly, I was on guard. I investigated the direction the noise came from. An owl hooted in unison with croaking frogs.

Something sped by me with unconscionable speed.

swoosh

swoosh

Swoosh!

With just the glow of the moon providing guiding light, my observant eyes surveyed the ocean, forest, brush, mountains, everything...

All was quiet.

It must have been my imagination...

swoosh

swoosh

Swoosh!

Sw o

osh

There it goes again!

A *bluish-red mobile blur encircled me.*

I was caught off guard by a school of sparkling swans that suddenly appeared in the regal form. Dark shadows dropped from the thunderous clouds above and settled on my shoulders, lifting me up. With ease, I was lowered onto an enchanted saddle atop a massive swan. Golden reigns formed in my hands. Once the shadows popped into sacred energy, I was floating on the ocean.

The Swan's vision became swirling worlds within my pupils and irises, spinning into one.

The sea of glow bugs returned and dressed me in a sheath kalasiris dress that swayed on the breeze. A lotus flower was draped over my forehead, and a perfume cone was atop my hair.

A legion of swans formed their leader, King Swan. When I landed on this isolated beach, I thought I would rest on my laurels until the dawning sun, but I was wrong.

The King quietly observed me. I remained on the elegant Swan observing him. What a gorgeous Negus! His dark skin was tried and true. I was caught inside his high-level frequency.

He had two sets of hypnotic eyes. His human eyes and swan eyes were on either side of his temples, laced with fragments of copper and topaz.

The way he gazed into my soul had me wet with lust and zeal. I didn't give it up that easily, yet I started to perspire. He managed to smile. "Our meeting is necessary, Alicia."

I gasped with surprise, running my hand through my mound of unruly nappy hair. "How do you know my name, yet I know not yours?"

He narrowed his third eye. "Your reputation precedes you." My third eye formed on my forehead but refused to meet his.

"You must know that I know you not, nor do I know who you are. Why are you disrupting my peace? What purpose does this unsolicited meeting serve when I'm no one's slave."

"You're in bondage. What freedom lies in that young one?"

I snarled slightly. "I don't have the energy for strangers. I should be on my way."

Brutally, he struck the salty waters with his crown, and the still waters spiraled to either side of him. He levitated above a hidden city in complete barren and ruin. The massive Swan beat her wings, hovering in place. I tightened my grip on the reigns.

It was truly a sight to see, but I remained stoic. I wondered why he felt the need to display his power when flights of fancy never appealed to my senses.

Yet I had to bite my tongue to stop my nipples from swelling.

Before I could dismiss myself, a green-faced witch appeared on the sand, gazing up at us. Fire funneled from her hair to her pitch-dark cloak.

All the Swans bowed to her except for the King. He never broke away from my gaze.

"Queen Mother Armona sends the Swan King to you with a message that only he can deliver," said the foul-smelling witch.

I floated from the massive Swan to the sandy shoreline while King Swan continued to levitate above a once-thriving ancient city that was buried by the ocean as punishment for their long-forgotten crimes.

"Queen Mother Armona?" I shook my head, confused. My feet found the sand. "I'm not familiar with..."

Her eyes enlarged. "Listen closely," she interrupted. She vanished and rose from the ground a foot in front of me.

"Do you have a name, stranger?"

"My name is Horishia Valiseah. I'm a 'borrower,' a witch, and a sorcerer. Queen Mother, Armona is the most vicious dictator you will ever encounter. In other words, her government rules over us and the supernatural at large. She's your leader as well."

I was in direct opposition. "I digress, witch. No one rules me!"

"Ah, but she does!"

"Are you trying to convince yourself with your psychobabble?"

"It is not I that needs convincing."

"You're wasting your breath. No one speaks for me."

"As the High Czar of the House of Dragonhead Ancients, she has the authority to kill you at will."

"She can try."

"You wouldn't stand a chance."

"Then I'm afraid this scene has gotten old."

"You are not permitted to leave...."

"We will see about that."

"Initially, we were sent here to kill you on sight. You were created into what you are without authorization from the Queen. There are consequences for such actions, Alicia."

I was attentive, to my surprise. "What changed?"

"Your potential."

Truth be told, I didn't know who the cold-hearted queen was, nor did I want to know. If this was meant to frighten me, then she failed miserably. I was the only Queen worth listening to, even though I had absolutely no political power. I was Queen of my world. What no one told me was how merciless I would become.

Being a sadistic individual wasn't what I desired. I was a vampire with limited power. It came at a steep price, especially when it was unauthorized, according to the hideous witch.

Before she could continue, I levitated towards King Swan.

He extended his hand. I shook it firmly. King Swan drifted to the massive Swan and settled on the glowing saddle. The golden reigns didn't form in his hands, nor did the saddle glow when I sat on it.

"Armona summons you, Alicia," said King Swan.

I thought to myself for a beat.

"Excuse me if I'm not quick to oblige..."

"Alicia. I urge you to come with us."

"This is where we part ways...."

"Alicia..."

I vanished and appeared on the sand.

"Nice meeting you. I'm afraid we'll never see each other again..."

Mid-sentence, an eight-foot being with dragon wings landed in front of me from a black hole in the sky. I was startled.

The instant his feet of bronze and alabaster made direct contact with the dust of the earth, King Swan and his pet bird became stone midair, and the barren city began to razzle-dazzle with sparkling lights.

It took my breath away. He leaned into my face. The ground shook with a deafening rumbling. Mysteriously, the witch vanished.

"As if you have a say in the matter, Alicia," he spewed. His deep baritone register made me weak. Uncontrollable fire cackled in his hypnotizing eyes. My guard went up.

"Who are you? I don't answer to you..."

"I am Khovahsh, the Queen Mother's Enforcer."

"That's nice. Now move out of my way."

He ignored me. "This is your official summons to the Queen. If you reject it, you will be severely tortured, then destroyed by my hands."

Before I could react to the Queen's lapdog, he grabbed me above the elbow, and the space around us turned to molecules and irregular atoms.

Once the dust settled, I stood before an elegant woman with soulful lips.

"Who are you, and where am I?" I asked her.

My stomach was in knots.

She held her head high. "I'm Armona, the Queen Mother. You're in my fortress."

I swallowed the lump in my throat.

There was no sign of Khovahsh, the witch, or the Swan Tribe.

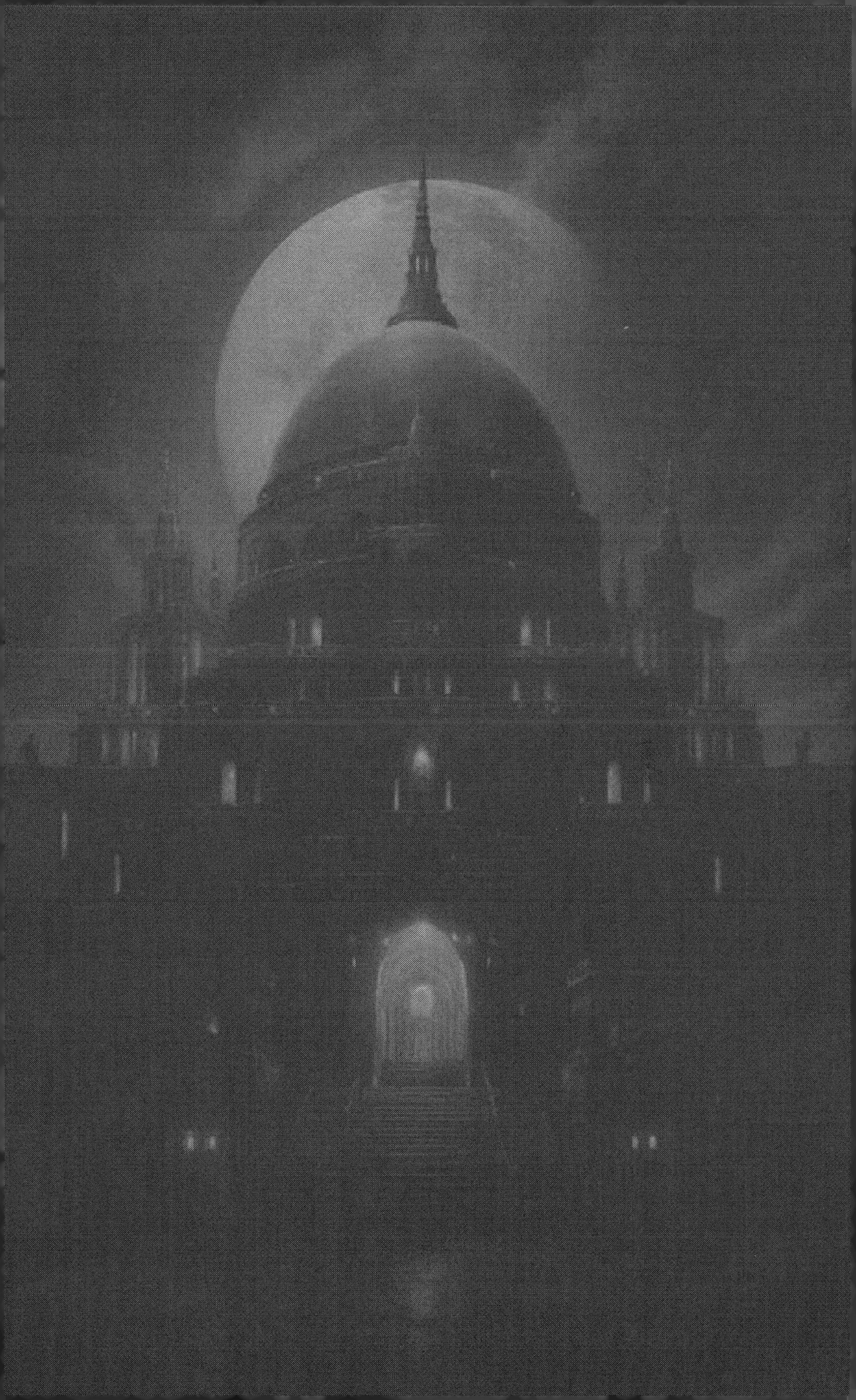

SEVEN
DOCILE CREATURES

QUEEN MOTHER, ARMONA AND ALICIA

I gasped at the sight of her resilient beauty. She was mesmerizing, gorgeous, and wealthy beyond the system of gold and monetary deeds. Her presence was extremely powerful.

Bedazzled in sapphires, black diamonds sparkled over her nipples, her curly bush and her amazing buttocks. The gems gave her intimate areas class and decorum.

She acknowledged me with a glance. Her majestically powerful third eye connected with my own. Only then did she speak.

"I'm going to ask you this only once, young one, a vampire created without my authority or say so..."

"And you are...?" I interrupted, annoyed. I had better things to do. A collective gasp escaped her reddish lips. Her eyes were black slits. "How dare you question who I am!"

I stared blankly at her. "And who are you again?"

"If you were a member of my staff, and you didn't know who I was, that everything starts and stops with me, I would torture you; then I'd throw you in the pit of unspeakable things just to torment you..."

"You're turning me on the more you talk," I lied.

Oddly, she glanced at me. I threw her off her guard.

"Keep your word," I continued. "Make sure you live up to everything you said and in that precise order Queen, or whoever you think you are. I'm quite curious. I'm not scared at all."

Armona squealed. "I'm going to slow down time and watch you burn. Fortunately for you, I have no desire to get my nails dirty. Servants just bathed me. I don't have the patience for it."

"Neither do I."

"Good, then we understand each other."

"Get to the point."

"There's something about you that I find intriguing," she said.

I yawned.

"Since you're ignorant to a woman of my caliber, I'll spare your life, even though you killed one of my cabinet members and took her castle just before this summons."

I was taken aback. "Is that right?"

"Yes. I used Queen Gree Lufu to lure you here."

I was thrown. "I work for no one, Armona."

"I've never summoned anyone to my private chambers. You're the first."

"Why was I summoned here?"

"That's for me to know and you to find out."

"I wish to leave. How do I get out of here?"

"When I say so, and not a moment before."

"Says who? You? I come and go as I please, Athena."

"My name's Armona. Let me educate you."

"I have an education. I don't need a teacher."

"Alicia, I'm a juggernaut, a steam roller. I have wined and dined with some of the world's most powerful kings. Such as Aktisanes, Aryamani, Kash, Piankhi-yerike-qa, Sabrakamani, Arnekhamani, and Arqamani. Kings, Alicia."

I stifled a yawn. "Sorry. I never heard of them."

She approached me. "You're deflecting," she went on, getting agitated.

I took a few steps back. "For good reason. You don't seem to take no for an answer. My mind is made up."

Her eyes widened. "You're useless."

I scowled. "That would be your weak attempt to show me you're the supernatural Queen of us all."

"Weak attempt?" She chuckled.

"And from the looks of it, you used salacious actions to gain some of your wealth, status, and power."

She grinned. "Lay with docile creatures, inherit fleas and ticks. Dine with Kings, walk away with all they acquired. That's the difference between you and me. I've never seen a flea in my life. I suggest you leave those hounds... animals, out of the equation if you thirst for power."

I narrowed my eyes, smiling inwardly. "You don't know what I want or desire."

She was enchanting. "Ah, but I do! You remind me of myself during the dawn after my transition."

"We are nothing alike, Armona."

"I was a complete wreck," she continued, ignoring me, "a vindictive savage creature with no heart. I carved out my own place on this great earthly ball of death."

"I'm getting bored."

"You are an alleged general scouring the earth mindlessly, wasting your talent on creatures we have dominion over. What vampire has pets?"

I grinned from ear to ear. "Weren't you bending over after you wined and dined with Pharaohs, sovereigns, and monarchs, as their pet in heat?"

"Something you do with no incentive or reward, I suspect."

I was offended. "Just because your intimate areas are adorned with glittering spectacle doesn't hide the hideous odor reeking from your worn-out hips."

Deeply insulted, Armona's face twisted into fury. After a pounding screech that made my ears bleed, she unleashed fiery chains that dispersed from her luxurious nappy hair.

They burned into every limb of my body with brimstone and sulfur embedded in metal hooks. Rapturous scorpions, leeches, and tarantulas dropped all over me from the baccarat crystal chandeliers shaped like immaculate beehives hovering from above.

As they pierced my skin, I released a battle cry of rippling effect that repelled her attacks. It knocked Armona to her knees in both shock and anger.

Unperturbed, she clapped her eyes.

Brusquely, she rushed up to me. I spiraled into pulsating dust, entering her body through her nostrils.

I wrapped my spiritual hands around the pulse of her soul.

"Why am I here, Armona?" I was serious. Coughing and gagging, Armona grabbed her throat with wide eyes. She slowly rose into the air, kicking her legs wildly.

With no sense of control, there was an urgent need to come out the victor. A nest of glittering snakes slithered around my ubiquity from deep within her.

As I did, she turned into smoke and rose from the floor with her hair in reddish-orange flames.

With a high pitch scream, she stomped her foot. Earthquakes separated her massive bedroom into a labyrinth eight hundred feet above her fortress.

I stumbled from her body. Ripples of her scorn held me captive.

"Is that all you got?" I teased, shaking off her attack.

She regained her composure. "I'm falling in love with you," she said, "but recreation is over. Honestly, no one has ever challenged my authority, until you came along. If you accept my offer, I will mold you in my image, granting you unlimited power…but if you decline, you will die."

I thought about her request. I never heard of her until the green-faced witch told me.

I had no idea about her eight-thousand-year-old reign of terror and global misery. She ruled within the Pre-Pottery Neolithic B Phase of the Early Neolithic, the second full millennium of the Holocene epoch. I was only two centuries into the vampire life. Everything I was, who I'd become, I'd learned on my own.

At this point, I knew what must be done. I smiled, but my eyes did not.

"I accept…"

She was pleased. "Good decision, Alicia."

Abruptly, I was whisked away by enchanted chains and connected to two totem poles in an empty field extending forty feet from the ground.

I didn't know what I got myself into, but I had a feeling I was about to find out.

As I dangled in the starry darkness of a sandy desert, it didn't dawn on me what was taking place until the first ray of the rising sun initiated what she referred to as "Daybreak."

I was on a deserted island. Alone. Underneath a darkened sky, I hung above the land like bait on a hook. I was a sitting duck plucked off her feathers, pride, and dignity. Every action was a reaction, but how did I react when I was bound against my will? What good was free will if I was forced to make an illogical choice for another person's security, peace of mind and benefit?

KHOVAHSH

When did I get to return to life as I knew it?

Why did I have to be a part of somebody else's decisive plans? I didn't enjoy hanging from totem poles. I had things to do, places to go, and an entity to run.

I missed my family of savages. Were they looking for me? I doubted it, but then again, maybe they were searching for me since they consistently fought each other for my love and devotion.

Men. They were worse than concubines.

There was always a pissing match between them. One couldn't just be there for the other.

I was lonely.

Nothing stirred. I wept for a moment. Crying wasn't going to get me out of this ordeal.

I had the need for companionship, even though I could live without it.

Who wanted to be a vampire with nobody to talk to, especially after you already lost a promising life?

Did that sound fun and engaging? I was extremely disappointed in myself.

Why didn't I fight for my freedom when I was on the beach, minding my own business?

It wasn't until I sunk into the waters of the ocean to clean my body of feces from my special treat-victim that this all transpired.

Why didn't I attack the king swan, the green-face witch or Khovahsh?

Why didn't I fight to the death?

Why didn't I join or die?

I did join, but why didn't I fight all of them for my freedom, even if it resulted in my death? I didn't know what was coming.

Was something going to rise from under me and eat me whole?

Was something coming from above or from the backside, or from all corners: north, south, east, and west?

It was the fear of the unknown that scared me. It was not a great feeling at all. I was living my life on my terms, until now. I was a World Builder. I found my own way. How did I end up in this predicament? How? I moved to my own beat, and I didn't answer anyone. Next thing I knew….on the 200th anniversary of **THE HOUSE OF THE HOUNDS** I was dangling 30, 40 – 50 feet above dark sand.

Only the sunlight could reveal its luster.

I didn't enjoy the beauty of it. I was numb. What was beauty to a person that was dead?

I couldn't remember my past life.

I had selective amnesia.

I choose not to remember. Now was not the time to think of it. My life was in danger. A seductive Queen manipulated me. That was my fault. I should've known better.

Was this retribution for all the wrong I'd done? I took a lot of lives. I drank a lot of blood. I watched my prey take their last breath. The Grim Reaper taunted, provoked, and seduced me to be something other than what I was, even though I didn't know who I was.

I was forced to go with the flow.

Did I embrace my past human self as a vampire, or did I let it go? I was no longer human. Maybe letting go would make it easier.

"Armona?" I called out with a thunderous voice.

Nervously, I looked around, yet nothing stirred. Inevitably, the blackened sky displayed purplish-pink hues as the sun began to rise.

The hair rose on my arms.

"No! No! *You tricked me!* I accepted your offer, you concubine! I was to be your right hand girl, your assassin!"

A thunderous growl silenced everything but my thoughts.

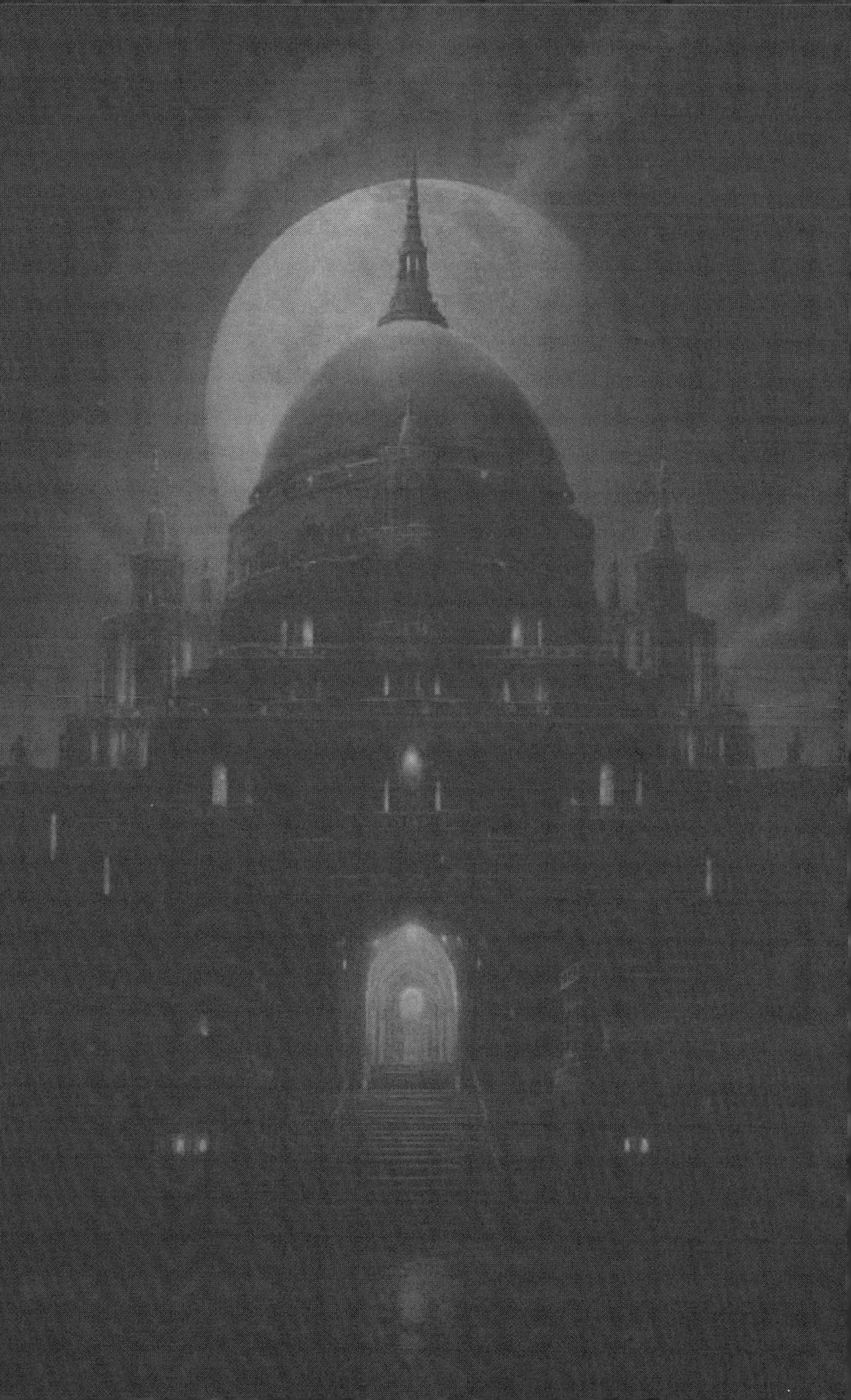

EIGHT
DAYBREAK

ALICIA CHAY

A mild earthquake rocked the turf as the totem poles expanded by twenty-five feet, putting me in direct contact with the approaching sunlight. It yearned for the darkness deep inside of me.

One I tried to subdue through my love for animals. Yet that love wasn't strong enough for manifestation. Because I was turned into a creature of nocturnal bliss against my will.

A dusty sand cloud spun into Armona's face.

Her black eyes bore into mine.

"Going through Daybreak is inevitable, silly girl."

The golden rays from the sun spiraled into Armona's majestic eyes.

I was strong in my views. "If you think I'm going to bow to you, you're sadly mistaken."

"If you want to live, you must obey, Alicia."

"I bow to no one! I never heard of your name in my supernatural life, yet you're the Queen Mother? Kill me if you must!"

"I'm disappointed in you, Alicia. This is your final chance."

"I am my own Queen! I bow to no one!"

With a screech, Armona formed from dust, sand and flames. She repelled the sunlight towards me with her saddened eyes.

I was set ablaze, along with the totem poles. My life was over. I screamed from the pain. I plummeted towards the earth below. My powers were invalid. There was nothing I could do. I was dying!

When my body hit the ground, a huge sink hole formed.

The sun roasted me.

I died as a human, but as a young woman with power and immortality, I thought I was going to live forever. As a vampire, I enjoyed two hundred summers, only to be murdered by a queen I never heard of.

Had I resisted Khovahsh and the Swan King, I'd be free, traveling the world, drinking blood at my leisure.

Instead, I was in bondage. Even though I was on fire, rusty chains and locks were around my wrists. As my skin fell from my bones, I rose from the sink hole, reborn and pure.

The chains turned to dust.

It took a moment to realize that I was like new. Laughing out loud, I eagerly touched my hair, my beautiful dark skin, my arms and legs. I hugged myself, spinning in circles. I glanced at the sinkhole. I gasped with surprise and wonder when I realized we were in a forested area, shaded from the sun by towering oak and redwoods. "I don't understand…"

Armona, the Queen Mother, cupped my face with adoration. Nine barbaric vampires, wearing black wool and linen, guarded every entrance and exit of the forest. "I'm still breathing! How is this possible? I was on fire! I felt the flames!"

Armona looked me over, brushing dust from my shoulders. "Daybreak is a form of purity, to see if your decision was of sound heart and mind. Had you been untrue, the flames would have destroyed you in an instant, Alicia…but since you were being truthful, I can now trust you to be my general, my executioner…

"I give you full authority," she continued, "over my government and the vampiric barbarians protecting our secret meeting. Run my empire as you see fit while I remain occupied with my private affairs."

In an instant, I was the second most powerful supernatural being in all four hundred realms. Carved on stelae were my terms and conditions. Animals were protected under my rule. Without Armona's permission, I implemented the "Treaty of Animals." Signatures from the Animal Kingdoms were required. I preoccupied myself before I lost my mind. I was thrust into a system I couldn't quite comprehend.

For years, we walked through her gigantic Fortress, learning things every day. Remembering the ins and outs of her government was tedious.

I had the respect of her staff and her government officials. They either respected me, or they died instantly. They were once human, so to die a second death was not on their agendas. Being Immortal was the best feeling in the world.

Armona taught me the Dershakney, a vampire constitution. I was extremely focused. To much was given, much was required. I learned to be careful what I asked for.

I put that out of my mind.

I took my time getting to know her. I didn't force anything. I barely spoke. I went with the flow; I trusted the process.

Someday, I would be the Queen Mother and run her government the way she never could. I believed it with everything in me. I slept thinking about it. I awakened thinking about it.

It seemed unattainable.

I kept it in the abyss of subconscious.

KHOVAHSH

Everything wasn't about Armona. I was figuring things out. I was still coping with being a creature of the night. There wasn't a time limit on how I dealt with it. Would I ever accept it?

The Queen's position came at a price. Armona gave me my first assignment. I had to seek out those that were in her debt and execute them.

Within a few weeks, the task was done. I carried out her demands, but my eyes remained on her throne.

If she made one wrong move, her empire, her life, and her identity would be mine.

I was crafty so Armona didn't suspect anything.

She had eyes and ears everywhere.

She knew what was going on in her empire. Every nook and cranny was under her control.

She approved everything. She was a very detail-oriented woman. I admired her business savvy. I also admired her discipline. Everyone obeyed her strict rules and dictation.

She didn't accept excuses.

The price was death, without a trial.

When she issued an order, she expected borderline excellence. Other than that, she killed at the drop of a dime. She slaughtered her prey like it was a hobby. She murdered humans with her powers, never with her hands.

She slept with Kings as if it was the thing to do.

I commend her for being exemplary.

One day, as the summer was ending, she approached me.

We were in her Ballroom that was closed because it wasn't a season for social gatherings.

"Alicia, something troubles me."

"I'm all ears, Armona."

She accused me of not paying attention to the security detail when I wasn't trained to govern the vampires that guarded the forest after *Daybreak*.

She didn't know about THÈ HÔUSE ÖF THÈ HÔUNDS, and that I had it built by slaves I hypnotized behind her back. Fortunately, none of that mattered. I didn't know she existed at the time.

She was a sly fox. She had the ability to talk you into your own death if you let her. Everything and everybody around her catered to her every need.

I must admit that I was one of those people as well. Doing what was required to be on her list of favorite people.

Maybe I wasn't one of her favorite people.

I was her favorite supernatural being, I should say.

Armona wasn't a very likable Queen. Anyone that worked for her held their tongues so they could live. They never talked badly to her; they did everything they were supposed to do. They didn't tarnish her name in private meetings.

If she gave an order, it was fulfilled expeditiously. The only thing I didn't like about Armona was the way she started torturing animals, considering I had a treaty created out of love and peace.

How did I fight the Queen against the very thing I was against when she didn't authorize my Treaty, nor did I need her approval?

I was summoned to an underground Coliseum that I never knew existed. Her voice found my ears shortly after I took a walk through the Courtyard of the Queen after the midnight hour.

I paused by a row of statues bearing her likeness.

I just wanted to be alone. I was regretting my decision to be at her beck and call. I was caught up in the moment. Now, I was in too deep.

Alicia, meet me at the Coliseum underneath my Fortress....

I was being tested.

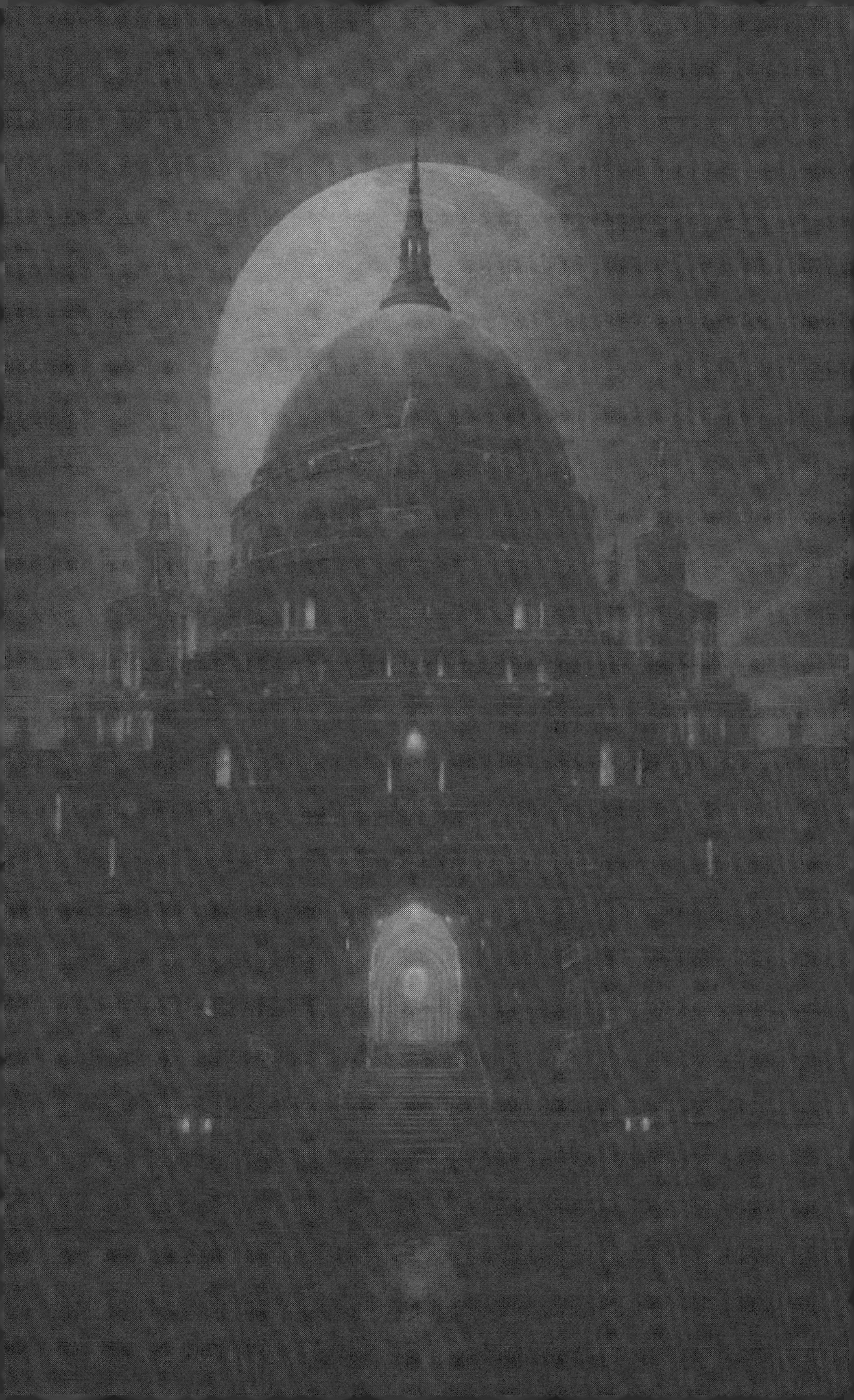

ALICIA CHAY

Armona and I were the only two in the 500,000 concrete seat infrastructure. Down on the main stage were huge iron cages with lions, tigers, leopards, zebras, and a hippopotamus. I didn't understand what was going on.

Caught off guard, I floated down four hundred and ninety rows of stairs before I reached her on the Queen's platform, built on a pedestal. The Queen's Throne was draped in gold. "There's only one way to get rid of your attachment to animals." She spat a stream of flames at the cages, setting the animals on fire. I fought the urge to kill her, but I couldn't. I was seething with rage. It killed me to watch them burn to death, but I took an oath.

What kind of woman was I stand by and do nothing? Even if it resulted in my death, I should have done something to save them. The wails of torment broke me to pieces to the point I couldn't sleep.

I cried blood the whole night.

I mourned their deaths. Deep inside, I began to hate the Queen Mother

KHOVAHSH

Armona.

I loathed her. She had my heart until she burned those innocent animals. I was going to destroy her, but in due time. I couldn't act on emotion alone. I laughed at her jokes that weren't funny. I was there for her, when I'd rather be somewhere else.

Taking the throne was going to be quite a task to achieve. I was up for the challenge, no matter how impossible it was. I was going to take her down. Yes, that was unheard of. I was writing my own death wish. I was on a suicide mission.

Armona was always protected by security and other vampires of a higher status that served as her council members. They were unapproachable. I didn't waste my time speaking to them. I was never introduced to them; all I knew was that I suddenly became their Queen.

I studied how Armona walked and talked. Her style of dress was otherworldly. Her sex appeal was undeniable. I was envious of her charm. I smiled at men in power that begged to bed her with the promise of gold and lavish gifts.

I visualized that they were coming to see me. In my mind I wore her ballroom gowns and her lavish dresses. I imagined that I had her luxurious nappy hair that hung down to her feet.

Whenever she hunted for blood, I collected information. When she visited Kings in neighboring countries, I slept in her bed. I smelled her scent on the sheets. I modeled all of her gowns in front of her enchanted mirror, but my sadistic side wouldn't let me be great. I turned this way and that, tossing my hair. I tried to pile it atop my head, but my reflection laughed at me.

"You'll never be Armona. Never!"

Ignoring my inner-voice, I bared my fangs, feeling supreme. I thought about Queen Lufu modeling Coffey's hair.

I loved Armona's gray rhinestone dress with the floral bodice. My hair hung in beautiful thick curls past my shoulders, down to the start of my buttocks. I loved the way my hair brushed the small of my back. I tried on another gown. I put on Armona's footwear, adorned with crystals. Her jewels were worth more than the castle itself.

In her absence, I was the Queen Mother. I started calling her "Alicia" in my head. She was me, and I was her. I could run her empire better than she could. I had more wit, drive, and stamina.

I was the Queen of the Hounds. I kept it concealed while I became the acting Queen Mother of the supernatural realms. I quietly renounced my throne to become something greater than a community Queen.

When Armona returned from her journey, she always treated me to a special breakfast, lunch, and dinner. We lounged in one of the forty rose gardens surrounding the Fortress. We waited until after dark so the sunlight didn't turn us into flames. The rose petals blended in with our red eyes. We lay in the courtyard and studied the stars.

Then she'd leave again for many moons. I loved when she went away. "Absence makes the heart weep," she would say, but in my opinion it gave me a chance to explore her Fortress. I went through all of her things. I found hidden parts of the castle that were forbidden. I won over her staff. I hypnotized them into doing my bidding without her finding out.

Her council members gathered confidential scrolls and gave them to me so I could take the throne. I wiped their memories clean to cover my tracks. A bird couldn't eat if I didn't leave crumbs. I imagined that her castle belonged to me! Her bed was mine. I replaced her face with mine on her oil paintings throughout the castle.

I floated around her room. Delicately, I ran my fingers across her lavish comforters. I loved the smell of lavender and cinnamon. Thirteen fireplaces surrounded her bed from thirty feet away. The flames never went out. No matter if it was the summertime or the wintertime, Armona always kept the fires burning. There was a massive oil painting hanging above her bed. In it, she had green eyes,

KHOVAHSH

She covered her breasts without it being crass.

It was tasteful. I wanted to be her. I was her. Instead of thinking of myself, I thought about her.

I changed my thought process.

I was the Queen Mother. When I handled her affairs, I was her.

When I awakened at night, I was her.

When I gave orders, I was her.

I did it without making it obvious. I had to get closer to her.

An opportunity presented itself on the Queen Mother's birthday.

I stood behind the scenes, shortly before my Coronation.

TEN
ALICIA CHAY'S CORONATION

ALICIA CHAY

When Armona planned my Coronation, I was taken aback. I didn't care for one, but there was no way around it. I let it be. I knew about everything as she put it together.

I hid in the shadows of her bedroom and quietly observed.

Five hundred naked dark-colored men held up dresses that covered their intimate areas. They tinkled before her eyes. The men stood like statues, too afraid to move or look at her. No one acknowledged her birthday, nor did she care. A bejeweled crown lowered itself atop her head from glittering dust. Armona looked over the first thirteen dresses, dissatisfied.

Once a dress was rejected, the male turned around and tossed it in the fireplace with his head bowed.

KHOVAHSH

She brushed her eager finger tips along their shoulder blades, in awe of their beauty. Abruptly, she paused before the 100th male. He gazed into her eyes, causing her to blush. "Happy birthday, Queen Mother, Armona."

With a Cheshire cat smile, he held up a multi-layered dress made from thirty shades of pure gold, with a baccarat crystal bodice. It was breathtaking! She found the dress for my Coronation. They couldn't stop looking at each other.

She instructed 499 men to turn their backs. "Queen Mother, you can do to me whatever your black heart desires. I taste like coconut."

As she rode his incredible member like a wild horse, he helped her put on the dress. Armona and her chosen lover were in ecstasy.

She exploded with delight atop him over and over and over.

Once she was done, she brought in 233 feminine castle cleaners of a pale ivory complexion to bathe the men. They were given a direct order from the Queen.

"You are prohibited from touching the men in an inappropriate manner."

One by one, the women were tempted to touch the chocolate, lick the swollen mushroom head, or fill every hole with meaty pleasure. The price was death by fire, but they didn't seem to care. Imagine being amidst the most beautiful, endowed men in the world and you couldn't enjoy them.

Twenty of them died instantly. The others turned to flames as well. There were four-hundred and ninety-nine dark-colored men, but there was only one pale ivory castle cleaner left that obeyed the Queen's direct order.

The Queen Mother approached her. I watched in silence.

"Thank you for following my directions."

She gushed with zeal. "My pleasure, Queen Mother.

"You are stronger than those that came with you. As a treat, I present to you four hundred and ninety-nine different options."

She turned in circles, like a dancer. "Really, Queen Mother?"

"You can pick one, you can pick four, you can pick eleven, you can pick sixty-three, or you can have them all. What will it be?"

The peasant maid looked the Queen deep in the eyes and gave her eagerly anticipated answer. "I desire the one you chose, oh gracious Queen Mother," she said. "Any man that can dress a Queen while loving her I much desire."

Armona smiled, grabbing her by the lower chin. "Only trash would want left-over meat that smells of my essence. Four hundred and ninety-nine untouched options before your very eyes, and you want whom I chose."

"I want to be just like you, my Queen. Is that such treason?"

I smiled from within the pale peasant maid as she buttered the Queen Mother's bread without wine or recourse. Armona granted the peasant her left-overs.

With the servant's body, I loved all of the men for the next four-hundred and ninety-nine days, individually and secretly. I gave each one of men in Armona's security detail endless orgasms without letting them inside of the servant.

I enticed them with her bedroom eyes. Once they were possessed, I squeezed her thighs tightly together, making them think they were dancing inside the gushy cervix of the Queen. Out of the five hundred, the one Armona loved was the only one that felt how warm and fuzzy I was, as Alicia. He danced inside of my tight, wet walls all night long.

ALICIA CHAY'S CORONATION:

For miles, there were decorations and statues of me created by the Queen Mother's staff. She recruited peasant slaves from neighboring communities to build a stone and concrete infrastructure that shaded the entire parameter of the back of the castle just so I could enjoy my coronation during the daytime.

KHOVAHSH

She spared no expense to make me happy. I appreciated the gesture, but I didn't ask her to do those things. I had no love in my heart for a woman who forced me to a summons and burned thousands of animals for sport.

Had I been able to go about my merry way when I encountered the Swan King, I'd be free, but that wasn't to be.

So, why didn't I reject the fancy trinkets that she presented? They stroked her ego but did nothing for my benefit.

She flaunted her power to remind me who was in charge. She was doing those things to pacify me into her way of thinking and understanding.

She didn't want a woman who thought as her own.

She didn't desire a woman who knew how to get what she wanted; she wanted someone she could mold in her image.

I was a replica of her in power when she let me take control. I was called a Shadowing Queen by her constituents because I was always in Armona's shadow. I had a problem with that. I was the Queen of the Hounds at one point. I had my own identity. I went through hell and high water to have my palace of blood built at the hands of peasant slaves.

I had a savage family I thought nothing about. I had love in my heart for them. I didn't care to see them again. We used to drink blood, hang out, travel, and hunt together.

We were inseparable.

We hosted events that cost human lives. That was the point of humans battling each other to the death. It gave us blood to drink without them trying to fight us off. It was a win for us, but a loss for humans.

I took off the Crown of the Hounds to ascend the throne of another woman's power.

I wanted her life as my own.

If that was what it took to take the throne, then so be it.

Was I selfish for thinking that way? As a human, I was taught to be grateful for what I had. I was gracious, humble and giving, but as a vampire, those morals went out of the window.

Now I was in the middle of my Coronation. The start of it, at least.

A whole program was planned for my ascension to active Queen Mother status, while the real Queen Mother privately fulfilled her agenda, whatever that was. If it kept her away from her castle, her council members, and her business dealings, I was all for it.

Breathtaking artifacts from countries from all over the globe twinkled like gold, glistened like diamonds, and glowed like rubies. *If you can see it, it's already yours, Alicia.* I thought, smiling. Wow.

When I decided to take over the throne, I took the time to plan my method of attack.

Alicia wanted to sleep with Armona's Greek-ruler-friend after a conversation she had with her about him before her coronation to power. While she rested on a bed of roses just after the sun rose, she dreamed about her legendary rise to power after surviving "Daybreak."

Her mountainous mound of organic hair was a series of thick curls piled atop her head, beautifully intertwined with her dreadlocks, adorned with specs of gold.

Armona looked over the parade of wealthy elitists that made respective grand entrances to her star-studded event, 1 BC style. Armona gushed, clad in a multi-dress affair. It was not the dress she handpicked the night before. "Oh my, I see my ex-Greek lover answered my invitation. And they say one night never has two good strong legs to stand on." Alicia brushed lint from Armona's shoulders. "Well, he's standing sternly. He's a looker."

"A looker?" Alicia repeated under her breath.

A throaty chuckle. "If only that was true, my friend."

"We're friends?"

"Seriously, Alicia. You must acknowledge your place in my world now.

KHOVAHSH

It is also yours."

"I will, Armona. This is happening fast. I can hardly think."

"You'll be fine, young Queen-to-be."

There was applause for the dark-skinned supernatural and powerful Greek czar and his procession of guests. His eyes were strangers, but his smile...

A thousand slaves carried him on a wheel-less chariot adorned in silk and jewelry. When Alicia dismissed herself, floating behind the concrete platform, the Greek ruler floated up to Armona, kissing her hand. His black skin glistened.

Her face flushed with delight. "I see you made it, Suh'Kyng Drykaten. I didn't think you would come."

Two piercings on either eyebrow sent lightning into his mesmerizing grayish eyes. "When the Supreme Queen of the Dershakney sends an invitation through a school of crows to the Valley of Caves, surely I can make a grand entrance. It's not every day I get to…see you in any capacity."

"Today is not about me. It's about a special moment in supernatural history. Surely you know the heads of hundreds of countries are in attendance."

He lowered his eyes, keeping a smile. "In that case, I'll leave you…"

Alicia strolled along in a dress of silk and diamonds that trailed behind her by one hundred feet. When she reached the main balcony, she took in the damp air. Dark clouds loomed above, blocking the sunlight. A loud trumpet sounded, followed by harps and soft violins. The satin train wrapped her hair in a pile atop her head. She briefly thought about THÈ HÔUSE ÖF THÈ HÔUNDS and a hidden history she had never told Armona about.

Appearing next to Suh'Kyng was the pale servant that obeyed Armona's orders. Alicia was stunned that she wore the multi-layered dress made from thirty shades of pure gold, with a baccarat crystal bodice.

She wears the dress the way you wore her body when you possessed her, came Armona's voice, taking her by surprise.

As the melody calmed everyone, Armona appeared on the platform in mind-blowing royal garments, taking Alicia's breath away. Her dress was gone.

"Members of my Council at the round table, please stand. The peasants in the upper balconies, those in my Cabinet of the order, please stand."

Twenty elite vampires with unspeakable power stood at attention.

"Today is a remarkable day. A day I never dreamed would come. Up until this very moment, Khovahsh was my Enforcer and Executioner, but his role in my government far exceeds what I have set forth. He was only a temporary solution, a stand-in." Thunder boomed, and lightning flashed through the rolling black clouds. "He is a Dragonhead Ancient."

Alicia held her throat.

"I know you're nervous, Alicia," said a voice in her sub-conscious.

"You can't begin to imagine."

"Just go with it. I'm sorry we weren't formally introduced."

Alicia tried to remain stoic but wound up blushing.

"Are all dark Greek men this engaging to a person they don't know?"

"I can only speak for myself," he said through telepathy.

Armona's next words took everyone by surprise.

"Today, Khovahsh renounced the throne of Executioner to return to the foundation of the very hierarchy I am Queen."

Members of her cabinet were in a state of confusion.

"Armona, Queen Mother...without *Daybreak*, how can one take the throne of the Enforcer and the Executioner."

"Ah, but someone has successfully made it through Daybreak. And she is here, now..."

"I'll leave you to your thoughts, Alicia; maybe when you find the time, you can pay me a visit. Let me entertain you."

"Maybe, Suh'Kyng"

Alicia opened her eyes and rose to her feet.

"Ladies and gentlemen, she's not only the Executioner, but she's also your new Queen. Alicia Chay, come stand by me."

Alicia casually floated along a thousand-foot platform.

Her dress sparkled. She was greeted with a standing ovation. As she settled next to the Queen Mother, Armona raised her arms in the air and brought the place to order. "Do you accept the role of Enforcer and Executioner?"

"I have to decide right this instant?" Alicia asked, backing away. She was getting cold feet. She was about to fly away and hide for the rest of her life, but even she knew that was absurd.

"Yes, Alicia. What is wrong? Are you not excited about being a Queen?"

"That I am, Queen Mother."

"Then it is done. Alicia Chay is the new Executioner and Enforcer to the Queen Mother."

Hail to Alicia. The Shadowing Queen Mother.

After a few moments, Armona faced Alicia. She was fond of her. Her eyes glistened. Alicia hesitantly kissed her cheek.

"Now that you accepted your role, there is one more thing I must do." Armona faced the assembly. "Not only has Alicia passed Daybreak, but as of right now, she is now your active Queen Mother."

There was a burst of joy from the eager crowd, but Armona's cabinet and council members grew dark. Armona took the black crown from her head and placed it on Alicia. It spun into a vortex of glittering light.

"All hail the new Queen! In my absence, you will do what she instructs, or you will all die. Do I make myself clear?"

The cabinet members frowned, but nodded in agreement.

ELEVEN
HOW I TOOK THE THRONE

ALICIA CHAY
Thirty-Three Years Later

This was a hard account to think about. It was one of the hardest things that I ever had to do.

I meant, I didn't want to betray the Queen Mother, Armona. She had herself to blame for her ultimate downfall. As ruler of the Supernatural Realm, she had a Council, a much different one than I would have chosen. One that was terrorizing, one-dimensional and had one vision: Armona's way or suffer the death by fire.

I carried out all of her orders as her right hand girl. I did whatever she wanted, no matter what. I made love to her body the way she asked. She was beautiful, wealthy, and elegant.

But then I got tired of being called the Shadowing Queen behind my back by her Council members. "She is a shadow of the real thing, a doppelganger."

On the eve of winter, she summoned me to her Main Study. There were two hundred shelves of scrolls, kish tablets, maps, and treasures.

It was a library within itself. As a matter of fact, it was called *The Library of the Mother*.

She was an amazing beauty. Her smooth skin rivaled alabaster. She had high cheekbones and pearly white teeth.

Her lips were reddish pink.

It was a succulent color that caused my nipples to swell with abandon.

I studied her with fear, trembling….and some sort of magical adoration. I couldn't take my eyes off the woman that made the Seven Wonders of the World pale in comparison. I was moved, emotionally, to tears when I was in her presence. She was a gorgeous woman, a vicious vampire, and a whorish murderer.

She never killed a human with her bare hands. She sent an army of foot soldiers to do the job for her. She hated the thrill of the hunt and the adrenaline rush that accompanied it. She was immune to the law. She commanded others to risk their lives for her safety.

The day she replaced my soul with hers was the day everything changed.

She trapped her soul in my body and transferred mine into hers without my permission. I didn't know how I felt about that. We made love from two different perceptions. The way she tricked me into soul-swapping was an act of deceit, and that prompted me to betray her.

I loved and trusted her as my Leader, and as the Queen Mother. I looked up to her. I loved the way she once stood on a mountain top and read her laws to thousands of vampires in the supernatural realms as a supreme demigod.

They adored her out of fear, but my adoration was separate from the other vampires.

I genuinely loved my mentor.

They were "possessed." They had no choice but to oblige her. I thought about my past life while we bumped pelvises.

My body containing her soul touched me from limb to limb.

There was poetry in her lips.

"I adore you," I lied, using her lips to kiss mine. If my soul was in my body and her soul was in hers, I wouldn't have gone this far. I was attracted to her beauty, not her body.

Why did she trick me. If I was inside myself, I would resist her. I pleasured her body out of obligation, not attraction.

Eagerly, she cupped my breasts and suckled on my neck. Her fangs extracted, but she didn't bite me. She set me afire; my salty rose wept with envy. My body ached. I'd never been vulgar in my life.

Tenderly, she laid me down and stroked my hair. "You adore me? Do you mean what you say?" she asked breathlessly.

Her voice made me tremble. I was stuck, utterly stuck.

I was tongue-tied.

She slid her fingers inside me as my body arched.

I was wet with fear, longing and frustration. Moisture engulfed my pinkish lips.

I was lost within her kisses.

"Yes," I said breathlessly.

"Why?" she asked, putting her lips on mine. She rode my face. I held her amazing buttocks and massaged her insides with my tongue. She narrowed her eyes into mine, pleasured.

"You like the way I taste you?"

She smiled at me and said, "We can't let anybody find out! Keep this between us! Can I trust you? Do you like those other harlots out there? If you give it to them, they'll tell everyone. If you keep your mouth closed, I'm yours, anytime you want me..."

She was powerful.

I wanted that power. Her power. All of it. And leave her with nothing. Aggressively, sweet Armona pushed my legs back and tasted me. I gushed with zeal. "Okay, I had enough!"

After we came together, I made my move. It was now or never. I waited decades for this moment. She didn't expect it or see it coming. I sunk my fangs into her neck, momentarily paralyzing her.

I backed away. "I adore you, but your minions and your cabinet members do not respect me! "

She couldn't move. "How could you betray my trust?" she asked. "After giving you the world, this is how you show your gratitude?"

"Khovahsh forced me into your world after your obey or die summons that came wrapped with swans and a green-faced witch. I was called a Shadowing Queen Mother, a replica. You burned animals with fire."

Golden dust encircled her with flashes of lightning.

"After all I've done for you, I had to find out about your betrayal and your deceit this way? During an act of passionate love making? I want nothing to do with you! I will run your empire and make it greater than you ever could. I mean exactly what I say! It is now mine. I will destroy your Council of imbeciles! I will eat all of their hearts!"

Armona began turning to porcelain.

I was in her body!

Her resilient body!

And I made her a prisoner inside my biological flesh as punishment for forcing me into a supernatural life, and for her unforgivable crimes!

Her body was my host, mine to control.

Armona glared at me with hate, anger, and frustration! For an instant, I wished I was human again, so I could forget this ever happened!

But her body felt good. Her veins, bone structure and her mind superimposed into my essence. I was her, finally!

She wasn't herself. She wasn't the queen any longer. I was no longer a Shadowing Queen.

I must bury her body.

When the golden light vanished, Armona was a marble and granite statue with sapphire eyes. I wrapped my arms around her and rose in the air like dry heat, numb inside. I flew to the the Nile River, dropped deep within its depths and buried her under the turf the waters rest upon, for the rest of eternity!

Once I rose from the waters of the Nile, I flew east.

In instant anger, the Dragonhead Ancients dug her up, but I intercepted and buried her in a forest three hundred feet in the earth. I released her from her marble prison, replacing it with poisonous thorns in a coffin magically sealed shut. I was the Queen Mother now. I jumped in the air, flying away, but I was struck by lightning and knocked from the clouds by a mind-boggling sound wave.

After I crash landed on an empty field, the ground opened with a deep rumbling. Leaves draped me. Restraints made from roots and soil grabbed both of my ankles and locked themselves, burning into my skin!

I screamed from the pain. Ghosts escaped my mouth and turned into ashes! Dark clouds parted and a ghoulish hole of blue and orange flames burned in the center of the sky.

Sulfur fell on my hair, turning parts of it to ashes.

A portal opened up, swirling with abandon. Roots restrained my wrists. I was being granted the power of the supreme Queen Mother.

On my naked frame appeared a sheath dress made of beads.

The head of a cobra was my crown.

Repulsed, I was against it, even though I was a lover of

animals.

The Queen Mother detested them!

A lump formed in my throat!

The ghosts that escaped lunged forward from my gut.

Animal souls cried for mercy in my veins.

Animal souls!

She never killed vampires or humans. She killed animals. Her council members abused their power of social world order. They pushed her agenda, but they didn't think of the opposite of that system going into effect.

Everything started from thought. The soul of the animals returned Heavenward, or was it really heaven?

Did animals die and return to the Father?

The Queen Mother never believed in the Father I once had, but as Aten, the Sun God, something I couldn't see, but I knew was there.

A wicked being flew from the hole in the sky of ghoulish blue flames, and the face of a vampire dragon peeked through the Portal of the Roots!

The Dragonhead Ancients!

I gasped when I saw Armona's spirit beside me in judgment.

Both of us, together.

"How dare you break the Oath, Armona!"

"I deeply apologize, Dragonhead Ancients!"

"You are not to switch souls with another vampire as the Queen Mother. You disturbed the natural order of things."

"I am in love with her!" said Armona's spirit. I knew she was, and I used that against her. "I was going to ask her to be my wife! We were going to rule together!"

I was in shock!

My soul seeped from Armona's Body, enough to form a beautiful ghost, a replica of me, in flesh form. I touched my face, the face in front of me, framed with the skin of the former Queen Mother.

I had Armona's tongue, her eyes, and her power. My essence was still drying on her lips. The memories rocked me senseless. I was held captive by the turn of events, and the hostile exchange of power.

I swore!

This was overwhelming!

To be given this experience! Ah!

I was breathless, wondering what the forbidden fruit between her legs tasted like. I had a burning desire to find out.

The dragon spat fire at us. I did my best to knock it away, but it was too powerful.

When I fell back towards the earth, Armona's spirit vanished. I braced myself as the fire connected with Armona's skin wrapped around my soul.

The next thing I knew I crashed through the domed ceiling of the Grande Bedroom of the Queen Mother.

It was my bedroom now.

With debris and stained glass all around me, the Dragonhead Ancient's voice filled the room.

"Armona has been put to rest as her punishment. Her body is your burden. Your flesh is her dungeon, sealed in a wooden coffin of thorns baring her face, but we must know where you buried her."

"I will never tell you!" And the voice was gone.

My flesh was Armona's dungeon, buried deep in the earth.

I'd never tell the Dragonhead Ancients her location.

KHOVAHSH

Forty Centuries Later….

THE CONTINENT OF VENCREASHIA

My three-structure-empire was on one thousand acres of land, located in Vencreashia. It was my empire and my empire alone. Violent thunderstorms spewed from poisonous clouds.

Twenty-inch acid rain provided a barrier around its seven-billion-dollar foundation derived from the coral of the sea.

Protected by mountains that stretch thousands of feet with astronomical peaks. The continent itself was hidden from humans and the supernatural eye. Majestic alarms guard its existence, as well as the massive landscaping of its one hundred and forty-four forests.

Forty centuries ago, I overthrew Armona, Queen Mother, took her paradise as my haven, and turned my back on **THE HOUSE OF THE HOUNDS**.

It was a split-second decision that cost me dearly. Turning my back on the humans I robbed of life was hard. I turned them into the damned and cut them off when I became Queen Mother. I never thought of them again.

I replaced her signature with mine on every deed she ever owned. In my possession was ten million square miles of the earth, from the supernatural side of things.

May Armona continue to rot.

May she never rise again.

Declaration of The Dershakney
Supernatural Constitution

As the acting, officiating Queen of this Supernatural System of Things on a planet wrought with evil, systematic stigmas and mentally crippled mortals thirsty for wealth and prestige, I put into order a crime of treason if any vampire, ghoul, witch, mutant, so on and so forth, inhabits any human body without my authorization, shall die without judgment or trial...

Number one. No host bodies. Number 2. No vampires should live in another vampire body without the authorization from the queen. Number 3 to speak ill against the cabinet, or my council members was treason, and espionage, you must be burned at the stake, and your ashes dumped into a pit of fire...

HIDDEN CHAPTER

ALICIA CHAY

Present Day

I settled down in the corner of a small diner in Naples, Florida. I pulled a hat low over my eyes as the server approached me. I ordered a coffee, black. Once she brought it, I opened my purse and pulled out a pill bottle of human blood.

After I popped the security cap, I poured it into my coffee and used my nail to stir it in. I had a lot of things on my mind but not enough time to exhaust anything. The place was an unusual blend of local patrons, an out-of-town couple, and an undercover meth head.

Once I took a sip, I closed my eyes and grooved to the blues music that filtered into my ears from the radio. It relaxed me. My mind opened up. I saw myself when I was a human. I had to be about seventeen-years old, a time in my life I was extremely happy, or so I tried to convince myself...

3 BCE: Chad, Africa

There was a big celebration, marking the 105th Anniversary of our village. My family and friends were celebrating. Meh-Yok, my Elder, informed me that we were granted immunity through the government, but the Elders and the adults were shipped into town to work for their "masters," even though they weren't forcibly in slavery.

I was happy that I wasn't of age, but when I turned eighteen, a day I dreaded, I would automatically be sent to work.

Like the women before me, my smooth hands would become callused and hard-looking, like reptilian skin.

My pretty face would grow tired, and my thin body would become worn.

You see…women had no stake, no claim and absolutely no rights. It was told to me that women were considered property. We were not looked at as people or beings with simple liberties in life.

Everything was monitored by the Elders, a group of thirteen old men that were meddlesome. I didn't speak to them unless I had to. It wasn't a requirement.

As an introvert, I didn't say too much when I was younger. The men took advantage of us every chance that they could. I had my share of mishaps, especially after getting my first menstrual cycle in the middle of my twelfth birthday, in front of a sea of people.

The music stopped. I stood there, embarrassed, dressed in soiled cloth that smelled of resin, cinnamon, and olive oil while my peers poked fun at me.

Sometimes, I didn't know how I got through the day.

Living in the village was depressing, but I had more good times than the bad.

Since I was not of age, I didn't go through the atrocities the Elders and the adults had to when they were at the marketplace for labor.

The men were respectable, but they only respected women because they were trying to get between their legs.

Fortunately, I wasn't ready to give out firsts, seconds, and thirds. I saved myself for the man I would fall in love with.

I was an immensely popular girl in the village, but I wasn't loose or whorish.

I had thoughts and desires but never told anyone…

KHOVAHSH

I was a private person. I enjoyed my own company. My love for people died outside the gates of the Village.

My life was all about love, my family, friends and the Village of one thousand people.

By law, we could have no more than that; we didn't have many sources of water, but all of us (men, women, and children) had to bathe together in the Great Bath twice a day.

Once, when the sun rose on the crowing rooster, and again when the moon began her trek towards the stars.

We had black linen over our eyes. We bathed and washed the day away from our exhausted bodies with resin.

Once we were done, we held hands and felt along one another's arms and fingers to find the missing links, and we formed a great line. The Elders entered the waters barefooted, holding the bottoms of golden robes that repelled water.

One by one, the Elders handed cotton to us. We exited the Great Bath and dried off by rows of towering trees. We never saw one another's body. I hated the Great Bath. I hated when the gates of the Village closed after sun down, just after the last of the working men arrived back from grueling labor in the Marketplace.

Young adult women were required to return to the Village before sundown, and the middle age working women had until the sun disappeared, or they were beaten by the Elders with sugar cane. Very seldom that happened. The women were well trained by the Elders, who were suppressed by a government of Pharaohs.

Women were submissive to their fathers, brothers and male friends; when a woman or a girl walked by a male, he must lower his head, and she must keep her head high, and avert only her eyes. That was a sign of respect. I accepted life on its terms until my 18th birthday was on the horizon.

JA'BREEL LE'DIAMOND

I was in the Grand Bath with the other women. Our breasts were bare. Their men were naked, turned the opposite way.

A moan escaped the group, alerting those that were watching over us. When the soldiers of the Village discovered that Larshaw was the culprit, having relations with one of the males under the water, they were seized.

Meh-Yok ordered four tribe members to nab the male criminal and tie him up. He put up a fight, but the men overpowered him. Once they tied him to a tree, facing forward, Meh-Yok spat in his face and castrated him with a sharp object. I vomited in the water from shock.

He bled to death. Blood trailed from his wound to the waters we bathed. Absent-mindedly, Meh-Yok tossed his penis into the river, and the current wash it away.

Larshaw was tied to an oak root. She kept her head high and refused to cry. After one of the tribe members put black linen over her face, the other three tribe members held her arms, legs, and her midsection.

Seven king cobras were in place all around her with a spell put on them by Meh-Yok.

The snakes would strike her if she tried to escape.

Meh-Yok used sharp objects to ensure she would never bear children.

It was then that I realized all of us, women, would be castrated so we could never have babies. Anyone over eighteen was already sterilized.

And now that my 18th birthday was on the horizon, Meh-Yok suddenly had his eyes on me.

Closing my eyes, I shuddered.

I put on my garments and made my way back to the Village.

I'd kill him dead if he tried to cut out my tubes....

TWELVE
MEGA CHURCH

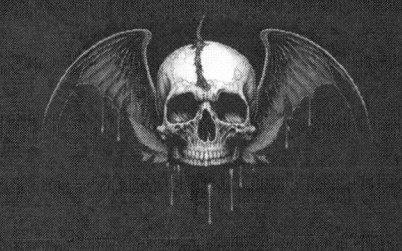

KHOVAHSH BURGOOS
Spring of 2002

A hidden fortress under the sands of Egypt, Africa

Khovahsh Burgoos was a nine-thousand-year-old relic, stuck at the age of twenty-five, the age he was when he transitioned to a life of complete misery and darkness.

He had regal skin of lacquered chocolate with tea-colored antique eyes. Khovahsh was a notorious body-shifting reincarnate that had a black soul with no sense of self or happiness.

He'd reincarnated himself so frequently that he was still aware of who he truly was. As a result, his addiction became the human hosts he randomly occupied without their knowledge.

He didn't care about his life. When he was human, before the shadows, he adored his mother, but he didn't love himself.

Hey, that was me. Enough of the third-person lingo. I never cared about myself. Being born to inevitably perish sealed inside me the death of life. Right after I was born, I began to die.

So why was I here? I was a lost soul that looked tempting to the ladies when I was in a male human host. I wanted to forget that I was a cursed vampire with various imprints. I toyed with humans like it was Christmas.

I was talented at many things, yet I couldn't bring myself to believe it, believe in it, or believe in my ability.

Those were three strikes against me that changed me for the worse. At one point in my life I was approached by mafia types with billion-dollar entertainment ties to be their "Star Killer." This gig didn't last long. I wound up killing off the entire Don Milia Dynasty after meeting an artist named Ajani.

Humans didn't tell me what to do or how to do it. I did my best to stay in a murderous blood bath of terror so I never had to be reminded of the time I was human. I didn't miss being submissive to a system designed to keep me oppressed. Being a demi-god came with its perks. I was wealthy beyond measure.

I was a member of the Dragonhead Ancients, a trillion-dollar enterprise governed by me, Raynedrakin, Don Sharps and Doppelganger, my brothers.

Nonetheless, my past haunted me in unspeakable ways. Skeletons with the flesh of my flesh and blood of my blood were neatly juxtaposed in my subconscious mind.

It reminded me of a time when life was simpler, back during the time of the Roman church and an empire that changed the Sabbath from Saturday to Sunday without God's permission.

I didn't know how true that was, but it was something I heard over time.

I killed those with countless false idol worshippers who put the rich and their flesh before their needs of themselves.

I'd come to realize that the weakness of the flesh was the kryptonite to mortal thought, fantasy, and desire.

The distractions humans created for themselves in a system of control fascinated me. Humans were born into a devilish matrix of social security numbers and subliminal conditioning through regularly scheduled programming.

Quite honestly, my inner self talk felt aimless. I didn't mean that in a harsh way.

As I lounged in my quarters beneath the sands of Egypt, random thoughts came to me that failed to connect. Many topics occupied my brain, from the government to society, to religion, to conspiracy theories. Was that my fault humans preoccupied themselves with the very things I brought up?

Why was I enslaved by the government and turned into property when I was a mortal? I was waste in an aquarium that others must clean up. Forced to become something outside of myself. Supernatural beings were slaves as well. I floated around elegantly, inconspicuously, careful not to bring attention. I was mischievous, but I disliked drama. I remained colorful and free.

The scent of fresh blood flaked toward me like snow because I believed it would. I'd dash towards my food option and flap my tail, famished, hungry, needing, feasting…laying, spent, tiresome, resting, and waking up in hell, a nightmare.

To repeat the process all over again. That was my existence. I was too tormented to enjoy life, even though I was dead, but alive… if that made sense.

It didn't matter if you understood or not. If you were into numbers, one thing was evident, two things for sure. I did not like people. If I could kill every human at the drop of a hat, I most certainly wouldn't hesitate. I'd jump to do so. I enjoyed draining them of blood. Honestly, I stopped caring about people when I witnessed the slave trade.

The beginnings of it, the preliminary stages. I observed thousands of dark-colored people being taken from their families. We had the same complexion.

They were beaten, chained, branded, and shackled with hundreds of others—in a state of traumatic shock.

Initially, I didn't care about mortal affairs. I didn't ascertain the thought of helping any of them, despite their cries of misunderstanding and pain. I drained numerous victims of their precious blood.

I wasn't into love, so eating their hearts simply turned me off. I didn't break bread with them.

Never had I visited their grieving mothers. I never sent flowers in their memory, nor did I want to.

Enslaved people were placed on the lowest levels of the cargo ships. I remembered The House of Dakar. It was a reception area for transporting the enslaved all over the world, not just to what would eventually become the United States of America.

Huge sails struck fear throughout the region. Expensive material and large sums of money was the foundation of those rugged-looking cargo vessels. I watched from the shadows. I was hungry and dying of thirst. I wanted to feed on them, but I couldn't bring myself to go through with it.

The slaves were already at their lowest. I hated myself for being weak. If my brothers found out they would destroy me. I wouldn't make it easy for them if it came to that.

Moneyed men with black hearts symmetrically and strategically aligned the slaves side by side.

They were trapped in the worst nightmare of their lives. For some, it would be the last nightmare they ever had.

To die in misery says a lot about how people lived their lives or were forced to live therein.

The enslaved were innocent bystanders caught in a web of expansion, sheep prepped for slaughter, expanding unseen kingdoms. The slave trade as a whole was about controlling humanity. Getting man and society to do what the laws of empires and kingdoms required.

Through excessive force, society's free will was disabled, taking the choice away, influencing humanity to submit to the authority of a crooked system. The ones in power dangled tortured humans before the natives for them to obey.

In the darkness of foul-smelling ships was precious cargo.

Above them were a few galas on the upper levels. Moneyed foreigners wined and dined under the moonlight as those ships cruised the friendly seas.

The stars shine down on them, playing on the cuts of their expensive diamonds, diamonds stolen from Africa.

Below, the slaves cried out with everything in them, everything they were as people, as a people enslaved, as a kidnapped people, to God, Aten for most, to help them. To free them from bondage.

Slaves were forced to read a bible when they were ignorant of education and forbidden from participating in it.

They were considered property.

Since the new covenant was activated when Christ was crucified and drew his last breath, the Devil hath been building his paradise here on earth at a breathtaking rate, according to a random Pastor I watched on television. I started to turn the channel, but he was fascinating. He took my mind off of slavery.

"The evolution of it all, from where we came, to what we see now, is nothing short of extraordinary," according to the man of the cloth, "not that I'm praising the Devil because I am not and never will," he concluded amidst cheers from the audience. It was a packed house. Every seat was filled.

It fascinated me how programmed the members were.

JA'BREEL LE'DIAMOND

I didn't believe in anything. I'd been to hell and back. I only had myself for protection. I loved rainbows, it didn't mean I believed in one.

Wasn't I a demigod? If I had to make a choice, I would lean towards the life of Christ if I was still human. It was better to choose the winning side over the side that used musical deceit to program the world, except in places without technology or outside communication.

Yes, I just might believe in Christ since the darkness tried too hard to deprogram society from its own wit and confuse them enough to influence how and when they use free will.

But as for now, that wasn't on my list of things to do. The television pastor, selling faith, was doing well. A toll-free number scrolled across the bottom of two projection screens, and televisions in fifteen million households.

"Right now, America, we are hurting. Homeless people are living in their cars, the poor can't catch a break and the less fortunate needs your help."

He faced the audience with a crooked smile. "If you can spare just a dollar, or a thousand, I urge you to call the number on your screen. Its important to be a cheerful giver. We must understand that we are all one paycheck from being homeless ourselves!"

The phone lines were lit like fireworks. People from all walks of life filled the collection plates with an impressive amount of money. Pastor Dacra pulled out his checkbook and pledged a thousand dollars on a fake check.

The crowd roared with praise. He readjusted his earpiece, and continued to read from a TelePrompter.

"I just received word that we have reached our goal. It amazes me how America can come together for an incredible cause. Until we get the final numbers, I'll keep preaching. God is right on time, ladies and gentleman and in that, his presence is limited.

"When you're the Almighty, you don't need to make a spectacle out of thy power. He exercises it at the right moments and on his timetable. He is a chief that sits back and observes his tribe from his throne; so powerful is his staff. Your pledges and donations are appreciated."

The crowd chanted their praises.

I closed my eyes as the Pastor's sermon filtered into my ears.

The Devil was banned from heaven, and out of anger he did the finest job he could do; convince the world that he didn't exist to justify axing "God" from public schools and the pledge of allegiance, separation of church and state. Francis Scott Key wrote the most racist song ever, The Star Spangled Banner. Read the lyrics!

I knew who everyone pledged allegiance to and what god they trusted, as printed on the back of paper currency. The Adversary sought revenge and vengeance. He was forbidden from ever entering heaven again.

Through a blinding rage, he began laying the blueprint and shaping kingdoms. He granted prestigious power to overachievers and free thinkers. The side effects spread like wildfire throughout the world today, with project computers taking over in Y2K, the real end of the world.

As cool air blew over me, I opened my eyes as a member of the congregation. The energy was through the roof. I witnessed Pastor Danny Dacra's knack for sensationalized worship for profit. Like attracted like. It transitioned me here from my Egyptian chambers. I applauded Pastor Dacra for effect, to remain inconspicuous. Since his evening service was after nightfall, I blended in with sanctified humans nursing a thousand untold secrets without fear of the sun bursting me into flames.

His image protruded on two wide projection screens.

"We are nearing the end of our privacy and 100% human thought; let's test the human mind after interaction with machines and computers via the Internet, the whole nine. Release it all to them. Lab rats we are, scapegoats we become, of all kinds and all races."

With hundreds of others, I rose to my feet, clapping and whistling excessively.

Clad in a black suit, I adjusted my reading glasses, even though I didn't need them.

"Let's keep humans in debt. Release Trojan horses (viruses) on computers they used their hard-earned money to purchase—identity theft, the whole nine."

His darling wife, doubling as the church secretary in the great old state of Texas, brought him a hand towel and a glass of water for his parched throat.

He took a swig and ignored the towel. After a quick kiss, he continued.

"Everyone involved cashed in on their eagerness to buy things that keep them distracted, so the powers that be can work together and plan public ruin; when the time is right. One World, One Government will be a reality. Bibles will be banned."

His fans exalted him, a pathetic millionaire that robbed them blindly through the collection plate and the phone lines.

"Preach, Pastor!"

"Say that, then!"

"They don't hear you in the back and upper balconies, Pastor!"

He gripped the microphone and descended four stairs onto the lower level of the auditorium.

He roamed the aisles, shaking a few hands here and there. "Humanity has lost its soul! Introduce machines into the workplace, integrate them into regular society, I should say, to make it all plausible. Allow humans to become dependent on them.

"Spend the next ten years using computers, the year 2000 through 2011, quite possibly, it's too early to tell right now.

"Once this is done, the powers that be will observe closely as they put everything online. We are social experiments. We will be allowed to shop from home, talk to our families and reconnect with long lost friends and relatives. Over time, we will run a business or make our own videos, even publish own books from computers, the digital pulse of mankind."

I didn't know what came over me, but the instant I sneezed, thirty framed religious photos of white Jesus fell from the walls and shattered on the floors. Everyone fell silent. The Pastor's mouth vanished. A great flash blinded us. With a piercing rumbling, the ceiling above the main assembly caved in.

Chunks of brick rained down on the north end of the assembly, crushing people in the audience. A centuries-old vampire landed behind the Pastor. He shoved his fist into the Pastor's back. He donned black tar and gold. Lava and volcanic lightning energized his crown; enormous ivory horns curled from his skull down to his ankles.

His eyes were traces of brimstone. Thousands of frantic people ran for the exits, screaming and shouting. I remained where I stood. I didn't run from war.

"Khovahsh..." The unknown vampire spoke via the Pastor's voice, like a ventriloquist. It was deeper than an abyss.

"Who are you, and how do you know my identity?" I asked.

The vampire's face swirled into the Pastor's with devastating accuracy.

"That's not important. I have a message for you."

"My business hours are closed for the evening. I'm too powerful for messages, surely you must not know who I am."

His natural black face returned, more resilient and refined. "Very well. I leave you with this. Either destroy Alicia Chay and her animal treaty, or I will."

As he transitioned into a half vampire, half gator, he bit off the Pastor's arm and chomped it down his throat. Dragon wings exploded from either side of my shoulders. My black suit turned to dust, revealing a cloak of leather and sharp blades on my waistline.

"You won't touch a hair on her body, that I can attest to."

"Ah, you say that like it'll come to pass."

I jumped from the second tier to the stage, a few feet from the pulpit.

"She is the acting Queen Mother. Under the Dershakney, she will be...."

My mouth vanished from my face, erasing the rest of my words. He grunted, amused. "Pardon my manners. My name is the same as your missing lips—Muzzle. As you can see, I piss on the Freedom of Speech and censorship."

I stumbled all over the place, holding on to the pews to keep my balance. I was depleted and weak. Muzzle floated over to me with his fist still in the Pastor's back.

"What, sir...? Are you trying to say something?" Muzzle dangled the Pastor like a rag doll. "Remember what I said, Khovahsh."

He released the Pastor, using an elongated blade to chop his head off. Jumping backward, Muzzle sprinted up to the Pastor and kicked his head through the stained-glass dome above.

Before I could react, Muzzle became an enormous crocodile. He used his natural speed to gobble up as many humans as he could by biting their heads off.

I flew at him, and set him on fire. After a screech, Muzzle burst into glittering particles that left the Pastor's mega church filled with worshipers burning to the ground. It was complete chaos. People lay dead, screaming and running, pressing their hands over their mutilated ears. I didn't care about their pain. I flew towards the Pastor's wife, a woman that abused her children.

After I drained her dry, I was rejuvenated. I took pleasure in watching the light slowly diminish in her eyes, silencing her untold secrets. "Your children will be better off without you!"

I kicked her through the burning hole of the dome. I flapped my wings. A dragon snout formed on my face. The flames tore through the mega church. I debated whether I should inform Alicia that her life was in danger. I flew through the fire, and continued to let the place of worship for profit burn. An enormous cloud of smoke polluted the city in a matter of seconds. I had a bird's eye view as I flew east.

News crews and choppers were headed towards the mega church.

THIRTEEN
FLASHBACK

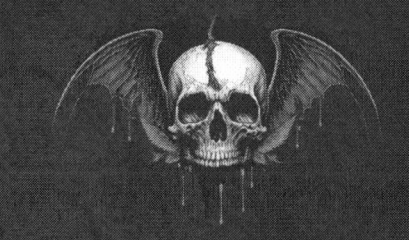

ALICIA CHAY

I had a flashback. It came out of the reddish blue. After a long, grueling night of hunting, I closed my eyes. I was haunted by reflections of my past life.

Instead of fighting it, I embraced it. To see change, I must do something different.

To get a different result, I must change my mind. When something became familiar, it became dangerous. I played it safe without taking risks. I did that once upon a time. I tried to walk, talk, and think like a mortal when I was a vampire.

I couldn't become great if I didn't learn myself all over again after I was turned. I remembered my first home, before THÈ HÔUSE ÖF THÈ HÔUNDS, before I was Queen of anything. I resided with golden-crowned flying foxes: bats.

I discovered the cave by accident. It was covered with immaculate moss and magnificent lavender. I slept in the cave upside down with vampire bats of the Chiropteran Order. For the first seven months of my vampire life, I foraged with different classes of them.

I took a liking to vampire bats. They fed on blood. I wasn't a fan of insects, nor did I enjoy feeding on nectar. I didn't know how to fly, so I watched them soar. I studied them like I was a scholar.

Unbelievably they were more agile in flight than anything I'd ever seen. I'd seen the eagle, I'd watched owls, even though they were lazy birds; they like to who-who-who-ooh! on tree branches with big wide eyes under the moonlight, and I needed more action in my life.

After four months of living with them, the bat king revealed himself. He slept right beside me the whole time, laying dormant. I didn't think bats had a leader. He taught me how to sprint on open patches of land through his incredible skills. He was patient with me.

At first, I tripped and fell on my face. He laughed but didn't utter a word. I was enraged.

"What is so hilarious?" He pointed at me, squealing with delight. I got right back up and tried again. I became faster as time went by. I was a vampire. All I had was time, so I mastered it.

The Bat King and I made love every night. He was one of the most handsome dark-skinned specimens I'd ever seen, yet we never spoke a word to each other, nor did we care.

Our moans and cries of ecstasy were enough for me. His lovemaking kept me sane in the scheme of things. We were attached to each other. We were beautiful together.

I remember jumping in the air. I was flying and lost my wit. I plummeted toward the earth. I nearly died from fear, but I refused to give up.

I was drained. I couldn't stop my body from its impending death.
Before my body could make an impact, the Bat King appeared out of thin air.

He caught me with his extended wings and brought me to his arms. We stared into each other's eyes.

We rose fifteen-thousand feet into the stars.

As we levitated, he blushed and looked away from me.

Beneath us were dark clouds. Above us, the moon cast a ghost light, causing us to glow, glitter, sparkle, and shine.

"If only you can speak. That would complete a moment I shall never forget."

I closed my eyes in his arms. He began to hum, taking me by surprise. I opened my eyes. We were dressed in gold regal attire. He lowered us unto silhouettes embedded with specs of stardust. We stood on them. Diamonds adorned every part of my body. The glow from the moon lit my hair with undeniable abracadabra. "You've been hurt when you were human," he began, humming with soft tempos. We slowly danced above bloodshed, wars, murder, and poverty.

I touched his face. "You can talk."

"Yes, I can, Alicia." It took a moment for me to say anything. I didn't know how I felt. "I only speak to those that think of others before themselves, which was no one in my centuries-old life, until you."

He took a few steps back, waving his hands.

Clouds of glittering dust formed a table before us. Next to an orchid centerpiece were two golden goblets of blood, sweetened with the richest minerals the earth had to offer. His captivating eyes glittered dangerously.

"Only the best for you."

I took a sip. "This is very good."

"What do you taste in the blood?" he asked, taking me off guard.

I smacked my lips. "I taste hints of grape, mint, pineapple, orange, resin, basil, cinnamon, spices, and watermelon."

"Life, Alicia. Those elements were fertilized shortly after the Persian military invaded Kush and robbed its inhabitants of their resources and gold, enslaving its people. Our people, Alicia. The soil absorbed the bloodshed and bared the very crops you…enjoy."

"Our people, how, when we're both vampires."

"You never asked for my name, Alicia."

"What is your name?"

The gold-crowned bat shed his DNA, body, and features, rising as a half human owl. Still retaining his human features, he stood ten feet tall.

"My name is Reinkarnation. I take many forms."

"Truly magnificent, Bat King."

"Unfortunately, he is no more, but my heart and humbleness remain. After this moment, you will never see me again, but I must warn you, Alicia. You have only been a vagabond for a short span, but your path will be wrought with great loss, deception, and peril. In the blood, Life, I gave you is your mustard seed of faith that only you can muster."

"Why are you telling me all this?"

"I saw you moments before you were turned. You ran through the scary woods of your village after a man that didn't love you. I saw your face when you caught him and your best friend love making under the moonlight. I know what was on your heart…."

"But, how? How do you…" My eyes welled with tears. I said I would never look back, and the words from a stranger I fell in love with looked back for me. I gazed into his eyes. He made love to me above the clouds, where we had privacy. He was slow and tender. His warm kisses made me tremble.

It was everything I could have ever imagined. When it ended, he rose to his feet, helping me rise to mine. He was my height now. My neck hurt from looking at a ten-foot-tall owl.

"I didn't mean to interrupt what you were saying just before we made love."

"Interrupt me how?"

"You said you knew what was on my heart."

"Yes, I do," he answered. I immediately asked, "How?"

"I knew what was on your heart when you caught your loved ones deceiving you because I was the bat that turned you into a vampire!"

The breath left my body. I began to shake with betrayal and rage.

"You're my Maker…?" I was in complete shock.

"I still feel the ice of your eyes as I flew into your mouth and into your heart. My intent was to slaughter you, but the weight of your pain and heartbreak won me over. I let you live, Alicia. Meh-Yok was going to sterilize you!"

Impulsively, I slit his throat and pushed him off the clouds. It was an automatic reaction. Flashes of lightning ferociously lit the sky. As his blood rained down below, he fell into a volcano to his death. Even if I had extended wings, I would have turned a blind eye.

Now that my Maker was a charred owl, the Bat King single-handedly turned me away from animals. It was something I didn't wish to get into, but I must. I was filled with blinding hatred from his betrayal, and his confession.

The Treaty of the Animals wasn't always a dream of mine. I didn't always love them. Reinkarnation played on my ignorance. After he revealed that he was the one that killed my human self, it sent me on a murderous rage. I slaughtered any and every winged creature I could get my hands on. I hunted them down. I adjusted my filter and fed on rabbits, possums, deer, and other creatures. If it had blood I fed on it to the brink of gluttony.

The next few months were filled with death and blood. I didn't know if I was heartbroken or if my heart was in pieces. I drank the blood of owls and became mentally inclined. I drank the blood of the reptiles and became a blind savage. I ate frogs and mastered the art of movement. I drank hippopotamus blood for strength and endurance.

I refused to feed on humans during that phase of my life.

A zebra was my method of travel. Riding one was thrilling. His black and white stripes against my dark skin was soothing. My breasts bounced as if my hair had more volume and class.

The way the zebra galloped over the wet grass just after rainfall was my absolute favorite time. The air was moist and crisp.

I walked away feeling brand new, until the dawning sun reminded me of who I really was.

Breaking away from the bat family was extremely hard. We bonded, we hunted and we slept upside down together. They were my family, but not anymore. The entire time my Maker had been secretly watching me. A connection I didn't know I shared with him lured me to the cave when I first discovered it. I was being observed while he blended in with the other bats.

Unfortunately, their Bat King deceived me. I felt I should be the Queen. They were birds of prey. Long story short, I killed all those furry mammals faster than I could wink.

I drank from forty-thousand bats as if they were only one, without a drop of blood wasted.

FOURTEEN
GENOCIDE

ALICIA CHAY

I was resting in a heavily forested area just before the morning's dew covered my tired body. I didn't want to move. Being a vampire was what I made it. I attracted the energy and the vibration I sent out. I was about to witness the sunrise. I was nervous, but I faced my fears. I waited until the first hint of pink penetrated the darkness, before I drifted above the waters, the grass, and the trees. I wished I could forget about Reinkarnation, my Maker.

I wept like my best-friend died. There was a connection to him I didn't understand. It felt like I murdered my father. Bouts of nausea hit me like a ton of stone. I wanted to go higher than he took me. I rose further than fifteen-thousand feet.

There was enough oxygen in my lungs to keep me alive. The instant I saw the arch of the sun, I flew towards it. I was shaded by the tail-end of the night.

The sun was midway past the horizon.

A few moments later, the sun passed the threshold of the mountains and the sea. A trace of smoke rose from my left arm. It stung a little. I was addicted. I wanted more. How much could I take?

I wanted to test my limits, find my boundaries.

The sun was ninety-eight percent in the sky.

Blisters appeared on my forehead. Black smoke covered my body.

I burst into flames. I closed my eyes and opened them in a heavily-shaded forest, in an unfamiliar territory.

I was healed.

I had a bout with the sun, but I barely escaped. The sun was the victor. Light smothered the dark. Without light, there was no life.

I put it out of my mind and went hunting. I sprinted around trees and jumped over enormous pot holes in the earth. I drained a warrior that slept by a waterfall. I was revitalized. I didn't kill him, but I left him panting with confusion.

Once I burped, I lay on a mound of fallen Spanish moss out in the wilderness and fell asleep. I dreamed of an African sunrise, but I was prohibited from escaping the sunset.

I awakened to the glow of the moon, my coat of arms beneath a glittering sky. I wished I never spent time with my Maker or gave him my heart. I felt foolish.

Again, I wept. The blood I drank from his golden goblet filtered out of me through my bloody tears. I remembered beauty. I remembered strength; I remembered the people that I loved in the past.

And now that I rest on the Spanish moss, I thought about my mother. Unfortunately, she died shortly after giving birth to me. Her eyes remained a permanent gaze on a scattered sunrise rot with doom. I didn't know this until after I became a vampire.

There were some discrepancies that I never cared to investigate. If I was afraid of the answer, why search for the truth? The truth was not always what it appeared to be.

KHOVAHSH

It never sets you free. I was bamboozled, and brainwashed.

The truth caused problems; the truth broke up relationships and pushed people away.

How did the truth free you when it enslaved you?

How do you pluck truth from the depths of blackness when only light can penetrate it? Sometimes I didn't care for the truth. It hurt too much.

Mysticism was a thing I had no interest in, only because of the life I was thrust into.

I didn't remember as a human giving worship to anything.

I was born into oppression at the very hands that had the same shade of color as mine. I never understood why, during those times, my own kind hated me and the Villagers.

Why were we oppressed? Why didn't we have the freedom to do what we wanted, and to come and go as we pleased, like I did as a vampire.

The only relief came after nightfall when the master and the Elders retired for the evening. We were owned by dark skin folks.

I used to cry myself to sleep at night. Why was I born into a system of deceit and corruption? Why did I have to deal with the aftermath of a game I never chose?

I dealt with it. On my 18th birthday, before Meh-Yok could castrate me, I was turned into a vampire by Reinkarnation.

I was forced into another system of oppression, a supernatural system. I was the walking dead. I was the air I breathed.

I thought about bursting into flames when I battled the sun. I transcended to smoke that stung my eyes and made me cry.

I was what I was supposed to be. I chose not to be anything I refused to see.

I wouldn't let others dictate my destiny.

I vowed it on my life! I refused to become anything I may

fear. Fear was a mishap of joy that took a wrong turn when I was supposed to be happy. I remembered when I used to read scrolls.

    I would sneak into the master's room and I educated myself.

    I studied his lips when he read something.

    If my master read a scroll, I pretended to be cleaning.

I matched the movement of his lips to the hieroglyphics on the scroll. Drawings of animals and objects fascinated me. I educated myself so no one could take advantage of me.

    Now I was the enchanting ruler and upholder of the Treaty of the Animals. Animal tribes followed my rules of governing.

    We had one common goal, and that was to maintain the balance between good and evil within our realms.

    I created a Treaty I was proud of.

    It served two purposes.

    The signatures I collected meant that I mastered three things: my thoughts, power, and discipline.

    I honed my skills by killing those who illegally slaughtered animals and I spared humans that loved and adored them.

    The alliance I formed with the animals, creatures, and creepy things of the earth, the reptiles of the forest, the fowl of the air, and the creatures of the sea, for their protection, was a constitution of sorts.

    We must all survive in this life among each other, tolerating each other for our differences and playing the hand we'd been dealt. Staying in their lanes was necessary. The Treaty was an exceptionally beautiful thing.

    As much blood, gore, pain, and disappointment I'd seen in life, I still found beauty amongst the living.

    The origin of the Treaty came forth centuries after my encounter with a reptile. I forgot when it happened. I was a regular mortal. I chased behind someone, a woman named Larshaw. We were headed to the sacred forest just after dark.

She was much faster than me. I had trouble keeping up. I ran, and I ran, ignoring the terrible pounding in my head, bouncing from my skull. Blood pumped as fast as it could. It matched the vibrations of my bare feet pounding against the earth.

I was panting, using agility and stamina to keep myself moving forward. I held the top of my dress made from resin-based cloth. Narrowing my eyes, my hair swung this way. My left foot slipped, and I tripped at the sight of a gator.

A full moon hovered above us, covered with cumulus clouds.

The enormous gator snarled. I shrieked in horror. I ran past it, and it snapped at my right ankle. One of its teeth tore the skin, just on the surface! Ah!

You see! When you penetrated the surface, what lied beneath rose to the top. It was all one unique design. I was learning from my wound and the gator. The laws I disobeyed. The rules I broke. I didn't care. I was rebellious, tired of being controlled.

I lost respect for every adult and elder I had in my life, even those I loved more than life, but not more than I loved myself.

They tried to change me into what I was not. I was my own person. I made my own choices.

The gator roared and chased behind me, gaining speed. Who knew those reptiles were that fast? I jumped over a huge log and the gator slammed into it. The log rolled and threw me forward. My head broke open on a rock by a tree trunk, lined with mold, moss and other fungi, organism, and mushrooms.

I sunk my hands into the earth. It was wet like mud, stuck in a cycle of transformation. It was cool against my pale skin.

My breath came in gasps.

I refused to move. The gator snarled. Stinky saliva fell on me. Viciously, it leaned into my face. The reptile bared its teeth. I screamed in horror, stunning it briefly.

The gator didn't know what to do. With a sharp will to live, I drove two sticks into its eyes, fell forward with my weight, and pushed the eyeballs so far in its head that it convulsed on the ground. I staggered to stand up.

I looked around for Larshaw. My heart dropped. How did I get out of the belly of the forest? I was lost and alone. I looked around wildly, weeping. I turned and walked towards a clearing draped with pink moss.

I gasped at the sight of a legion of gator eggs and baby alligators. I broke apart in an instant. The mother gator was only trying to protect her young and her eggs. She wasn't exactly targeting me.

I invaded her home, her territory.

Grief-stricken, I looked over her young.

They had no idea their mother was dead. I placed open palms on either side of my face and balled. I noticed a stone cage that kept them inside, deep in the ground.

I would later give them refuge at my place once I became a vampire, shortly after I killed their mother when I was human. I was changed into a dark creature against my will as karma and retribution for my ultimate sin.

My secret empire, THÈ HÔUSE ÖF THÈ HÔUNDS, had been around for two hundred years, before I worked for Armona.

It was a remotely hidden place shaded by trees that scratched at the sky, surrounded by waterfalls and rocky bridges. It was not on the continent of Vencreashia.

Through telepathy, I communicated with the baby alligators. Oddly, they remembered me from my scent.

With supernatural power, I used replicas of myself to move all the baby eggs to my castle, a castle I acquired after killing its owner during a hostile takeover.

He was a human, and I was thirsty. Once I became the Queen Mother, Armona's right-hand general, hundreds of years later, the Gator Tribe protected the ocean and seas, but resided on my land.

THÈ HÔUSE ÖF THÈ HÔUNDS I gifted to them when I gave up the Glittering Throne, in hopes that my savage family looked out for them.

With my council, we created the Treaty of the Animals, my personal action in honor of the mother gator I selfishly killed, leaving her descendants without her presence. And to honor all the animals I slaughtered.

This was how the Treaty came to be. Somewhere over time, THÈ HÔUSE ÖF THÈ HÔUNDS became a vampire slave house run by the evil Emperor Ferdinand Demarest, a legendary vampire known for changing his last name because he hated his father.

Ferdinand came upon it and took it over. He bedded women and fed them to his male victims. He stored their blood, every ounce, in special glass containers imported from Mesopotamia. He labeled and categorized them by color, race, status, and creed.

When he reigned, around the time I was the Queen Mother's fledgling, he was a tyrant—a cold-hearted vampire with the soul of darkness. He infamously created a supernatural genocide. He lured four thousand newborn vampires, adult women pregnant with wolves and vampire children in a gigantic chamber. A rain shower of contaminated water slowly filled the dungeon.

Terrified, they screamed and scratched at the walls, finding nothing but stone. They turned on each other, scratched each other's faces, and fought each other as the filthy water filled the stone dungeon. Catastrophically, they drowned.

Redirected matter into the product of death.

The unbearable pain was traumatic.

The stone was blackened by a sulfuric glowing inferno that followed once the watery dungeon was drained. In the darkness, they were bound.

A few minutes later, their hearts were burned to a crisp. Emperor Ferdinand Demarest was pleased.

After the genocide, he saw me standing in the silhouette of the moonlight. It took him a moment to say anything. He rubbed his eyes like I wasn't real, but I was.

I was drawn to the pain and suffering of vampires illegally breeding with wolves.

Into his arms, he engulfed me.

"You are mine, all mine, whoever you are!"

It took a moment for his words to sink in.

Being back in THÈ HÔUSE ÖF THÈ HÔUNDS felt weird, but I was on a mission.

FIFTEEN
SOULLESS EYES

ALICIA CHAY

I wanted him for two reasons. One, I wanted to bed the man Armona once loved when he was human, breaking the laws of the Dershakney.

Two, I wanted to feel his power and his arrogance. See if he was as passionate a lover as he was a tyrant.

We were enchanted by one another. When he found his cadence, he said that I was the most beautiful woman he hath ever seen. I corrected him. No matter what person, first or third, the story was told. I *was* the most beautiful woman you hath ever seen, or I *am* the most beautiful woman you hath ever seen?

I was in marble statue form, functioning like a moving painting.

I lowered my garments…showing a breast. I then covered up my unwavering bosom. That's what I was to him, this magnificent tyrant, this evil man that loved dictatorship—a wavering bosom, full, and firm. Waiting to be suckled and milked.

JA'BREEL LE'DIAMOND

He once possessed nineteen thousand vampire slaves, connecting metal rods to their brains via red dots, using the power of thunder to read their minds as a collective whole. He seemed humble in appearance. The ice of his soulless eyes didn't agree.

He was fascinating. When he touched me, marble met marble, and a smooth tread to the forbidden vulva seemed evident, but it wasn't on the docket just yet. I wanted to give him instant access to every hole on my body. To be uninhibited drove me crazy.

I was on fire! Flames danced with infernos too smoky for my eyes. They were wet with longing. He pressed me against the wall and slid up inside me by eleven inches.

I arched my back. My pleasurable flower stroked the length of his throbbing passion.

I loved him, but only for the moment, and for the love of wealth. It started and ended there. I was on a mission for the Queen Mother, to take out the man that was her ex-lover.

A man she left for dead when he cut ties with her. For centuries she ruled the world unchallenged until whispers of a tyrant, Ferdinand, found her ears by the Dragonhead Ancients. An amnesia spell prevented Ferdinand from remembering how he became a vampire. So long ago, he met Armona by sheer chance.

She was hunting through a forested area when she came upon him. A blue-eyed chocolate warrior, he dived into a river for fish. He was a cannibal, but his immaculate beauty showed through. He was trained to survive in the wild. Droplets of water glistened on his body in the moonlight and its uncanny ghostly glow.

After hunting for blood in various territories, Armona paused in sweet surrender, bound by his innocence. Her nipples swelled with honey, and her hips yearned for attention. Her feminine scent and his swinging vine overpowered her need for the hunt.

Blood covered part of her chin. Her hair was long and thick. He had a mother, sister, and father he adored. He always tended to his father's crops. Nakedly, Ferdinand walked onto the shore from the river, dropping a net filled with fish for his family. She shuddered with longing, wanting him. She rushed up to him as if slowing down time. In a snap, she inhaled the scent from the nape of his neck. As her hand graced his collarbone, he glanced over his shoulder.

Licking her lips, he turned to grab his fresh catch and came face to face with her. Captured by her beauty, they made love as if they were long-lost lovers from another life. They would make love for many moons, meeting in the same spot by the river under the glittering stars.

An addiction that eventually had to end. Around the time of Cesar's rule, Ferdinand met up with Armona. As she caressed him, he cupped her hands and brought them to his lips.

"My sweet. I really appreciate the time we've spent together. This has been something of a dream."

Armona, clad scantily, agreed. "You are a dream, an escape from the reality I face every time the sun rises."

He cupped her face. "If that reality dispels your passion, then I'd rather keep thinking you're a dream."

"Let's discuss this later. I need you, Ferdinand."

He grew pensive. "No, we must talk now. I'm afraid tonight is the last time we'll see one another."

Her eyes turned black. Startled, he started moving away from her.

"This can't be! Who…what are you?"

"Your end. If I can't have you, I'll turn what you love into what you will never experience again!"

The hairs stood on his arms. "Leave me alone! This is the end of us!"

Hissing, Armona bit into his neck, temporarily putting him in a deep sleep. She turned him into a vampire against his will long before he became a tyrant, long before he ruled THÈ HÔUSE ÖF THÈ HÔUNDS, long before she sent me to destroy him.

He used to be Armona's human lover until she wanted to own and possess him. The sun rose on Ferdinand in transition. He was dying from exposure to the sunlight. She awakened him.

His body started turning to ashes at a horrifying rate.

The Queen Mother rose in the air without a sound. He was in grave pain, rendered speechless. He twisted in the air. Armona cast a mobile dark shade over him, protecting him from the rays of the sun.

His fingers were contorted.

Blue and white hazel lightning reconstructed his face. His arms and legs fell to the floor. They melted into each other like paint.

His reconstructed limbs returned to the missing places of his exhausted body. He opened his eyes and screamed for dear life. He escaped, flying to a home he shared with his family.

After he arrived, his fangs and ghoulish features sent his mother and sister into a screaming panic. Ferdinand slaughtered them.

Shortly after, Armona fell on top of her ex-human lover and tore through his flesh. She threw chunks of membrane this way and that.

Blood was on her face.

Her fangs gleamed, poisonous at the tips.

There was a loud crash, startling Ferdinand and Armona.

A pack of lions leaped at him, shifting into four strange creatures. They had irregular bodies and cock eyes.

He rushed into his father Jahja's private chambers, wanting blood. One of the strange creatures chased behind him, and the other creatures followed suit.

KHOVAHSH

The chambers were dark. The foreign creatures saw everything in a foggy-looking display of images.

The Queen Mother Armona ate one of the creatures from the inside out. Loud banging sounds spilled through the walls. Three ghoulish creatures rushed over to Ferdinand and bit into him as his body continued to rejuvenate from the transition. Ferdinand's eyes were wide with fear and pain. He was sent into convulsions from shock alone. Jahja awakened abruptly.

He screamed from the sound of horror, but he couldn't see a thing in the darkness. Light was trapped on the opposite side of the closed curtains. Ferdinand's eyes rolled to the back of his head.

Armona swung her arms, and the thick curtains fell from metal hooks.

Sunlight ravaged the creatures. They shrieked as their bodies became ashen. The last of the ripple effects of fire sizzled over their ashy fangs just as Ferdinand's body rose in the air.

The room was illuminated with a kaleidoscope of light.

The rush of power and murder was strong on the Queen Mother's breath. It consumed every thought that popped into her head. She tried to take it all in. She tried to figure it all out.

"I told you I'll turn what you love against you, Ferdinand!"

Ignoring her, he smelled his way to his father.

Before he could reach him, the Queen Mother ran through the stone wall, taking Jahja into her arms.

She bit into his neck in the dead of the dark, drinking uncontrollably.

He couldn't see a thing!

Gone was the kaleidoscope of light.

Outside, the sun was about to set.

"You're going to die...and take the secret to the grave with you!"

Ferdinand bit into the opposite side of his neck, challenging Armona.

After slaying Jahja, she ripped a hole in Ferdinand's chest and decided to flee. She left Ferdinand for dead. She jumped through the glass by the back of the dwelling.

Chunks of glass fell onto the grass. She sprinted across the land, She scowled at the moonlight. Two rows of black feathers formed on her arms. Wings extended from either shoulder blade. She had a breathtaking bone structure. She jumped into the air, plummeted onto her chin, and slid a few feet, eating the dust of the earth.

She flapped her wings, rising five feet in the air. She flew higher, to fifteen feet, twenty, one hundred feet, ah! Progress came faster than she realized.

Her sense of smell and sight intensified. She flapped her wings in a clumsy execution that improved with practice. She was a determined specimen.

Devastated, Ferdinand burned his father's palace to the ground.

He never mourned his loss. He focused on his anger. He wanted to kill Armona. He would get revenge for the death of his family.

He was close to his father, adored his mother, and loved his sister until Armona selfishly took them away. She destroyed the love he had for his sister after becoming a vampire. That rage turned him into a gruesome dictator.

He spent centuries dethroning the world's wealthiest and most powerful rulers and inherited their Kingdoms. He merged forty-five of them into The House of the Hounds, sitting on 122,000 acres of land, and hath 897 rivers, 19,000 damns, 456 canals, mountains, plant life, and vegetation.

Ferdinand took what I started and revolutionized it. Breathtaking mountains rose via erupting underwater volcanoes, and the base of the rocky mountains dipped into the Vatican-inspired Underwater Kingdom, the supernatural's best-kept secret.

It was carefully hidden. THÈ HÔUSE ÖF THÈ HÔUNDS was the most powerful kingdom the world hath ever seen, unknowingly overshadowing Ђe Queen Mother's empire; Armona thought she was the most powerful ruler in the world. Ferdinand set up the game. He never sought her out. She assumed that he perished.

He wanted vengeance, but she had to choose to challenge him, or else it would mean nothing. How could she do that if she didn't know he was alive? Unless she sought him out, her death would be in vain, and he'd never have closure. He detested becoming a tyrant. He hated making vampires his slaves.

For centuries Armona never left his thoughts. Well-paid spies, now vampires, kept tabs on her whereabouts. An Army of 34,000 military vampires guarded his estate and marched around the parameter of the land at thirty-second intervals in groups of 1,000, each armed with deadly weapons.

Every time she left her castle, he knew about it.

For centuries she never took her mind off him. She attended concertos and balls, masturbating in the shadows thinking of him. She dined and made love to Czars, thinking of him.

The love of gold turned her into a classy Jezebel. She ruled by marrying wealthy men while in female human guise form.

She did away with them during Carnival, a festival celebrated by millions of people that get naked in the open fields.

I embellished the whispers on the wind, and those whispers told me that her Σmpire wasn't the largest and most powerful.

Ferdinand, her ex-lover, lived and wanted her dead.

Unfortunately, he was the King and Ruler of THÈ HÔUSE ÖF THÈ HÔUNDS, a place I once owned.

A place I turned my back on after becoming Armona's right-hand assassin.

It was a wicked place where records were kept, and people of all kinds were bedded and screwed; a place where skulls from victims were kept as statuettes and artifacts. The Queen Mother grabbed her neck, stunned by the revelation of the universal winds. The power of the Dragonhead Ancients danced before her eyes, then vanished without a trace. "Ferdinand lives?" Not for long. The Queen Mother called on me, her right-hand girl, her lieutenant, to take care of her... lightweight.

"Kill my past lover and bring me his head and heart, will you?"

I obliged, doing what needed to be done. Ferdinand used to be good and now represented evil. Armona betrayed him. He was unemotional, closed, and heavily guarded. Armona used to be evil and convinced herself she was good, killing Kings for nourishment.

Ferdinand never killed a mortal, not even his father, though Armona burst through the wall and tried to take his father's life.

He wanted control over a continent. He enslaved vampiric beings at secret prep schools that trained young vampires into programmed killers with faulty morals. THÈ HÔUSE ÖF THÈ HÔUNDS was a world within a world that had its own resources.

Armona wanted total world domination.

She thought she was the biggest fish until her past lover came out of the dark of night and knocked her off her pedestal. And there I was, making love to him, tasting his fleshy lips. His fangs glittered like diamonds. His touch aroused me. My flesh was weak. My blossoming rose gushed with rainfall, staining my garments.

He entered the opening of the treaty between my vaginal lips.

"I am about to release," he said, shuddering. In that moment, I punched into his chest and ripped out his heart. I ran to his eating quarters, grabbed a sterling silver platter and sprinted back to him, before he could fall on his bed, which was a huge linen sack filled with hay and leaves.

I started to tremble. I snapped his neck, snatched his head off, and put it on the sterling silver along with his heart.

I took his brain and heart to Armona.

She examined it with a smile.

It was pleasing to her, the Queen Mother.

After officially having the most powerful Dynasty, she gifted THÈ HÔUSE ÖF THÈ HÔUNDS to me, not knowing that I was the original owner, freeing the vampire slaves.

She granted the elder vampires immunity, closing the House and the Institutions inside it. Armona learned that her rise in authority was covered with the blood of the past.

And eventually, the emotion of it would be the way to take the throne…

SIXTEEN
ALICIA CHAY

PRESENT DAY

"Come!" said the eerie voice...

I blinked a few times, making sure I was not hear things. I was reluctant to answer this unsolicited summons, not knowing what to expect. I quietly studied the massive chamber of the unknown.

I strolled past the first row of black-crystal shifter-ghouls with four-inch emerald eyes. In deep awe, I floated along a concrete bridge that glittered. An elongated rack of sterling silver gates glowed like a moon's hue three hundred feet before me.

Suddenly, the gates opened.

"Cooommmeeeee!"

From the peak of nine thousand black granite stairs oozed a life force I didn't recognize. My heart beat like pistons. I covered my ears.

There was an enormous explosion that rocked the place.

KHOVAHSH

After a hiss of hatred, a crooked-back ghoul shifted into an ugly creature.

He grabbed me by the neck and squeezed. I screamed in terror.

Panting, I awakened from slumber behind an abandoned building in San Francisco, California. It took a moment to realize that I was having dreams, nightmares, or visions again.

I stood up without effort.

One of my high heels was missing, but the other was still on my foot. I audibly sighed.

When I turned to leave, my reflection in a dirty, broken mirror took my breath away. My sadistic side chuckled, throwing me off guard.

There was blood all over my classic blue jeans and a dead body behind the dumpster.

My other high heel protruded from his forehead. His face was yesterday's stew. I gasped, trying to keep it together. Yes, I killed him. It wasn't until I leaned over him, licking blood from the nape of his neck, that I found out he was a vampire living in a host body for ten years.

That was a direct felony in my government. The price was death.

Well, he paid for it in full. He was dead, right along with the wealthy human body he lived in.

I squatted, then jumped into the air, flying toward Germany.

SEVENTEEN
COMBUSTIBLE SPARKS

ALICIA CHAY

As the leaves began to brown and fall, signaling the death of summer, I dreamed of something poignant.

I felt like a pampered queen. A faceless being demanded things of me.

Things that only a vampiric supreme queen could do. To his delight, no one did it better than I could; I pleasured him beyond anything he ever imagined.

I had the sweetest taboo on earth. Hell, none of those other powerful women he bedded compared to me.

I was worth seventy-billion dollars. Money longer than any bitch that reigned before me and longer than the fourteen inches he desired to have inside the womanly folds of my deliciously blossoming cauliflower.

KHOVAHSH

When he departed, he'd tell his other lovers about me. They would hunt me down to suck his residue from my softened lips.

Whatever my dream lover asked for, I was obliged. I told myself I would do anything to keep his shaft buried six feet deep in the coffin of my cervix. If lovemaking felt this amazing, then I didn't want it to end!

With a jolt, I was awakened in my bed by the call of the wild! To hunt! To kill! To feed my ego with the shenanigans of annoying mortals. The very ones that didn't value the gift of life. The feeling was so powerful that I found myself levitating above the middle of the Bed of the Queen Mother.

I was startled by wicked ghosts that spiraled around my body with faces unfamiliar to my senses. Yet, something about the blueish glow struck me as odd...

"I'm Chanteuse," said one of the ghosts.

"I'm Zulu," said the other.

"I'm Mama Reshma," said the third ghost.

Wrought with fear, my eyes turned ghostly white. The trinity of ghosts formed into each other. I was now naked deep in a heavily forested area.

There was destruction all around me. Huts burned to the ground; trees were engulfed in ravenous flames. A soul-lacerating hiss grabbed my attention just as a gust of wind blew me fifty feet backward, bringing me face to face with two tombs.

Remember The Village of Opus and the Grand Forest...!

Two names were on the tombstone, blurred out.

On my knees, I attempted to touch the tombstone amassed in mildew.

"Wake up!" came the distorted voice. Slowly, I gazed up into the fiery eyes of an eight-foot angelic being.

"I'm the Raynedrakin!" As he morphed into the most hideous creature I'd ever seen, I awakened eight thousand feet above my estate.

Startled, I plummeted with no sense of control. I closed my eyes. I landed on my bed without pain or harm. It took a moment to gather myself. I tried to remember the name of the ghosts. Frustrated, I rose to my feet. I gazed at the mirror.

The words *"I will find you!"* appeared on the glass in a shade of red lipstick. Something or someone was hunting me, yet I hadn't a clue who that may be. I needed a change of scenery.

I dissolved into the air and appeared behind my castle. I rubbed my arms. The scent of rain caught my attention before the torrent befell everything around me.

Suddenly, a witch appeared from a burst of combustible sparks at the start of the forest, a hundred feet in front of me. Only then did the acid rain stop.

She was cloaked in a chilling dampness that rubbed off on me in an unnatural way. I released an incorrigible scream that made a large school of fowl caw away in fear.

My nails extended seven inches. I put up my guard. Why, I didn't know, but it was better to be safe. I was annoyed, endangered, and threatened all at once only because I encountered her before I met Armona forty centuries ago.

With astral projection, she vanished and reappeared through blood and ash, more powerful than before. As she mumbled chants, I remained nonplussed. The ability to create her own spells was impressive but not influential. She radiated wickedly from the dirt path. A golden arc predicated her presence. I'd never encountered a being with this type of power since Armona.

More importantly, why was she here? Dressed in a velvet cloak wrought with sapphire, she removed her hood. Her gorgeous face was unique and enchanting.

She had upright triangular ears. Her nails were poisonous snails that emerged out of their shells.

Her long hair was twisted into tarantula legs.

They crawled over each other, giving her hair a moving painting effect. Creepy!

Her mysterious doe-shaped eyes were reddish orange.

And those curved canine teeth were a muddy green. Sheesh.

I was on guard. "I know who you are."

She cocked her head to the east. "I know you do, Alicia. Long time no see," the witch mocked.

Her voice was a fit of high pitches mixed with an unconscious echo that made my skin crawl.

EIGHTEEN
UNDER ORDERS

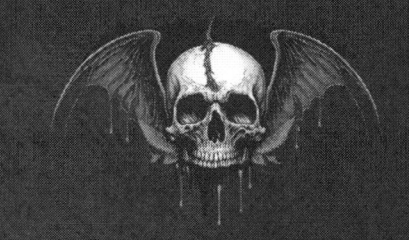

ALICIA AND THE WITCH

I was floored by her arrogance. "Obviously, you wanted my attention." I didn't have time for somatic jargon. I didn't give a damn who she was.

She grinned. "Pleased to meet you again, Alicia."

"I'm displeased to meet you. Now leave. Solitude I seek once more."

A sly expression curled her chapped lips.

"It's imperative that we speak, Alicia. This isn't a summons."

"Say what it is you have to say, and go on about your merry way, witch."

She gazed at me for a moment. A smile followed.

"At the time of my birth many moons ago, Humasch was the King of the Elephant Tribe. Talmod the Tyrant and Syr To'Rah were the Emperor Kings of the Panthera Pardus in Europe."

"Leopards."

"Correct. Sir Majesty Negus Nula was the King of the Cheetah Tribe in

Africa. The most powerful of them all. Menorah was his Queen, and my mother, Court Jester, was his scroll keeper and secret lover. Armona, the Queen Mother, was in possession of those territories, but I need to locate her body for this to happen. And I need your help acquiring what's rightfully mine."

"How did she acquire them?" I humored her. She glanced down at her intimate area with a coy smile.

"She slept her way into power and inheritance."

"That doesn't surprise me."

"She lay with nearly every Czar and every ruler of the various territories in the world."

"Interesting…"

"After they signed over their land, resources, and empires, she summoned the dark ghoulish spell of the banished and sent over five hundred thousand faceless ghouls, goblins, and evil spooks to their respectable lands."

I fought myself to stifle a yawn. "If you want sympathy for humans, you've darkened the wrong threshold."

My comment was ignored. "Let's just say the ghouls, goblins, and spooks inhabited the bodies of the people and ate every authority figure alive and still thirsted for more."

She grew painfully quiet. "Fortunately, my mother, Court Jester, managed to escape long enough to put me in hiding with the Animalia Tribe before she was killed. However, as a curse, I was sentenced to the life of a banished witch."

She was holding something back, and that something usually wound up being the thread that unraveled deception.

Absent-mindedly, I floated towards her. Growling, she covered her face. It shifted into the striking features of a side-striped jackal. Embarrassed, she ran into the forest.

Why did she flee? How much of what she said was true? Was the witch a jackal…? Against my better judgment, I went after her. Expertly, she leaped over broken trees, large ponds, and lakes.

Many hidden geographical treasures lay deep inside the woods, enshrouded with shadows and mystery. The crepuscular creature moved with spellbinding agility.

A deep snarl. "He's coming for you," she hissed, grabbing my undivided attention. The witch sprinted faster than sound. I was right on her tail.

"Who is coming for me?" As half-witch, half-jackal, she glanced over her shoulder, leaping on a huge lake via her fused leg bones, running on water.

"Khovahsh Burgoos. He wishes to destroy you. I had to distract you with the story of my mother to get you alone."

"Why didn't he destroy me when he was Armona's Enforcer?"

"He was under orders not to."

"I will kill you with my bare hands!" Challenged, she hurled five flaming balls of smoky tar at me. I knew how to handle witches. They required immediate focus to perform spells. I squinted at an enlarged branch and it careened towards her.

Once she was distracted, I deflected all five fire-tar balls back at her. They quickly made direct contact.

The witch slammed into an enormous redwood.

I vanished and appeared behind her, punching through her back. Her beating heart was in my tight grasp when I held it in front of her.

"So much for spells and potions, witch. Now talk. I was enjoying my solitude until you ruined my evening."

Wide-eyed, she gasped for air. "Khovahsh is an immensely powerful vampire that hath caused havoc amongst the supernatural for nine thousand years. He hath the ability to shift and re-shift into anything with a nucleus."

I squinted. "Why is he pursuing me?"

She turned inside and out, facing me as her black heart remained in my grasp.

"Can you please put my heart back in its place?"

I squeezed tighter. "Talk!" Her eyes fluttered.

"I had to lure you into the forest for privacy, as I've said before. If Khovahsh finds out that I'm giving you a warning, he will kill me."

I winked, and she was completely whole once more. She fell to her knees, covering her face with her greenish hands.

I grew weary of the scary woods, so I took her by the arm and rose from the sands along the shoreline.

It took a moment for her to meet my accusing eyes.

"Thank you for sparing my life. I don't have much time, so I will make this quick. Khovahsh hath three sides. Each version of himself is wicked. He wishes to trick you into...."

Twelve horseshoe-shaped knives sliced her into chunks of meat. Her blood splattered on my face.

Where did they come from?

I was uncomfortable.

It was time to go.

NINETEEN
MONEY AND PROMISES

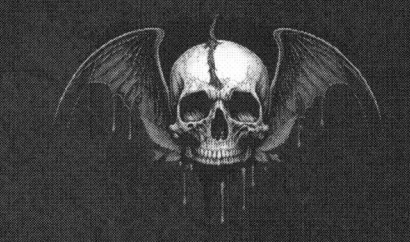

KHOVAHSH BURGOOS
2002

Paying bills on computers was the norm and the great ole American way. I must admit that randomly living in those annoying humans was a pastime of mine and the only way I could walk in the sunlight without becoming last year's pot roast set out in the sun.

A business man named Clifford parked his Porsche in a reserved spot at a software company located in Dallas, Texas. It was a quarter past ten p.m. He hopped out and made his way to a heavily-guarded private entrance. While he looked for his badge, I grabbed him from behind, startling him. I bit into his neck and drank uncontrollably. Once I was satisfied, I possessed him. It took a moment for him to get his bearings. "I must be coming down with the flu."

He swiped his badge and entered a secret conference room.

KHOVAHSH

"The man is here! *Congratulations*! LonCha Tech opens tomorrow!"

Two investors and a Pastor cheered him on. His computer company went public, one he stole from his father just before he drowned him in a bath tub. "The company uniforms arrived yesterday," Clifford said. "We will pay our employees peanuts on the dollar while we cash in on the results!"

Pastor Ford slammed his fists on the conference table. "But the staff is black. I don't like the sound of that."

"Come on, Pastor Ford! You're on the winning side!"

"As the rich gets richer, the poor gets poorer. Jesus died for this?" Pastor Ford asked. "and you all want me to participate?"

"Why not, Pastor Ford? The world is headed towards the digital era."

"I didn't sign up to underpay my own people."

"But its my company. The old way is out. Not all of us are religious."

"And the new way is better?" asked Pastor Ford.

Todd Gripes, a computer science major, chimed in. "Pastor Ford. We understand your concerns, but we are providing people of color with stable jobs that will make their lives easier, as well as our own."

"By underpaying them?" Pastor Ford grimaced. "You do know that LonCha Enterprises is built on top of a cemetery."

Clifford chuckled. "Yes, Pastor Ford. We are aware of that."

Pastor Ford glared at him. "And you sleep easy at night in your three story homes knowing that families were hurt from your greed."

Clifford folded his hands in front of him. "I sleep soundly."

Todd smiled. "They seemed to like the money we gave them in exchange for their silence."

"No wonder Pastor Dacra's church burned to the ground after he invested in your father's *private* company, one you inherited after his death."

"No offense, but what does that have to do with this meeting?"

"Steve, your father, wanted his company to *stay* private"

"It doesn't matter, Pastor. I don't understand the sudden resistance."

"You are no better than a man selling slaves on the auction block."

"You would know," said Sampson Hones, an investor from Dubai. "Didn't your kind sell themselves to that system of slavery as well?"

Pastor Ford grew pensive. "That may be the case, but ivory-colored specimen spent hundreds of years tearing us down while we built this country."

"Pastor Ford, you're wealthy. You don't have to work a day in your life. You invested in us."

"We're talking about seventy million dollars," said Pastor Ford.

"With a guaranteed nine hundred million dollar return," said Clifford.

"All money ain't good money," said Pastor Ford. "I see that now."

Clifford poured a tonic. "Yet you attend this secret business meeting. Listen, Pastor Ford. I offered you a seat at the table because you knew my father. He was your editor and agent. He used you as his play toy when he built your brand. I made you a household name. I was a fan of your money. You are under a contract, a NDA, and a limited conservatorship. Technically, your life isn't your own."

Angrily, Pastor Ford stood up and grabbed his car keys from the polished oak-wooden table. The centerpiece was Steve's golden Urn. "Well, in that case, my time here has expired. I'll satisfy the terms of our deal."

"You're doing the right thing. You need to look out for yourself. When you worked two jobs to make ends meet, who helped you?"

"You and your father."

"And no one else. As a matter of fact, my father helped you launch your own church, before you became a multi-millionaire."

"Yes, he did. but he didn't underpay my people in the workplace."

Clifford frowned. "Thank you for your investment.

KHOVAHSH

I observed Pastor Ford as he looked over a presentation from his office a few hours later. His church was on the corner of an inner city. As a Dragonhead Ancient, I was addicted to religion. I was fascinated with what people believed in. He burned the midnight oil into smoke and mirrors. He was typing a sermon he was going to present to the congregation.

"Why did the devil show up after God created Eve? Was she plagued with demons when she charmed Adam? Is the vagina the forbidden fruit...? Why was she cursed with painful childbirth, unless she was pregnant?"

He thought about Clifford and his greed. *When you worked two jobs to make ends meet, who looked out for you?*

He pressed stop on the recorder and poured a tonic. "My people treated me like crap. No one offered me a meal or a dime. No one supported me. Steve, Clifford's father, was the only person that helped me. He introduced me to some people that made things happen. Then I met Clifford and he became my manager."

I approached him out of thin air, taking him off guard. He wasn't frightened or nervous. He looked me over, and yawned.

Quietly, he set the recorder down. "Who are you?"

I smiled, dressed in a suit. "An admirer of your work and your cause."

He was uneasy. "The church is closed for the evening..."

I held up my hand. "I'm in need of understanding, if you are a man of the cloth. Plus, your church has only been closed for fifteen minutes."

"Well, since you're here, have a seat." I sat down.

"What is your name, and how can I help you..."

"My name is Khovahsh Burgoos."

He chuckled. "That's a rather odd name."

I smiled, baring my fangs. "I'm sure it is, Abrams Sicily."

Pastor Ford sat up straight. "How do you know my real name?"

137

"Is that important, Pastor Ford?"

He sprayed Holy water around the parameter of his desk. "Yes, it is."

"You are into make believe. You enjoy toying with religion, don't you?"

Pastor Ford shuddered, looking over my shaded eyes and fedora.

"You don' t know what you're talking about. You don't know me!"

I took the nozzle from the spray bottle and drank the Holy water.

He began to tremble as I licked the moisture from his desk.

"I know a lot about you, Pastor Ford. I know more than I care to know, but that's besides the point." I crushed the spray bottle and tossed it in the trash.

"Did Clifford send you here? I already invested in LonCha."

"No, he didn't send me here."

"What can I do for you, Khovahsh?"

"I'm curious about my beliefs. Maybe you can help me out."

"Ok...."

I floated to his cabinet and opened it. "Why do people pay for religion?"

"I'm sorry, I don't follow."

There was five rows of Holy water. "For instance, you're a Pastor."

"Yes."

I grabbed a bottle and closed the cabinet. "Jesus is the Son of God."

"That's correct." He looked down at the pistol in the top desk drawer.

"He wore sandals, healed people and started a ministry when he was thirty years old."

"Correct."

"Yet he never required the general public to pay ten percent tithes, nor did he dress in golden robes lined with silver, like the Pope."

I had him. I sprayed the Holy water on my tongue, then in his face.

"Why is God celebrated on Sunday, when he created the earth in six days and rested on Saturday, the seventh day?"

"You'll have to ask the Roman Church."

"Who authorized the Vatican to alter the Sabbath day? Did they have the Lord's permission to make such a significant change?"

We stared at each other. "I refuse to say. Certain things I don't discu--"

"Why was John Huss burned alive for spreading the gospel of Christ in the Roman tongue on July 6, 1415?"

He averted his eyes. "I'm not the person to answer those questions."

"Was John Huss singing Psalms when he was set afire by the Council of Constance, after they united Western Christiandom?"

"Yes. The Emperor promised his safety, but it was a trap to silence him."

"So its safe to say that he was a messenger of the Word."

"Yes. He was a martyr, along with Jerome of Prague.".

"Why was he against church reform at the time?"

"I don't see what this has to do with me."

"It has everything to do with you, Pastor Ford. Answer the question."

He jumped up to his feet. "I think you need to leave! Now!"

"I'll leave when I get ready to. At least John Huss didn't die in vain."

Pastor Ford fell to his knees when I took off my shades.

"Clifford, is this some sort of game?"

"No, its not, Abrams Sicily. You are a paid actor doing God's work for profit. I don't understand men like you. There are thousands of idols and gods, but only one devil. Why is that, Pastor Ford?"

"I'll call the cops! Khovahsh, hell. Your name is Clifford!"

"Through prayer you play the role with thoughts of collection plates, purses, cash, and checkbooks on your mind."

I fed on him until he passed out. I had to warn Alicia about Muzzle, but we haven't seen each other for centuries. Muzzle caused me to expose my dragon side in a public church, compromising the Order.

Alicia may have taken Armona's Throne, but I was obligated to protect her at all costs.

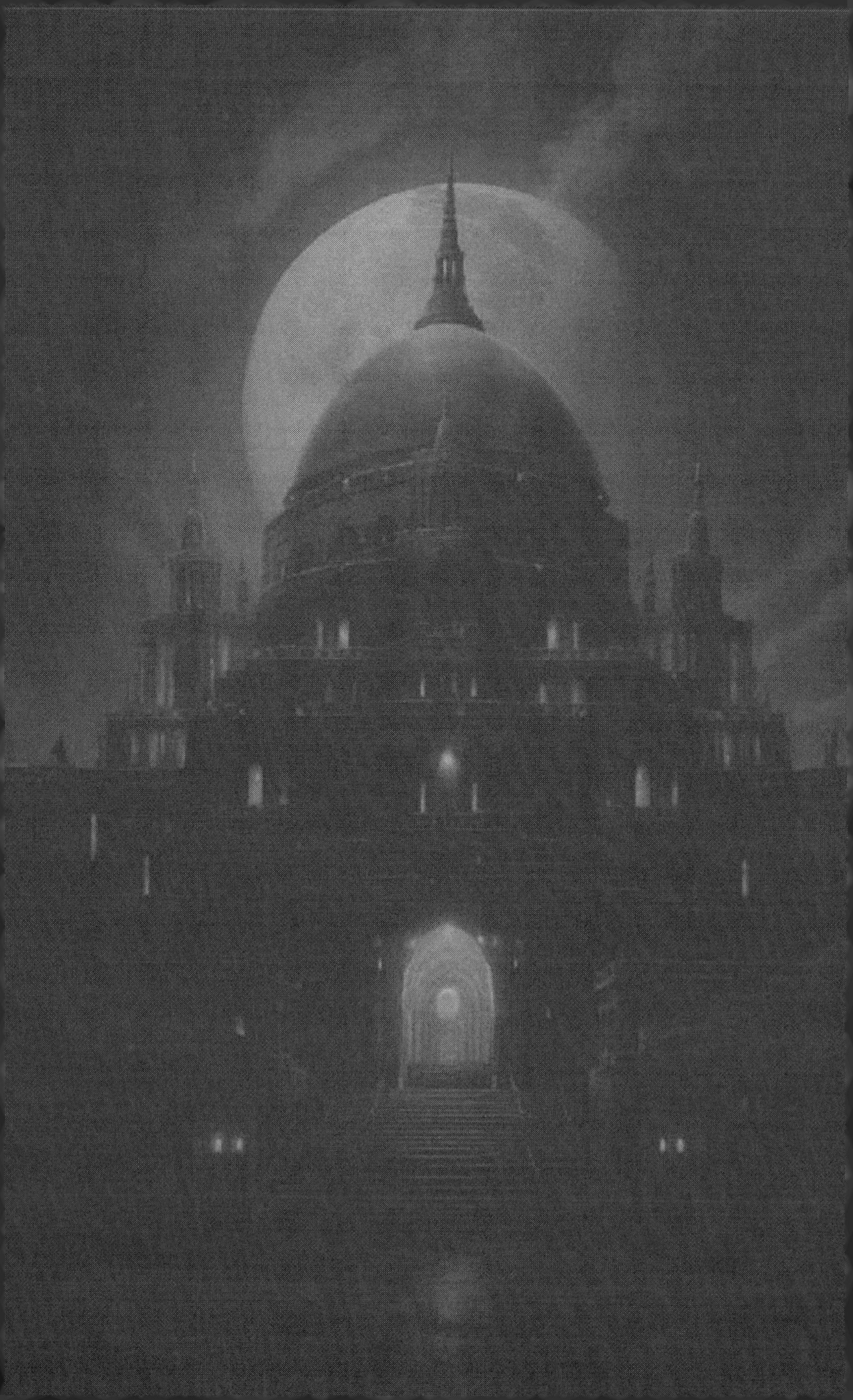

TWENTY
SECRET MEETINGS

HENRY FORD
Dallas, Texas
August 19th, 2002

Only when he had the Bible did he forget it all happened. As he preached his sermon, he ignored the scantily clad women in the crowd, and he really showed off for the men. What an entertainer!

For Pastor Henry Ford, a mid-forties law student, worldwide fame was his obsession. Back in 1997, when K-Ci and JoJo's "All My Life" was the number-one song in the country, and the Monica Lewinsky scandal was the trending topic, he had the number-one book in the world. It was written under Abrams Sicily. Steve LonCha, his editor (and agent) convinced Abrams to change his name to Henry Ford, denounce his Negro heritage, and made him a brand. They had an affair. Unfortunately, Steve was found dead in his bathroom shortly after hiring Steve's son, Clifford, as his manager.

Pastor Ford had a Proverb's wife. Her only purpose was to mask his same-gender attraction. He paid her handsomely to marry him; his grown children weren't of his DNA or his genetic makeup, and the children didn't know it.

However, after he found out about his wife's affair with Clifford, his advisors forced him to continue taping his overly successful gospel talk show that was just renewed for a fifth season. The action saved his brand at face value, but behind the scenes was brutal. He signed an iron-clad contract. Information leaked about blacks being underpaid at LonCha and he was publicly humiliated as an investor in the company that banked nearly a billion dollars. Then he was hit by the IRS for not paying taxes out of the money.

His brand brought in four hundred million dollars a year. To jeopardize that would mean instant death. His face was planted on all the merchandise, even on his Grammy-winning spoken word Album, *I Am the Way to Heaven*. On the credit page he was the author/producer, but in black and white on the contracts, he owned only fifteen percent, yet he did all the work.

During secret meetings before his humble debut, he became the carefully put together Pastor, an atheist. Faith for pay. He had a passion for public speaking and theatrics. He never wrote a word in his number-one books that had been stolen from broke authors with no desire to make a grandiose thing out of it. He owned a Concorde plane.

He was a generic celebrity with a staggering net-worth. Pastor Ford was addicted to money. He'd do anything to get it. Since the age of eight, he wanted to preach, but a Pastor killed his mother. He turned his back on God. He sold faith and drugs on the side.

What does an atheist on top of the Pastoral World of Wealth, Control,

KHOVAHSH

and Church do when he has it all?

Nothing. He had no power.

He had no authority or say so.

His handlers never let him do anything on his own. Conservatorship was his reality, and he hated it. The fact that other people, by law, could manage his money and daily life, regardless of his desires, made him feel powerless.

He was not the one making the decisions, yet people slept with him thinking that he could open doors for them to have a life of prosperity.

A ghostwriter remained his confidant. What was important about this ghostwriter? He felt normal with this person under his conservatorship.

This was the only area he had control of.

From a dark corner in his office sat a chocolate-colored marble statue. She faced his desk from forty yards away, by the private latrine.

She had red ruby eyes. They sparkled incessantly. His lamp was on; the dim lighting ceased just at the start of the oriental carpet, next to his trophy case.

The fabric of the oriental carpet was ten feet before me. I remained in the dark. On Henry Ford's wall were the heads of animals I didn't protect or represent. Slaughtered animals! I covered my mouth in shock.

I suddenly wanted him dead.

I hadn't shown myself outside of the marble statue. Henry was in a heated discussion with someone on the phone. He was drop-dead handsome in a money green suit.

His hair was cut low to the scalp.

He threw a liquor bottle. "Hell no! I won't do it! I hope you're listening. I'm not going to urge the people in my congregation to support microchipping their pets. Endorsing this would tarnish my image, and deliver a blow to my brand. Are you testing animals before you place them in humans?"

"You have no choice but to do it," the voice said over the speakerphone.

"It's bad enough that eventually, chips will be on debit and credit cards."

"You will do what I ask. Everything that you have, we gave you. We marketed your material. We got the public to have faith in you. You take $30 mill after Uncle Sam takes $90 mill off the top of your gross pay."

He rolled his eyes. "Yea, yea, blah, blah. I'm not doing it, and this time I don't care what you do or how you do it. I will not tell them a thing! I will not read your pre-written sermon today. I preach my own for the first time."

The caller was apprehensive. "Are you ready to die and lose it all. Your kids will be stripped of their inheritance when we publish reports that another man fathered them and not you. You're not even a sperm donor, atheist! Fake pastor."

Pastor Ford was unbothered. "Is that what you bullies do? Threaten people?"

"No, we love people and their last ten dollars. If they had light bill money and had to make a choice to buy your products, well, there ya go.

"It's a patron's free will choice," he continued. "We can't be responsible because a person is irresponsible with money. We're in the business to make money, not give it away.

"You're despicable!"

"Product in hand, money in ours, that's the only reason we gave you a daily show. It was for the revenue. The last thing on our minds was your status and public fame. We made you. We will break you."

"I will like to see you try."

"We own the industry, and your fame. You never wrote a word of anything. We pay you to get on TV and lie to the world that you wrote those movies, newspaper articles, and columns."

"Your insults mean nothing to me, you miserable person."

"You don't have an education, but we gave you one. We falsified your doctorates. We put you through theology school. We put you in law school. You never had to do the work."

"After all the money I made you, who gives a hoot, dude."

"Oh yes! Our gifts to you started early. Have you forgotten? You owe us, and I come to collect."

"One last time, your threats don't scare me."

"They should because death stares you in the face."

Nervously, his eyes swept the room. "Stares me in the face. What are you talking about?"

"Death! It wants you! It is there with you, in the same room, breathing like you."

"You're lying! My lights are on! I don't see anything!"

"Look outside of your window."

Pastor Ford hung up the phone. Hesitantly, he looked outside his fifty-six-story window, overlooking downtown Dallas, Texas. In a building directly across from him was a man in a black suit. With an alarming smile, he waved at Pastor Ford. He had char-black granite skin.

His eyes were black pearls, clear and cut.

Shaken, he backed away from the window, drawing the blinds. A masked man stepped out from behind the grandfather clock in his office and tried to grab him.

"No!" he shouted, near panic. "The Devil will not win! Not today! Not ever! I rebuke thee in the mighty name of Jesus...."

Unexpectedly, a cell phone rang, distracting him and the Perpetrator. For a few beats, they stared at each other.

Impulsively, the Perp knocked Pastor Ford across the head. In grave pain, he slumped to his knees. Reluctantly, the Perp answered. "Put the phone to his ear," said the disgruntled handler, Todd Gripes.

The Perp obeyed. "Your time's expired," said the demonic voice.

The Perp flipped the phone closed, pulled a huge gun from the elastic of his waist, and planted the start of the barrel on the Pastor's temple.

Pastor Ford cried out to God above, the one he didn't believe in, the one he robbed and cheated, for protection. He once committed blasphemy.

Yet none of that mattered. He cried out to God to save him with everything in his being. "Goodbye, Pastor! You're worth more dead than you are alive!"

Instantly, he pulled the trigger. The Pastor cringed as my granite hand covered the barrel of the weapon. The bullet ricocheted off my fingers, back into the chamber with the force of exploding gunpowder. I, Alicia Chay, didn't bat an eyelash.

It knocked the Perp and Pastor Ford on their asses. Eagerly, I moved in They screamed at the sight of me.

I blew a kiss at the window, and his curtains opened.

The handler, Todd Gripes, whipped out his cell phone and made a call. As if on cue, masked CIA men thundered up the emergency stairwell towards Pastor Ford's Penthouse to take me out.

I scowled at the caller, pointing a bejeweled finger at him, like Babe Ruth. I was coming for him. To make a point, I rammed my nails into the Perp's chest and ripped out his black heart.

I devoured it like a bum did an orange when he was dehydrated and famished. I hissed at the Pastor. He reverted to Christianity in five seconds flat, turning his back on years of dedicated atheist service for a chance at eternal life when he thought his life was over. It was a scary thought. I didn't know that bandwagon faith was a thing.

Frightened, he ran outside his front door and headed for the stairwell.

He was ambushed!

TWENTY-ONE
HAIR BECOMES THORNES

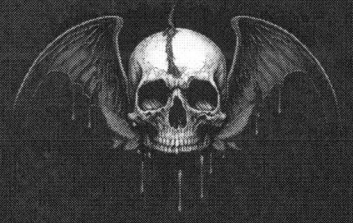

ALICIA CHAY

Five CIA men in masks screamed from fear when I leaped at them from Pastor Ford's unconscious body with blood in my eyes.

They opened fire from sophisticated weapons. I ran circles around bullets that spat at me a mile a minute. I sprinted to one of the men and slashed his neck. Jumping over a spray of hallow tip bullets, I transitioned into invisibility, becoming air.

My fist came from the shadows, hitting another agent in the face. Running along the side of the wall and the ceiling, my hair became thorns.

Brutally, I slapped three other agents in their faces with my weaponized dreadlocks.

My feet gave way. I flipped to the floor, running a sweeping kick under another villain, snatching his soul through his backside.

After I tore his heart out, I shoved it down his throat. Boom, boom, boom! Snipers from the building across from the Pastor's penthouse shot at me. Windows exploded, but I was much too fast. I ran along eighteen flights of stairs to the roof. I was there in five seconds.

They tried to take me out, eight snipers in all. I spun in place, catching every bullet. My hands were extremely hard with granite.

The bullets didn't put a scratch. I was incredibly powerful. I put the bullets in my mouth, placed a finger on my temple and closed my right eye. I held my breath and spat rapid fire. I killed all eight snipers. Done.

As their bodies fell to the ground, their assault weapons fell with them. They were now lifeless without a user. An unknown supernatural being fell out of Pastor Ford's body as well. It took me by surprise.

With pride and defiance, he stood eight feet tall, glaring down into my eyes. He looked familiar. "Who are you?" I asked, knowing that he broke the laws of the Dershakney. No vampire or supernatural being was to inhabit a human host without the authorization of my government. "I'm going to ask you again. Who are you?"

"I am Khovahsh Burgoos! I must warn you about..."

"Khovahsh!" Did he have full control over the pastor? The pastor's refusal to do the caller's bidding seemed out of character for Khovahsh, especially after our first encounter when he landed in front of me from a portal in the sky back in millennium three. B.C. He forced me to Armona's summons.

After spitting huge balls of fire at me, they shifted into psychotic faceless ghoulies. His expansive black wings extracted from the muscles of his upper shoulders. He fled. I sprinted across the helipad after him.

He was trying to tell me something. I wasn't interested.

Twelve-foot ghoulies chased me. They wanted me dead.

KHOVAHSH

Did they know I was Alicia, the Queen Mother? As I thought it, the ghouls paused in surrender, falling to their knees. No time for apologies.

I blinked, and they turned to dust. I jumped in the air, flying towards a fifty-story window, dropping a few more floors. I looked for Khovahsh. The imbecile broke the law and had the nerve to openly attack me. As I flew past a few floors, thoughts from an unknown vampire funneled into my ears.

I inhaled deeply. It was Pastor Ford's handler, Todd Gripes.

He was a vampire? I hunted him down and ripped out his spine.

The creature I encountered before I accepted Armona's offer to run her government was toying with me.

The deceiver the green-faced witch warned me about was in violation of my rules. I hadn't seen him for forty centuries, the shape-shifting demigod. Why did he show up now?

For that, he must die! An unidentifiable vampire hired to kill Pastor Ford screamed when he saw me. Ah! Abruptly, he ran past the living room sofa, but Khovahsh's essence entered his body, transforming him into a weapon of mass destruction. Angrily, I flew through the window, shattering the glass. I attempted to kill the John Doe. Before he could attack me, I brutally punched him in his chest.

Khovahsh screamed as the host's face contorted in pain. The John Doe's name was Clifford. Khovahsh ejected himself from the vampire's body. I was a bit confused. He seemed different from the God-like specimen that I met so long ago.

Here, he was the opposite. Weak and cowardly. Then it hit me like a ton of bricks. Khovahsh was weakened when he occupied a vampire versus being fully charged after having a human host. I swung my hair like a lasso and entangled his wrists and legs, but he vanished without a trace. *Clifford is a vampire, always have been, so I didn't break the law!*

Damn it! Savagely, I ripped out the vampire's heart and put it on a silver platter that was on a shelf by a hidden door. I grabbed the Bible from the nightstand, but it burned my hands.

I dropped it on the floor, backing away.

Clifford and Todd were Pastor Ford's handlers. Clifford was a man with wealth and power. He was worth a billion dollars. He was also a film producer and director that owned LonCha Enterprises, a computer company.

After a deep sigh, I drifted through the ceiling. I knocked on a door of an apartment in another building. Pastor Ford answered . "You can come in," he said blandly. I entered. I had no desire to kill him.

I sat on his sofa "We have some things to discuss. Our meeting wasn't by sheer chance. It was fate. I saved your life."

He closed his eyes and swallowed hard. "How can I be of assistance to you?"

"I thought you'd never ask..."

Just then, a blinding light momentarily turned our eyes translucent white. An explosion rocked the entire region without bombs or smoke.

A massive earthquake swept through the city. I looked at the platter. The vampire's heart was red dust.

Off in the distance, Khovahsh squealed with delight.

"I used Pastor Ford to lure you here. I came to tell you that your life is in jeopardy, but you tried to kill me. Now we're enemies, Alicia Chay."

The silence that followed his sultry voice was deafening.

"What have I done?" I whispered to myself.

I was in danger of losing my life?

I wasn't worried.

TWENTY-TWO
BODY HOSTING

ALICIA CHAY

For the next few moments, news stations were on high alert. The earthquake injured hundreds of people. There was instant panic and paranoia. The world was at a standstill...

It took a moment to realize that we were no longer in Dallas, Texas. We had teleported to a massive forest! Disoriented, I was on my hands and knees, thankful that I was still alive. My vision returned like it never left.

Pastor Ford, the converted atheist, groaned piteously. As his sight was restored, the soft reds and purples and yellows and greens of a rainbow extended from the clouds.

I rose to my feet and took it all in. Pastor Ford turned in circles, ingesting the mind-blowing experience that was a sight for our sore eyes.

A winged creature walked down the glittery stairs of the rainbow.

His face was solemn and serene. Ah! The converted atheist was captivated. We stood side by side. It was magnificent. Who was this being? Khovahsh? If it was, then his entrance contradicted how he was portrayed during our fight. There was a drastic shift in my perception of him. If he was powerful enough to match me, then I was fooled. I had to question Khovahsh's sudden reappearance since I chased him off moments ago. He claimed that he came to warn me about something.

Khovahsh hath three sides, each side is wicked, the witch told me before Khovahsh chopped her to pieces.

The gold of his breastplate blended in with the colors of the rainbow. It was soft against his lacquered skin. His alabaster-coated eyes were on fire. His garments were black. After a loud explosion, Khovahsh lowered himself before us without warning.

We were on the balcony of Pastor Ford's Penthouse, overlooking the city. The forest was nowhere in sight. I glared at Khovahsh.

"I will kill you with my bare hands!" I promised.

He leaned into my face. "Your life is in danger!"

After he knocked Pastor Ford unconscious, Khovahsh sank his fangs into my neck. I turned to mist and rose from tar and flames behind him. I kicked him in the gonads. A loud shriek caused my ears to bleed. He fell to his knees. I began choking him from behind. I wanted him to die!

"You are guilty of illegal body hosting, assault against the Queen Mother, and for ignoring that I am the acting Queen of every realm of this earth!"

"But you are a puppet for the Dragonhead Ancients, Alicia."

He threw his head back into my stomach, sending me over the railing.

KHOVAHSH

I plummeted towards the ground below. My body reduced its weight, and I rose towards Khovahsh, emblazoned with rage.

After a hilarious grunt, he took Pastor Ford and flew thirty thousand feet above the earth. I soared past the clouds after him. "Do you want this worthless man? I've lived in his body since 1997, and now you choose to do something about it? You are guilty of illegal body hosting as well!"

I wasn't intimidated.

"You're going to die, Khovahsh!"

His eyes were flames. "You think so, acting Queen?"

"So, you do know who I am!"

He chuckled mockingly. "I know who you are not. You are not my Queen, ruler, or leader…nor do I seek one. Aren't you the egotistical narcissist bitch that overthrew the real Queen Mother, Armona, and took her identity?"

"And if I did?"

"Then. You. Are. A. Fraud!"

He dropped Pastor Ford.

"No!"

I snapped my fingers, and Pastor Ford appeared from dust in his bedroom. It was just enough of a distraction for Khovahsh to cast a sleeping spell on me.

Everything faded to black…

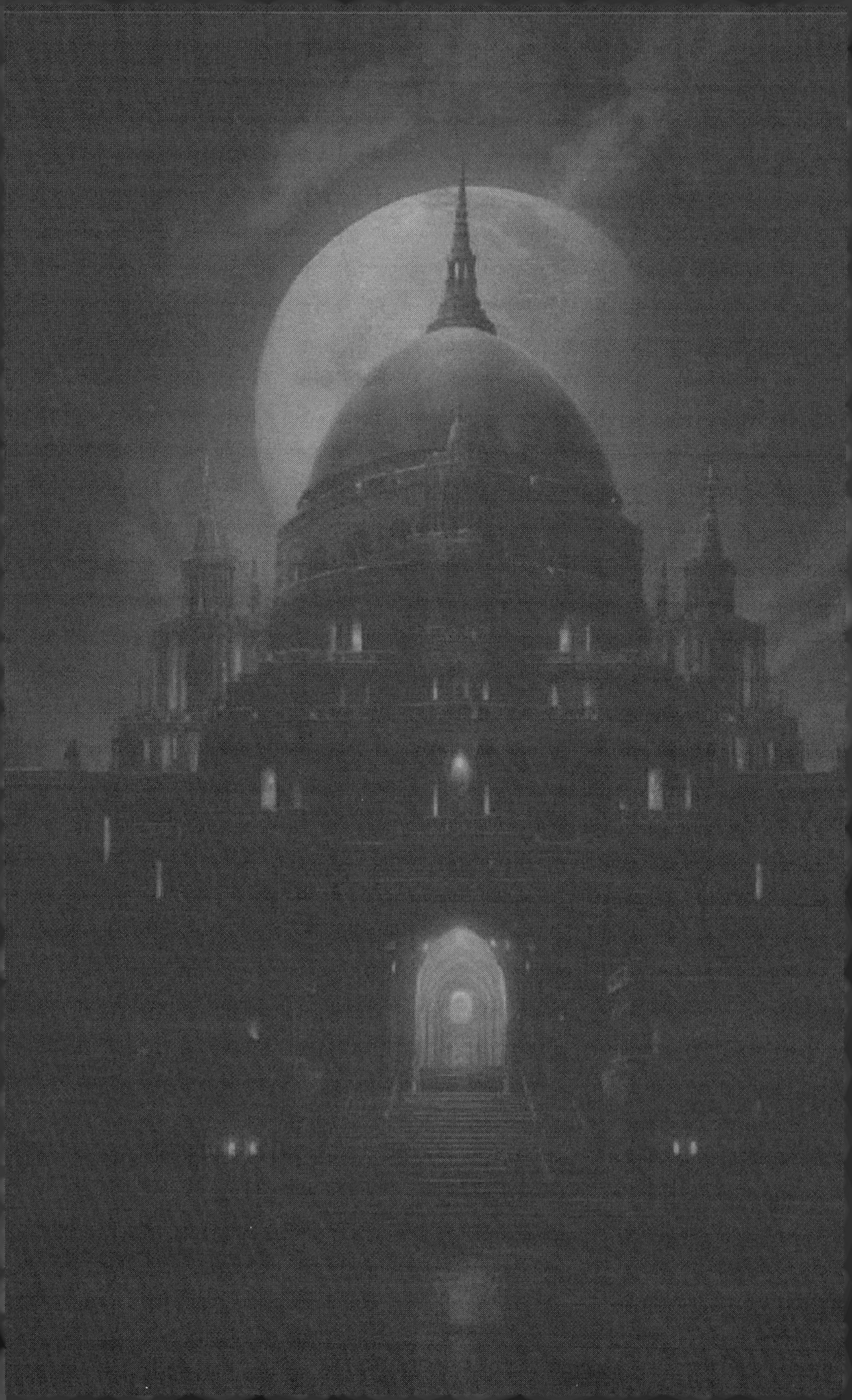

TWENTY-THREE
BUFFET OF TERROR

ALICIA CHAY

I awakened from slumber in the safety of my bedroom. Was it all a dream. Another dream that seemed real. Maybe it was a vision. No, It happened!

Or was it a glimpse of things to come? I looked at my mirror. Gone was the message written with my lipstick.

Now it read, *"Nice to meet you, Alicia. The next time we see each other, you won't remember who I am."*

I was baffled for two reasons. One, how was he able to see my invisible fortress on Vencreashia? And two, how was he able to locate my empire? Did he bring me to the comfort of my room for safety? At least I knew he wasn't trying to kill me. I was confused. I was infuriated!

I prided myself on being inconspicuous; now that was gone out the window like it was never a reality.

Bummer! I summoned the head of my security. He was a heavy set vampire ghoul that worked for me since 1 B.C.E., around the time I slept with a Greek ruler for ownership of his empire. I took a page out of Armona's book. In an instant, he was at my disposal.

He brushed his hair with his hands. "Yes, Alicia, Queen Mother?"

"Search high and low for Khovahsh Burgoos. He is number one on my most wanted list. Once he is captured, bring him to me, alive. I will deal with him accordingly."

Slush'shu nodded. "As you wish, Alicia, Queen Mother."

"You have twenty-four hours to find him. If you fail to deliver that traitor, you will die in his place. Do I make myself clear, Slush'shu?"

"Crystal." In an instant, he became a school of crows and flew east.

KHOVAHSH BURGOOS:

Drinking endangered animal blood was a delight I never passed up, despite Alicia's ridiculous Treaty of the Animals. It was much easier than chasing down imperiled humans. I enjoyed tasting their flesh. Some tastes you had to acquire like a vegetarian virgin eating olives for the first time.

All human blood wasn't worth drinking. In fact, I'd drank so much disease-infested blood that I switched to eating animals to curb my thirst for mortals. Nonetheless, I thought of Alicia, the so-call Queen Mother of the supernatural world, and the Treaty she implemented.

She punished vampires that legally and illegally kill animals. Phooey!

Not only that, what gave her the right to punish me because I wasn't aware of her policies and laws? Spitting fire at the bitch was a highlight, but I regretted it. I couldn't kill her even if I wanted to. Deep down, I laughed just thinking about dropping her atheist puppet from thirty thousand feet in the air. I was immune to her law. Armona was appointed to be the Queen.

Granted, I was quite disturbed that Alicia was drawn to him in the first place, a human I possessed since 1997. I laid low within him for years without controlling his body, until Alicia showed up on the scene, saving Pastor Ford's face before it become spaghetti on his office walls. I wanted that to happen so I could be free. Seeing her made my heart skip a beat.

She stopped a bullet with her bare hand. Casting a sleeping spell on her was worth the hassle. I had to keep her safe. Now it was time to feast.

I possessed another human body. A female, this time. I frowned at her taste in food. There was nothing that could stop me from turning every rain forest into my own personal buffet of terror.

How amazing was that? There was one rain forest that tickled my fancy. The Grand Forest. Centuries later, I recalled the Village of Opus. It was once located past the massive forest of beauty and deception.

I also remembered one of the villagers named Klĕŏphấ Achieng.

The gifted one, the chosen one; the one I would never forgot.

I had a lot of lovers, but I hadn't thought of any other woman in my life, but her.

My thoughts were on her and of her. She was different from everyone else. She had a unique quality about her that was destined for something bigger than the village that confined her, a village that misled her. The villagers hated her because, if it weren't for Klĕŏphấ's birth, her mother, a legendary champion of the village, as strong and as stern as the Elders, would still be with them.

The girl born in accordance with the sun and of the forest, the girl an entire village deemed a gift from their god, served a unique purpose.

The village betrayed her in the end, before the settlement was burned to the ground by supernatural forces, wiping them off the face of the planet.

Ḳlĕŏphȃ was a beautiful girl that fascinated me. She inspired me to change the way I looked at myself. She went against the rules, all the way to her death. She left a lasting impression, and we'd never met face-to-face.

Her soul was a powerful entity. Then Alicia Chay came into my life. Bullets, tasers, lasers, and guns couldn't stop me from thinking about her. I thought of her more than I should.

I wanted to warn her about Muzzle, but she tried to kill me. Her minion, Slush'shu, searched high and low for me. I observed him from ten thousand feet above.

I acquired my tracking skills so long ago…. I was once the vampire, the extraordinary vampire that walked through the civil war, dodging every bullet that careened passed me from the smoky chambers of powerful rifles.

While President Abraham Lincoln tried to save the Union with his dangerous men and not the slaves, I feasted on dead mortals. There was no needeth to leave all that precious food lying about for vultures.

Why should they have all the white and dark meat? I left the dark meat for vultures to devour. I feasted on ivory-colored flesh. After catching a flesh-eating disease, I began to die amidst thunderous canons. My life was over!

A bald eagle soared high above the war, the blood, the fallen warriors, and the gun smoke. I wished to taste the blood of life. I needed to ingest something alive and not dead, to distinctly separate the two tastes.

The latter appealed more to my senses. I couldn't die like this!

Gathering all the strength I could muster, I stood up. Snarling, I rose in the air, and then I began to fly after the bald eagle. It took a while, but I finally nabbed him. I viciously snapped off his wings and dropped them.

I ripped open his head and drank from the rich interior while levitating seven thousand feet in the air. The rush I experienced changed my life forever and for the better. My face reconstructed itself.

My body was comprised of black granite. Intricate etchings zigzagged along either side of my face. I was in rare form, enshrouded in color of all kinds, before limitations and boundaries were set on me.

I was split into 144,000 forms of polarization. My image was filtered through the eyes of 144,000, and then limitation, color and the yielding of color was transposed on them, individually and as a group.

The way the clouds unfolded empowered me. The sky transformed me into a beast of my own accord. I levitated, staring at the head of the eagle. His eyes were sunken.

I felt nothing for his death. I felt nothing for the kill. The dead eagle plummeted towards the sea of bodies below. I looked at the moon and saw a brief image of a rainbow. It made me shudder because I didn't know what it was.

Being a centuries-old vagabond, living as a young thirteen-year-old during the civil war was no easy task. I had to fend for myself. I didn't have guidance or a teacher. My only family were my Dragonhead Ancient brothers, but we had our own lives. We only came together when it was necessary.

Since the eagle's blood was on my hands, I'd been indifferent. I lived a long time feeling this way, with no desire to change. I withdrew into myself and left a bloodbath of bodies. I was a savage, with no feelings and emotions.

The blood of the eagle gave me the ability to do one thing, and that was the power to reincarnate myself.

I decided to do that with a slave in the south during the early 1920s.

JA'BREEL LE'DIAMOND

He was a feeble-minded man that was enslaved with his family.

When his master inappropriately touched his wife, he punched him in the face. Three other white men thundered into the room and grabbed him.

After hitting the slave with the butt of a rifle, the master assaulted him in front of his children.

A horse and carriage was being prepared. He was going to be separated from his family, forever.

Four dirty lads tried to cling to their mother as they were haggardly stripped away by the master.

TWENTY-FOUR
ABANDONED

KHOVAHSH BURGOOS

I remembered the event that changed the course of his life, the life of his family, the lives of the rapists, and inevitably…my life. Each of the men spat on him while the master shoved his member inside the slave.

Before his master could climax, I jumped into the slave's body.

I possessed him. I killed three of the four men before they could scream. I spared the man who wanted to violate the slave last; coming back for a second round of action was not his intention.

I tortured him slowly. The friends of the masters that abused the women slaves were all inside.

They met a horrifying fate. The instant I took over the slave's body, I began to feel the effects.

His arteries, veins, and membranes shackled me, yet his T4 cells attacked me, since I wasn't born with his body. I was a foreign object.

JA'BREEL LE'DIAMOND

They weren't powerful enough to kill me.

My glowing soul took away the pain of assault; the blood spilled from his anus suddenly snaked back inside him as he slowly rose in the air. His bones broke him down.

A thunderous cracking sound caused the master to run.

Before he could escape, I scowled. All the doors locked.

A force field enveloped the house, trapping him inside.

All hell broke loose. I was bloodthirsty. I looked at my wife and kids now that I was in his body, now that I was the slave. They were my possessions.

I freed them into the north, giving them an identity. They were no longer considered property. I freed them for a greater purpose. I abandoned them. If they were around me, I was going to murder them all, and I couldn't live with myself if that had happened.

As his body grew old and tired over the next few decades, despite my soul being in it, I knew something had to change. His seventies were about to close. He was about eighty years old.

I was tired of using his body to be a serial killer. I killed every participant in the holocaust that I could. I slaughtered over seventy-eight moneyed men that invested in the slave trade, an event that changed the course of the world forever.

An event that still placed a sour taste in many darkened ones' mouths. I couldn't say that I blamed them. Unfortunately, animals have attacked me for decades because of the brutal way I killed the bald eagle.

Yes, I drank his blood. I had the sense and the agility of a bald eagle. The concept of my powers was difficult to follow beyond human comprehension, so I wasn't going to explain it.

I could shapeshift at will, which was different from my reincarnation ability.

My arms shifted into an array of earth-toned feathers. They were soft. I didn't use one of two sets of wings that often. I could fly without them.

Despite the freedom I gained, rainbows caused me to be obedient. The day I basked in a rainbow's glory was the day my life changed forever.

It was on Independence Day, 1977. I decided to reincarnate myself, since the universe gave me the unlimited ability to do so.

Using hypnotism, I married a nun and had her expelled from a cathedral she was living in. We made love by the river, something she never experienced. I impregnated her. My soul reincarnated into the seeds I implanted in her.

The slave's body lost its luster and turned to ash. Screaming, she crossed her hands over her chest, marking an invisible cross. She inevitably gave birth me, a healthy eight-pound, six-ounce boy in an African forest.

She kissed me with adoration.

I had rainbow-colored eyes infused into balls of light. Once she held me close, the darkness swallowed the clouds, and a million stars spiraled into each other. Truly, it was a sight to see.

If it wasn't filled with rage and deception.

To my dismay, huge hands extended from the earth, taking me from her. Once I was engulfed by the stars, she was pulled, terrified and screaming, into the earth.

Five months later I awakened from a coma. I was five months old. I was adopted by a wealthy family in Florida. I grew up rich and spoiled. We moved to California. Everything was given to me.

Servants cleaned behind me and cooked my meals. As an introverted seven-year-old, maids and servants were at my disposal. I had the best money could buy.

When I turned eight, my adoptive parents hit rock bottom.

We lost it all and had to move from the mansion in Beverly Hills to a

Chicago project. I was a firm believer in God. And therein, was the problem. I only believed in him when we were rich. Once we became poor, I lost all faith.

I paid attention to the world around me. I was dealing with spiritual warfare.

Music and videos became darkened affairs used to program society. Entertainment itself conditioned me into a certain thought process that I had unknowingly applied to my daily life and those I loved most in the world when I was a mortal. Everyone was choosing a side.

I eventually had to choose one as well, and it came during my thirteenth birthday.

Them: the government and their sick needeth to control humans, no matter the continent, no matter the country or the state. Or.

Us: the ignorant, the fools, the ones with something they wanted to possess but never could. Still, they could certainly use the idea of free will to their advantage and for their benefit.

Free will was the most sought-after initiative the government wishes to hold the titles to at least.

The people needed to open their eyes, not that I gave a damn. People were just as evil as Armona.

All people thought about were themselves.

Humans would rather feed a dog than the homeless, and I'd drain the dog, the human and the homeless for blood because of what I was and what I would never be again.

The only interaction I had with mortals was when I used their bodies as my hosts to keep tabs on Alicia Chay.

For her protection....

TWENTY-FIVE
BUILDING'S ABLAZE

ALICIA CHAY

What occurred after I was placed under a sleeping spell still baffled me. Was it even a spell? There seemed to be a level of uncertainty as to the direction I was going in, especially after Khovahsh brought me to my bedroom.

As I came back down to earth, shaking away the memories, I thought to myself. I had a tough exterior. Nothing penetrated that cold block of ice protecting whatever heart was in my chest cavity. Unfortunately, I was this way for forty centuries until a bloody event eventually broke my cold-hearted, uncaring demigod Queen nature.

The Saint Louis massacre.

July 1917

The year was 1917. I was awakened from slumber in the bed of the Queen Mother in Vencreashia. It took a moment for me to catch my bearings. It was after seven pm.

I was hungry. I wanted to hunt, but I told myself that it wasn't worth the hassle.

Outside of a Council meeting with members of my elite government, I planned on resting.

Being that my eight-billion-dollar estate was the only residence on this continent, I kept to myself. My three-layer castle used to be cleverly hidden. Before I knew it, I floated out of my open window. I needed alone time.

On the way down, the smell of blood caught my attention. I had flown thousands of miles through four weather changes in five regions. My skin crawled as I sniffed.

The strong smell of blood vaporized into smoke. I appeared from tar and flames as I entered the state of Missouri. To my amusement, a mob had been terrorizing dark-skinned people.

They said Black people were evil, yet ivory burned in the sun. If ever there was a moment that humbled me, that was it. I was a demigod vampire that hardly got entangled in civilian affairs.

I regretted the things I did to become the Queen Mother. I truly wished I could have done things differently. It wasn't clear what the correlation between my regret and being involved with civilian affairs was. Maybe I hated the way blacks were being treated.

It was a side effect of gaining the Queen Mother's power.

It exposed me to destructive thoughts that led to me being sympathetic.

Why did seeing the mob make me regret how I went about taking the Queen mother's power?

At this time in my life, I did some soul searching.

I thought about how I overthrew the Queen Mother, Armona, and took over her system of things.

I was at the top of the food chain.

I was a judge, jury, lawyer, and executioner without courtrooms or taxpayer money. During 2 BCE and before that, Armona was the most feared being, in any form, in earth's history.

She was so powerful she never had a last name. Just Armona.

Fortunately, she was rotting away in an untraceable grave and had been for the past forty centuries.

As much as I hated seeing what black people were going through, I never intended to get sucked into the funnel of their problems.

I witnessed a white mob snatch Black folk out of their cars, purging a few before running off to attack more strange fruit. Enraged white folk set buildings ablaze. Illinois Governor called in the National Guard. It was like a big-budgeted Hollywood movie.

I had to look around to make sure I wasn't on set. The massacre was unlike anything I'd ever seen. White men in a black Ford Model T drove through a black area of the city.

The passengers fired several shots into a group on the street. Shortly thereafter, a Ford containing four people, including a journalist and two police officers, passed through the same area. Black residents opened fire on the car, killing one officer and wounding another.

The next day, thousands of white spectators gathered to view the bloodstained automobile. From there, they rushed into the black sections of town, south and west of the city, and began rioting.

The mob beat and shot Black people on the street indiscriminately, including women and children. After cutting the water hoses off the fire trucks, white rioters burned entire sections of the city and shot Black residents.

Even more, Black people were pulled off the bus by angry mobs and savagely beaten, while others were killed execution-style. For a Black family that worked tirelessly to maintain their humble belongings, they were met with a different fate amidst an all-out war against the alleged God's Chosen People.

Black people.

    Meanwhile, a few miles away from the genocide, James tried to save a stray dog from choking on a bone. The beauty of the opposing end of the afternoon hour couldn't get his attention, nor did the seven white men that crept up behind him. I watched James do everything he could to save the Rottweiler from choking. The passion in his voice as the dog was dying lured me to his bungalow. I looked at the precious animal, and the bone in his throat turned to sugar.

    After licking his lips, the Rottweiler hopped up to his feet and started licking James in the face. And that was when the racist goons attacked. An enraged perpetrator struck a devastating blow to the back of James's head, sending him to his knees.

    Four rednecks dragged him into his house with his beautiful, brown-skinned family. His wife was terrified. Once the men rushed outside, they locked the Black family inside. They boarded up the front and back doors. Once they finished, they set the house on fire.

    Amidst celebratory cheers from drunken lips, they assembled the perimeter of the home. They threw rocks until all the windows were shattered. The black family had a choice to be burnt alive or die by gunfire if they decided to jump out of the living-room window. I was in deep conflict. I hated humans.

    Seriously, if it hadn't been for the dog's pain, I would have never known James existed.

    I was the Queen Mother. I had nothing to do with this race war. I closed my eyes and jumped five hundred feet into the air.

    A mournful yelp after a gunshot stopped me, midair.

    I looked down at the wounded dog.

    Life began to slip from his eyes.

    I don't want to die! I want to save the nice stranger man that saved me from choking on a bone!

I translated the dog's thoughts. Dogs were loyal, even if you were not loyal to them. Glancing down into the soulless eyes of each mobster destroying Black home for blocks, their bloodline made me scream with thunderous affinity. Momentarily, the astronomical roar stopped everyone. White mobsters searched the sky and everything around them.

Ah! They were startled! I found it fascinating! "Screw that! Kill those coons, now! *And that's an order!*"

Meanwhile, inside the home...

James gathered his son and three daughters and ushered them into his bedroom. Joan, his pregnant wife, plugged the drain in the sink and bathtub and turned on the hot and cold-water full blast. She started a flood.

"Everyone in the bathroom! Now!"

"I'm scared, Mom!" said his oldest daughter, grief-stricken. Joan glared at her husband.

"What are we gonna do, James? What about our kids? We're gonna die!" Vaporizing from the sky, I rose from flames, tar, and smoke before the leader of one of the mobs, clad in body glitter derived from grinded gemstones.

My bluish-white hair of unheated flames was on standby until further notice. Ashton, the Rottweiler, was at my side. I smiled as I looked at him, patting his head four times. I couldn't let him die at the hands of an angry white man that cared nothing about life or the destruction of beauty. I decided to help James because that's what the dog wanted.

I gave a command. "Drop your weapons."

"Screw you!"

I winked at his men, and they aimed at his head. "Put out that fire, you vermin," I demanded.

He was a stubborn piece of carcass. "Those niggers are about to..."

I was tired of talking. Conjuring my strength, a replica of me exited my body. She screamed and blew ripples of ice toward the burning house while holograms of my infinite power formed a circle around every Black family on the block.

They were protected from the flames and smoke. Once they were safe, I raised my arms high. The ground shook. Seventy members of the mob lost their footing from the rumbling.

Hideously, flaming sulfuric arms expanded from the dirt and all the burning homes in a five-block radius, and pulled the screaming men into the fire. I smiled.

My polished porcelain fangs glistened in a way their frantic eyes never would again. Once they were dead, I leaped into the sky, exploding into a black eagle.

I was in the shower a few days later, washing blood off my tired body. Five slaves, with nooses around their necks, helped bathe me. They were ex-plantation owners with nail kilts piercing their hips. They were taking turns tasting me. Lust sparkled in their eyes. I'd experienced orgasms a few times already! Each was more powerful than the previous. They washed and scrubbed me from head to toe in the Bell De la Bell Latrine of the Ancient Queen Mother.

On their backs and faces were whelps and scars. They were punished in loving memory of dead slaves that were cold-heartedly thrown over ships en route to America and tortured at the hands of their ancestors.

So, I punished their descendants and the seeds of their sexual labor, wiping the sweat off my brow as I made them remember sins from yesteryear.

From a high-ceilinged, stained glass dome, a huge chandelier hung from a platinum rope chain. The stained glass dome was filled with snapshots of the Civil Rights movement in gilt frames and the Renaissance Era. Elder cherubs made love to nature on the silk wallpaper.

I loved this room.

Sixty feet in height, the walls lead into the foyer of my grand bedroom. The Torture Room was legendary!

The humidity was startling and intense; it was too hot for for my slaves that once sold slaves, spat on slaves and killed slaves after assaulting them.

The only thing worse than their incarceration was death itself. I couldn't imagine being taken captive by dark forces and forced to tend to their young and clean their homes.

One man's treasure had always been another woman's woes. The Torture Room was a room my slaves were never allowed to leave.

And the hell with the Emancipation Proclamation! The sacred document penned by Mr. Lincoln was invalid in my chambers. The government didn't care for my slaves anyway.

They were presumed dead.

The lives that they once knew were dead to them.

They didn't have any recollection of their birthright.

I stripped them of it.

There would be hell on earth for my slaves until they perished.

TWENTY-SIX
EVERY HEART I ATE

KHOVAHSH BURGOOS

I thought back to those naïve days when I didn't have a clue what was going on around me. I was a confused teenager, distracted by the wars in the ghettos.

I never studied a rainbow or cared to see one. I turned my back on a promise. God used a rainbow to symbolize that he wouldn't destroy the world with another flood. Man, instead, would destroy themselves. If you asked me, it was all a pissing match.

The civil wars in courtrooms all over the country divided darkened mortals into staggering groups, with child support being a booming business.

It was very profitable, not that it pertained to me because both of my adoptive parents were dead.

That was a lifetime ago. I couldn't say that I missed them. I really didn't.

That day I died in two diverse ways: with heart and soul.

Unfortunately, I never recovered. My reincarnated self died shortly after, around my thirteenth birthday.

I remembered who I used to be in a past life. I had the knowledge of the eighty-year-old slave I used to be as well, but not of him one hundred percent collectively. He was a birthday suit I inhabited for a bigger purpose. Using him as a host, I hypnotized a virgin nun, spent all night pleasuring her, and then I married her. Yes, I loved her. She gazed into my eyes. Her womanly folds fit tightly on my erected staff of sorts.

I remember the events before I inhabited the slave. I remember the civil war. I recalled the bullets I caught from the blow of the wind while Abraham Lincoln killed for a union he couldn't save.

So, he abolished slavery. The Emancipation Proclamation was the biggest lie told to the slaves. It was a signed document that was written by a president that denounced his Negro heritage before he took office.

For every fallen soldier I fed from, for every heart I ate, I left a bullet shell on the forehead. It was all locked in my subconscious.

I had a good childhood with my adoptive parents.

I lived in a home filled with servants. I was plagued with nightmares of the civil war, and of a president I hardly knew anything about. He certainly didn't abolish slavery. It was only modified. I never knew I was once Immortal.

I was reborn through the act of sin, despite being married to the nun. Her only purpose was to carry my reincarnated self to term. If it wasn't for the power of hypnotism, I would have perished. Mating with the nun was imperative for my survival. It was all or nothing. Unfortunately, if I was born a bastard, not only would I have never known I was an Immortal creature, but the sure way to the knowledge locked inside of me would have been lost forever, along with my seat with the Dragonhead Ancients.

I wouldn't have remembered that I jumped above the president, his troops, his foes, and the boom of powerful rifles, and ripped a bald eagle's head off without warning or apology. I instinctively poured its DNA into my genetic makeup when I was poverty-stricken. I didn't care.

My rich adoptive parents lost it all and was forced to move to Chicago. Rich Anglo folk on TV sang for my last dollar, and I barely had that. At twelve years old, leading to my life-changing thirteenth birthday, I knew we were "broken down" into three categories in the Pyramid of Life. The Rich. The Middle Class. The Dirt Poor. The Pyramid of Life.

Being a member of the military, having joined when I was eighteen years old, wasn't what it was cracked up to be. I did have an amazing career.

I knew this as a fact. My rich friends granted me immunity against the rules other soldiers had to follow because of my other life—the life of an assassin. I killed generals and lieutenants.

I killed men in positions of power that were beneficial to the policies of the Chain of Command. There were secret orgies. I took a blood oath.

I was axed from "the Circle" of the Chain of Command because I told the woman I married after graduating high school about my extracurricular activities. I couldn't deal with the guilt.

I answered every question she asked and told her every law I broke for the Chain of Command, things that could land us in prison, or dead. She was grief-stricken but she stayed by my side.

The truth about why I was sometimes gone for weeks at a time opened my wife's eyes. I was a murderer.

Still, I had another job, and that job was more important than my military career.

Fortunately and unfortunately.

It was about the Chain of Command.

KHOVAHSH

I defiled the secrets of my rich friends by talking about their secrets with my wife. They cut me off.

How was I supposed to know my home was bugged? Suddenly, the most popular one in "The Bunch" became a disgrace and took his place at the bottom of the totem pole.

I prayed that they didn't touch my insignia and ribbons. I earned every one of them, including the Purple Heart. I was wounded while saving one hundred kids from being blown up on a bus.

I'd be damned if I sat by and let them take my hard work because I confided in my wife. There were things I refused to forget about the slave I inhabited and the previous life I led—the vampire I used to be. It was a dangerous sport I engaged in, calling on an angel during times of trouble and conjured dark spirits once I became successful.

I thanked myself for my achievements. I convinced myself that I was successful because of my own labor.

I kept to myself a lot. I didn't have many friends.

During my freshman year of high school, that would soon change.

I grew up lonely, despite having two loving parents. They may not have been my folks biologically, but I loved them no less. I hated crowds because my beautiful adoptive mother loved crowds.

I loved privacy because my humble adoptive father, Bob, hated privacy. He was a garbage collector after he lost his wealth (drug bust by the Feds and the ATF) and moved to Chi-Town. Everyone loved Mr. Popular, and so did I.

He was a hands-on man that helped me with my schoolwork. He was a stern disciplinarian. My mother, Ginger, forty-five years old, was the most beautiful woman in the world.

She spent more time in church than at home, with her family, or with me, her adoptive child and her only child. I put nothing above my mother.

Not even God. I worshiped Mama. She was my pride and joy.

FORTY YEARS LATER

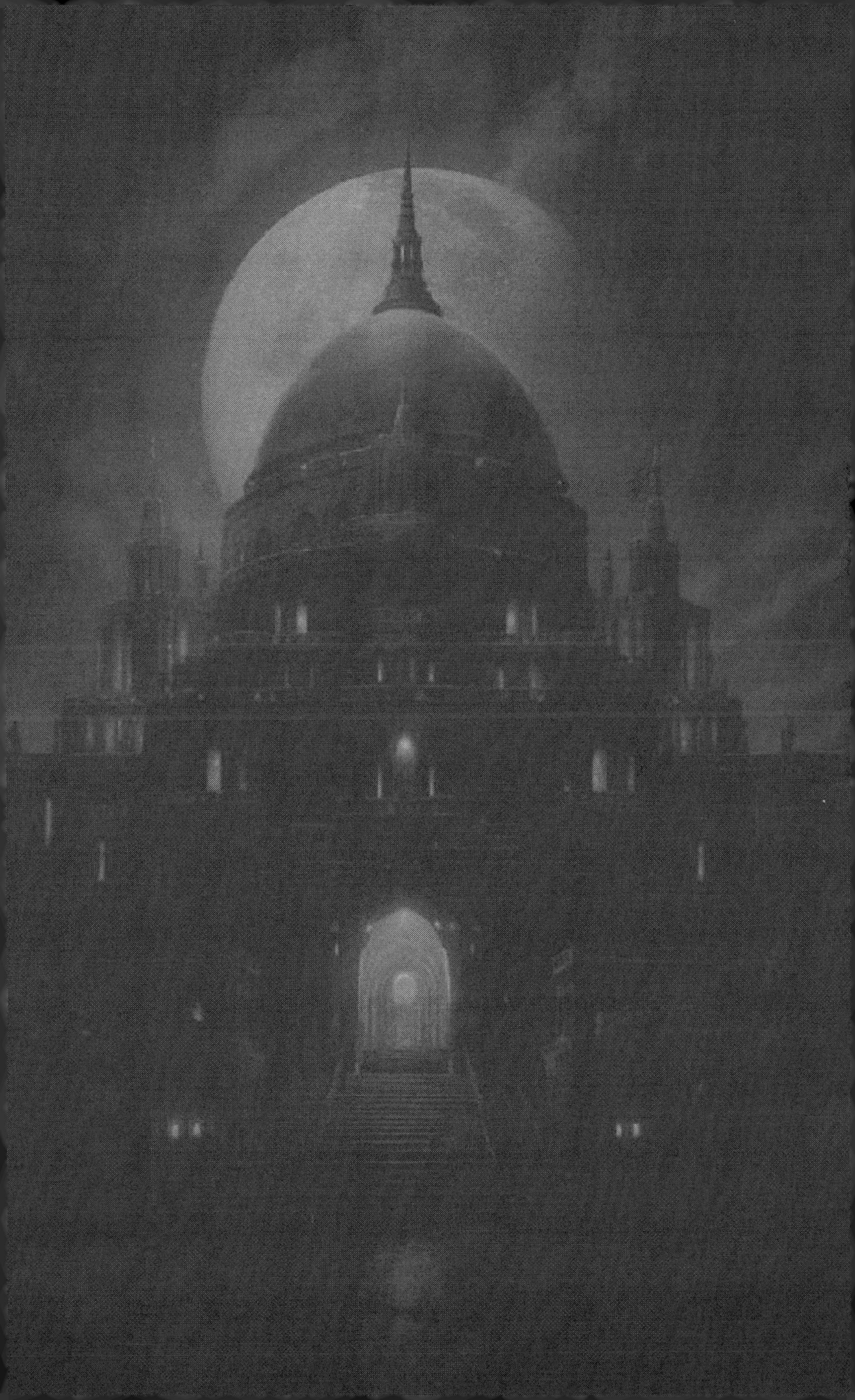

TWENTY-SEVEN
COUNCIL MEETING

ALICIA CHAY

It was a quarter past one a.m. I used telecommunications to summon an emergency board meeting with Armona's old board members.

I prepared the Council Room of the Queen Mother. One by one, they appeared before me. Thirteen cushioned conference chairs surrounded the polished oak wooden table. Seventeen chandeliers emitted fifty watts of light. It was easy on the eyes. Once they found their respective seats, I called the room to order.

"Roll call. At one-second intervals, state your name."

Golden...Boa...Android…Lydia, Digital, Soundbite, Gorgeous, Ramón, Sawford, Trumpet, and Jayshion. I informed them of my encounters with Khovahsh and put onto the docket the crimes against the Dershakney he committed. Even though he kept me safe, I didn't ask for his help.

KHOVAHSH

At the end of the day, I was Queen Mother. Digital informed me that Khovahsh was a part of the dominion that owned the Dershakney and my laws.

Golden interjected, "Unfortunately, he's immune from the law, Alicia, Queen Mother. He's a top regal ancient god-tier demi-shifting reincarnate with a life span of three hundred million years."

I stared blankly. "*Before* dinosaurs?"

"Yes, Armona," said Lydia, "I meant Alicia, my apologies. As crooked as he is, his actions are protected by the sura of the Dragonhead Ancients."

"The sura?" I repeated.

Snake gazed at me, clad in a beige suit. "We answer to the Dragonhead Ancients. Fortunately, they never interfere with our order of operations. They work for the one percent: themselves."

"But I am Queen Mother."

"A mere face on the brand," said Boa, "if you will. With unlimited godlike power. Yes, you are in place to run the supernatural realms as you see fit, but you are restricted to just that: Queen Mother and the boss of us."

I started brooding with defiance. "I'm not your labels or your myths."

Sound Bite tested my intelligence with offending negligence.

"Tell us, Queen. What consequence do you suffer for breaking Dershakney law? You are guilty of the same crimes as Khovahsh Burgoos."

I glared at him with bloody eyes. I wrung my hands, and Sound Bite levitated above the middle of the Grand table. After I paralyzed him, I set him on fire before his constituents and let him roast a bit, enough to remind him of his place.

I didn't like sassy men. It was not my cup of bloody tea. I looked at him, and the fire and pain vanished. He was in his seat again as if nothing had happened. I looked at everybody.

"Watch your tone." Sound Bite was relieved.

"Basically, Khovahsh is in place to secretly create supernatural havoc, cause the problem, and then he shows up with the solution," Digital informed me. "It keeps the supernatural communities loyal and obedient."

"Only then does he implement his own agenda," said Ramon. "There has to be a loophole in the Dershakney."

"It's air sealed tight by Armona," said Gorgeous. He had three eyes below a thick uni-brow.

"The Dershakney is the only thing you can't change, undue, or revise."

"So let me get this straight. Khovahsh can't be judged by my authority."

"No," everyone said in unison. With a loud noise, the enormous double doors to the Council Room of the Queen Mother flung open, startling us. Slush'Shu returned. I gazed at him. I knew I could depend on him.

"Is the job done, Slu'Shu?" He remained quiet. He never ignored me before. "Where is Khovahsh?" Blood seeped from his eyes. His head fell from his neck and rolled over my feet.

Attached to his upper garment was a note. Dismayed, I read it aloud.. *Come get me yourself, Alicia, the way you took the throne. Never send the help to find a demigod!*

His voice filled my ears. I grit my teeth out of frustration. I clapped my hands, and Slush'Shu's body turned to dust. After I scooped up his ashes, I poured them into the hourglass at the head of the table.

"I can't do this right now. Slush'Shu was my friend."

"Do we truly have friends as vampires?" Android asked with an irregular breathing pattern.

"I would think that maybe we have allies," said Sawford, "but alliances aren't genuine friendships."

"You make it sound so vague," I responded, thinking about my dead friend.

"Our suggestion…just lay low somewhere for a while," said Trumpet, pulling his long thick hair into a bun. Everyone agreed. Sawford grimaced.

KHOVAHSH

"The last thing we need is a visit from those that breathe brimstone. If you can turn your back on the Hound House, then lay low."

Jayshion remained quiet. Lydia said, "If you agree, raise your hands."

Everyone raised their right hands. Deeply upset, I vanished.

Once I appeared in my grand bedroom, I fell back on my mattress and covered my face.

I stared at the leaves. They quivered on swaying branches that reminded me of pom-poms.

After an eternity, they became blurs, ghosts…then I was out.

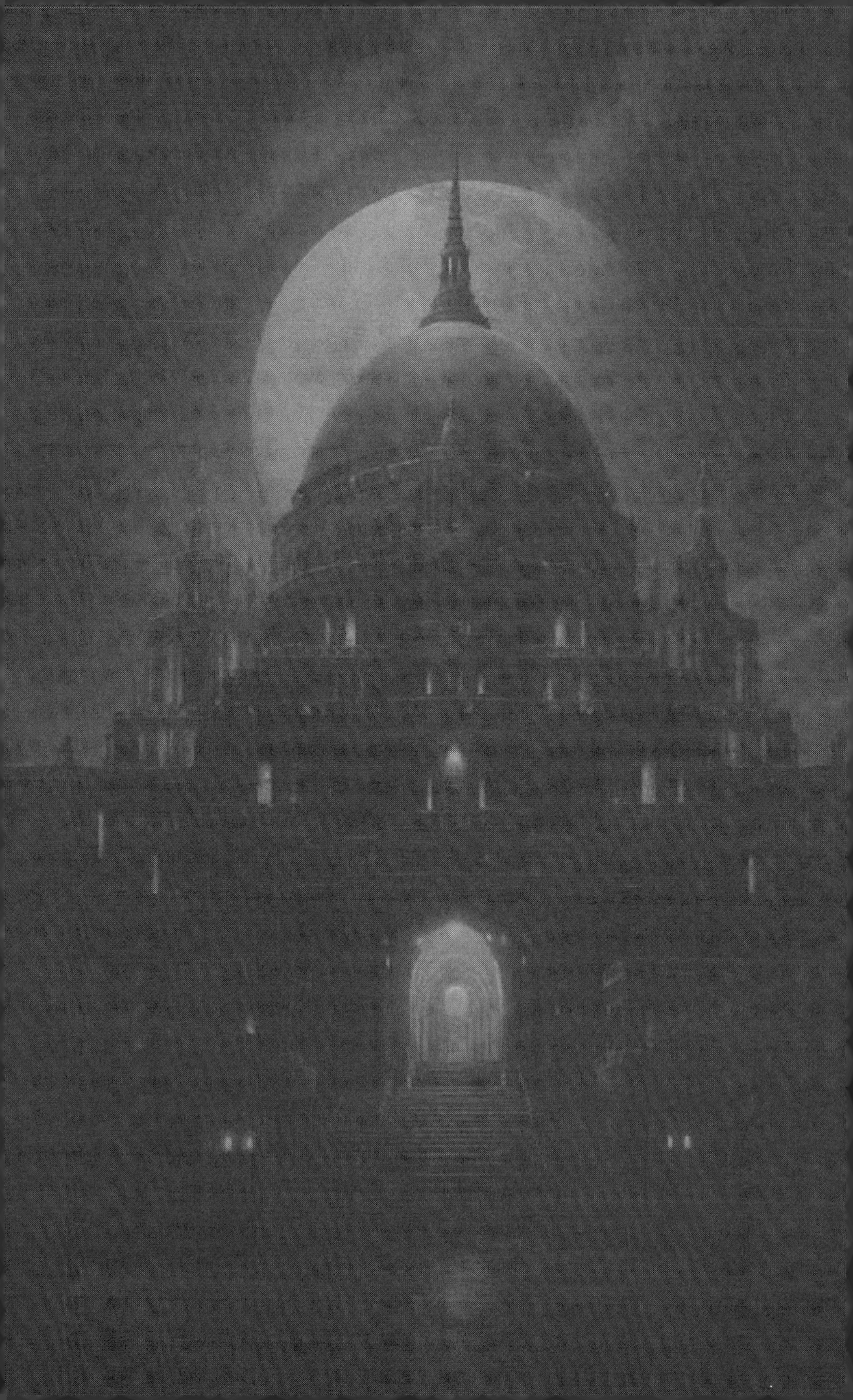

A YEAR LATER

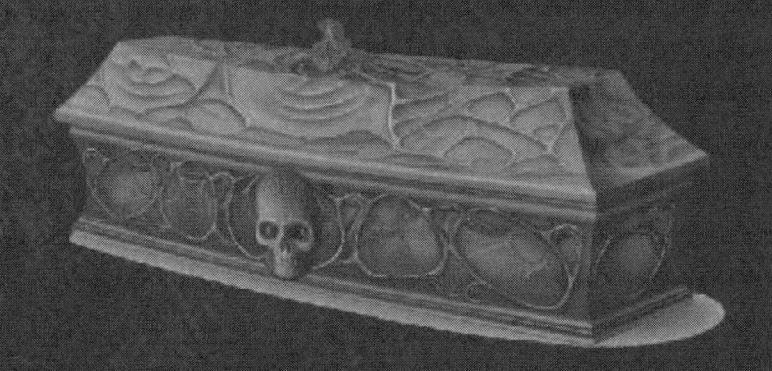

TWENTY-EIGHT
I HEARD OF

ALICIA CHAY

The gentle glow of the computer monitor shined in my face as I read over Brenda Seymour's essay paper from my quaint bungalow in Downtown Fort Lauderdale, Florida.

    Jesus Christ was one of, if not the greatest man, and the most famous man, that ever lived! In fact, he's the greatest man to have ever walked the earth.

    Nothing tops the ministry of the Son of God. His life have been one of the most talked about events in global history. His crucifixion was the basis of a few movies. When he rose from the dead, he became the gospel, and his human life had come to pass; Amen, so be it.

    Two thousand years ago, he once lived in Palestine. He was born in Jerusalem to a virgin woman by the name of Mary. God came to her in a dream and told her she was going to give birth to his son.

He pre-existed before her pregnancy and post-existed as well. In the beginning, there was the Word (God), and the Word was God (Jesus), and the Word was with God (The Holy Ghost). In mortal form, he lived for thirty-three years on earth.

He began his ministry when he was thirty years old, publicly performed miracles, fed the hungry, cast out demons, brought a man back from the dead, healed a blind man and a leaper. It all had a purpose.

He performed miracles to show he was sent by God and for spectators to praise God through his acts of love and compassion. But there were some stubborn hearts that still didn't believe. One man, Judas, betrayed the Son of God with an ill-suited kiss, and it would cost him his life, dying for our sins.

The only thing Christ lost was his life on earth, in mortal form. His crucifixion served a greater purpose; the main agenda was to die for the sins of man and bare all iniquity. His crucifixion put the New Covenant into operation and the Old Covenant out of order, but it was met with opposition. Written by Brenda Seymour. 12th grade.

Rollins High School.

Fort Lauderdale, Florida

I lived as a teacher/lecturer for the past year at the urging of my cabinet members. I laid low. Being Brenda's teacher was the escape I needed, but Brenda's essay paper broke my retrospective chain of thought.

Unfortunately, my student did a poor job. Her paper seemed rushed—copied even. It didn't meet the criteria. Just because she wrote about Christ meant she got an automatic A?

Despite a missing bibliography, her paper was informative. Yes, I heard of Jesus, but I was bound by the darkness and its terms of endearment. With that in mind, I found myself levitating through my ceiling and appearing from circulating dust on a stool at a local bar on NW 27th Avenue in Miami Gardens.

It was after nine p.m., and I needed a drink. Catching my eye, the tall, handsome waiter walked over to me. "No offense, but you're beautiful." I knew that. Who was I toot his horn, because I wasn't getting on my knees. "Thank you," I said, barely above a whisper.

"Shoot, do you know what...? The drink is on me since the bar is about to close."

"Appreciate it. No ice, please. The warmer, the better."

He turned his back and fixed the vodka and cranberry I asked for.

"I've never seen you in here before," he started, looking deep into my eyes. He handed me the drink. Now was not the time to tell him that he was in the early stage of diabetes or that he was going to die in his sleep after he found true love because his ex-wife killed herself after he had a child with her mother.

A few people stood up, dancing to salsa music.

"I never knew of this rooftop bar. I like it. It's very engaging."

He turned up the charm. I noticed the crucifix around his neck. His veins were thick and juicy, like his Johnson, but I wasn't there for a good time.

He cupped my left hand. "What's your name?"

"Becky Sims," I lied. "And yours?"

He chuckled. "Matt."

"So, do you believe in Jesus?"

My question threw him off, guard. "No, why?"

"I mean... you wear the crucifix."

He withdrew his hand. "It's more like a prop."

I sipped and observed. "If you don't believe, why even wear it? You don't find that offensive?"

His mood changed. "Listen, lady. I'm not into Jehovah's Witnesses."

I looked at him fixedly. "Never said that I was one. I merely asked a question, and your tampon went in the wrong hole." I killed the drink.

"You know what? Screw you, bitch! And that'll be twenty dollars for the drink."

I stood up and headed for the latrine. I wanted to wash up and splash cold water on my face. He was annoying. Mortals were predictable creatures.

His eyes were lasers. "Are you going to pay for that drink?"

I entered the women's restroom. "No!"

Matt abruptly burst through the rusty door, startling me. He grabbed the back of my neck and rammed my forehead into the wall. It cracked, and four mirrors and sinks fell to the floor.

He hiked down my panties, and I turned inside out. He was spooked. The hairs stood on his arms. "No means no!" I said.

I ripped off his crucifix, pushed him out of the bathroom, through the bar, and over the fifteenth-floor balcony.

For someone who didn't believe, he surely called out to Christ to save him as he fell into the traffic below. He shouldn't have laced my drink with GHB when his back was turned to me at the bar.

Once I was back in my study, moments later, Matt's "suicide" made the ten o'clock news. I could care less. I was going to tell you about my student Brenda Seymour, the baby of her dysfunctional family, to keep my mind off the dead bartender.

She was a nineteen-year-old reject that didn't graduate on time. She was currently trying to finish her senior year (for the second time) of high school. Brenda was the only one of her parents' children that didn't graduate on time. She was close to her lawyer/cousin, Jolie, a twenty-nine-year-old success story that always provided Brenda safety at her home. But when Brenda's parents found out, they forbade her from seeing Brenda.

This caused Brenda to loathe Jolie. She vowed to make her pay for turning her back on her, and cutting her off. Jolie changed her house phone number. Her eleven older siblings matriculated with honors and went on to graduate college.

Brenda was present for it all. She looked on with jealousy and envy. She witnessed each of her siblings walk across the stage of change over the years, mechanically shaking the Principal's hand. The stoic, broad-shouldered Principal handed each of them a 5-by7-inch leather diploma.

For Brenda, when she finally graduated high school, that stern handshake (the old way of closing a deal or making one) would serve a different purpose. She dissected the handshake. It meant one thing: the end of a business deal. The ignorant child had been educated through a well-devised educational system cluttered with lies printed in history books, blatant lies programmed into her psyche. It gave her a moment of confidence that would surely crash and burn when the lies of those edited history books began to sprout in the real world.

The handshake meant, "Thank you for using our flawed institution. It was paid for with taxpayer money. Now it was time to push you into the real world, a world of employment, taxes, and blood-sucking corporations, contaminating food and water to sterilize population growth.

"If you attended college, applied for loans, and other silent rip-offs, we're going to bind you to payment plans for the next ten years after you graduate." In fourteen years of school, she barely learned a thing. She was more focused on boys with testosterone problems, material things, and sexual exploits with raunchy men on trophy-winning sports teams.

I sat in my study. It was organized with bookshelves displaying various publications, a mini library. It was my sanctuary. I smiled to myself. Brenda hadn't graduated yet. I glimpsed into her future. She was headed for doom and STDs. Too bad she wouldn't be able to turn in her paper. I felt like being close to mortals when I occupied the body of their substitute teacher, Becky Sims. She was a white, blonde-haired person, too soft-hearted for her own good. I observed Brenda in her element. She would have gotten a B- if her heart was in the right place, but her heart wasn't pure. As attitudinal as she was, she bullied the first-year students.

During a cool spring night in March, just after Spring Break, was her breaking point. It was the night Brenda's heart turned black. She overheard her parents talking from their bedroom about how disappointed they were with her. They called her a whore. She was the odd one out of the family. When they said that her siblings wanted nothing to do with her, she discreetly packed her things inside three large suitcases.

Hurt, she called a fling to come and take her away from that loveless home. Uninvited, Brenda showed up on her favorite cousin's doorstep, a fake bitch that used to have her back.

Since Jolie changed her number, Brenda didn't feel like she should call before she showed up. Her cousin was a soft-spoken woman with a heart too pure for confrontation. Once she moved in with her older cousin, it wasn't long before Brenda's anger got the best of her.

Jolie had strict rules. It baffled Brenda. "You never had rules before, cousin. Why now?"

Jolie buttoned her extravagant kimono. After pouring a tonic, she sat on the sofa. It took a moment for her to respond. She was uneasy.

"You weren't living with me before you showed up on my porch begging to live here." Jolie avoided Brenda's intimidating eyes.

"Do you want me to leave, Jolie?" Brenda asked with deep sadness in her shaky voice. She shuddered, thinking about being homeless.

"And go where, Brenda? You are your own worst enemy. You're standing there, soaked and wet from the rainstorm outside, and your parents forbade me from helping you."

Brenda was crushed. *She hates me now,* she thought. *She once said that she'll always believe in me. The bitch is just like everyone else.*

"Why help me now?" Brenda asked. "What changed?"

"Listen, Brenda. Your stay here is temporary. You have three weeks to find a place to live."

Brenda's heart beat woodpecker quick.

"Come on, Jolie, three weeks? That's not long enough!"

"Twenty-one days. Your mother is my auntie, my dead mother's sister. *Don't* let your mom know you are here. You *better* keep quiet about it."

"Fine."

"You can take the guest room. Home by 8 pm, or don't bother coming back. When I leave, you leave."

"Ok, Jolie."

"When I have guests, you must stay in the tact house out back. Use this time to get yourself together. Nobody's going to take care of you but you."

I found it quite entertaining. When Brenda looked in the mirror behind Jolie, she was possessed.

A few weeks later, on the twenty-first day, Brenda had a psychotic break. As soon as Jolie asked for the house keys back, Brenda pulled out a rusty butcher knife and swung it, in a fit of rage, at Jolie a few times.

She then pressed the sharp blade against Jolie's neck. She was manic. She scared Jolie half to death. Jolie was never attacked in her life, especially not by a beloved relative. She slipped into traumatic shock.

Brenda was lost and determined to make something of her life no matter what it cost her. Brenda laughed into the dimly lit living room. "You have it all, bitch, and I don't have a thing! You flaunt your high-paying job like it's the Holy Grail! You are not at all the cousin I grew up idolizing."

Jolie was stunned by the attack. She was too afraid to move. She remained silent; her eyes widened with fear. Brenda scowled. "Therein, the problem lies. I am not supposed to have a false idol, and you were my false idol, my hero, and the woman I modeled myself after for the past five years. But no more! Do you hear me, bitch?"

Brenda stammered, forcing her cousin against the wall. Her confession fell on deaf ears. Was this just a young woman taking what she wanted?

Nowhere in her heart was the admiration she had for her cousin during the moments when I spoke about her family and their accomplishments. Brenda spat in her face.

"That is what I think of you and your job," Brenda said.

"You are a crazy bitch!"

"And your college degree doesn't make you better than me, Miss Perfect. Leading that feminist crap in the courtroom, but in the shadows, you have sexual romps with powerful attorneys in this mini-mansion. Your firm mates and you wear masks. You sicken me! That's why you wanted me to leave when you have guests, but I never left. I have it all on videotape. I need a car and a new wardrobe! You're going to give me what I want, or this tape finds your superiors and the news."

"And as I said," Brenda continued, "I need a new wardrobe. I'm taking your clothes, the good stuff. And you will not do or say a thing!"

With brutal force, she put her hand over her older cousin's mouth and footed her in the gut.

"If you call the police and report me, you will regret it! You will suffer! I have nothing to lose. So, try me!" Brenda cut her in the face.

Her cousin feared for her life, and I fed off it. I was leaner and stronger, blinking behind Brenda's eyes as she attacked her relative. Yes, I was illegally using her as a host, but I was the Queen Mother. It was my way or no way. My laws, policies, and rules dictated everything.

It felt good to be inside her body. I brought out her burning passions.

I gave her the power to manifest her reality any way she wanted it. I controlled her thoughts. She hadn't a clue. I found myself blushing from the display of Brenda's personality when she was behind closed doors. Brenda got her wish. Jolie eventually checked into a mental ward to escape her and to punish herself for being too weak to face her violent cousin.

Why hadn't Jolie stood up for herself? Sigh. Jolie lost her mind taking suppressants. Unfortunately, I witnessed it all. Registered nurses doped her up with psych meds that eventually fried her brain.

While she was being abused by wicked personnel, addicted to marijuana and institutional sex with out-of-it-patients, Brenda moved into Jolie's home.

She took all her accessories, shoes, heels, and clothes and moderated them to fit her whorish needs. Brenda became her older cousin, like I became Armona.

She took Jolie's life as her own without apology. Brenda walked, talked, and acted like the girl she once idolized. She took her cousin's men, drove her cars, and started taking her children's child support checks.

She used her cousin's I.D. to cash them. She neglected her cousin's children by spending the money on drugs, the best the city had to offer— top-of-the-line.

The state stepped in and took her older cousin's children, turning them over to the state. Her cousin signed a waiver to have Brenda remain in her home and signed over her bank accounts and her life to Brenda from the mental ward. Jolie no longer admired beautiful things or remained of the world. She disconnected herself from reality. She prayed to Christ until she took her last breath in her sleep six months later.

To create a diversion from her deception, Brenda attended the place Jolie was baptized. It was a place Jolie turned her life over to Christ, Mount Sinai Baptist Church.

It was the same place Brenda turned her back on being saved. She let Jolie dedicate her life on her own.

The day Brenda began to hate Jolie.

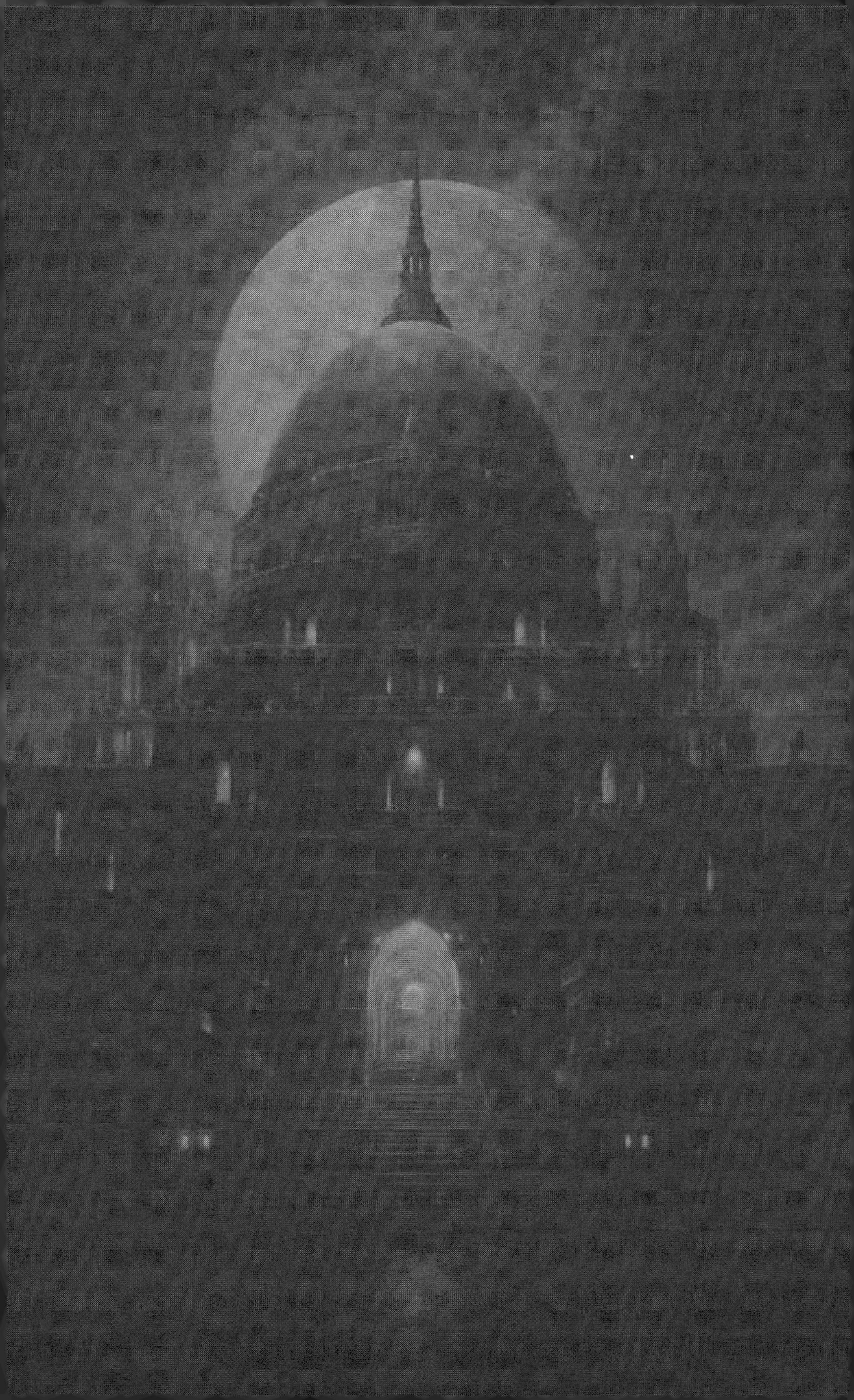

TWENTY-NINE
BRENDA

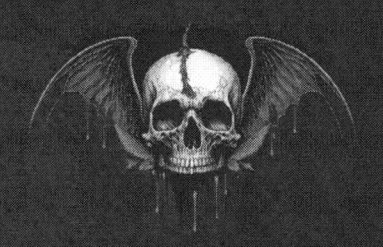

ALICIA CHAY

Brenda became the church's largest monetary donor, seduced the Pastor, participated in secret sex parties at his home hosted by his alluring wife, a beauty in her own right, and pretended like her heart was really in it.

Then she drafted her essay paper haphazardly. She prayed for peace in her oldest cousin's home, but she caused havoc outside of it. So, reading her essay paper seemed so blah, like, what was the point, hypocrite?

What she wrote and who she was didn't add up. Why did people pray for peace when they were hell raisers and kept dysfunction at the top of their Things to do Lists? Come to think of it, that was humankind concisely, if you asked me. Man has done heinous things to one another out of emotion and bitterness.

Men have used napalm bombs on themselves, gas chambers, slavery, Jim Crow laws, the holocaust, and flamethrowers. Arsonists burned down Black churches and concentration camps. The cries of the inner city and the unprinted bloodshed continued to be swept under the rug.

KHOVAHSH

The miserable, brutal sighs of the suburbs was overlooked.

All that glittered wasn't gold.

When I hunted Brenda, I didn't feel guilty about what I was going to do. If you asked me, anyone hurting animals deserved a little discipline. In my case, I went overboard.

I drained Brenda, my lunatic student, of blood an hour after she called her mother a bitch. In front of her screaming parents, I ripped Brenda's heart out because she kicked a cat in the stomach on her way home from school.

I happen to love cats! I gasped with fear. I wanted to take away the cat's pain. It wasn't the cat's fault she was in remedial classes. I could care less about her calling her mother a bitch.

Her mother was her own woman, a tax-paying zombie following an ant routine of life, love, cheating, and bills. All I wanted to do was scare her, but she was extra tempting that day, smelling of expensive perfume yet dressed cheaply.

Her essay paper, which I read Online, was enticing and informative. It had my overall attention, to my dismay. She touched on a subject I'd struggled with for years, decades, and centuries when I was a growing young woman.

For the past four thousand years, I'd been eighteen years old! And now that I was a vagabond, I was in direct conflict with the subject of religion, spiritualism, whom to believe in, and what side I should choose.

I struggled with one thought: did I believe in God? Or the devil? Or did I brush both aside and believe in myself? Become my own false idol and the replica of it? Was there a God and a Devil?

If being a vampire for centuries was any inclination, I'd say I still didn't know if one or the other existed. One thing was for certain. The way Brenda's dead body hovered up to me with something sinister in her eyes took me off guard. Her body morphed into Khovahsh, the eight-foot being I kept running into.

I hadn't seen him since our encounter in Texas. So much for laying low. He found me anyway. Glaring deeply into his fiery eyes, he smiled down at me. "Alicia Chay, we meet again."

"Yes, we do. Have you been stalking me all this time?"

"Maybe you should ask Brenda."

"I asked you."

"Dear, how does the Queen Mother flatter herself?"

"It's easy, really."

"You may intimidate others, but I am not easily fooled, Alicia."

"Is that right, Khovahsh?"

"Yes."

"But your name means fraud. You are aware of that, aren't you?"

He was amused. "I'm well aware of your limited power."

I was taken aback. Why hadn't I slaughtered him for killing Slu'Shu? According to the council members, he was immune from my laws.

"Limited? I could kill you at the drop...."

He waved his hand dismissively. "I think not. I won't spoil the fun of your rule since you are the queen and all, but if you think I'm going to fall to my knees, it better be worth it."

"Worth it, how, Khovahsh?"

He smiled inwardly. "Do you really need to know?"

"I only ask once, Khovahsh."

"Worth it in orgasms, of course."

"I don't lay with ticks, Khovahsh. I do have a question."

"I'm listening," he said. He sat on the couch as if he belonged in this mortal's home, as if he was a part of the family.

I certainly saw why Brenda led the life that she led and made the choices that she made during the past year. Khovahsh lived in her body.

Whenever I looked into her eyes, Khovahsh was toying with me. I hadn't a clue. "I have but one message for you, Queen Mother. I will only say this once."

"And if you say it twice, what are the repercussions? Should I be scared, frightened, because you are eight foot tall and pathetic, might I add?"

He grunted, then broke into a throaty chuckle that I found to be quite sexy and unique, to my surprise. If I was a regular woman, he'd be husband material, but I was a Queen. "I will not hurt you. It was I that returned you to your bedroom after the sleeping spell I cast for your protection. You must remember, I used to work for Armona before you learned of her existence. Have you forgotten?"

"How could I forget? The bird man…"

"The Swan King…"

"Peacock brains is a better description. What I say is what I mean, sir. I'm very aware that you used to be Armona's foot soldier."

He was offended. Ask me if I cared. "Foot soldier?" he repeated.

"Yes, do boy, they call it presently."

"You know what…I came here to warn you that my brother, the Raynedrakin, is out to deceive you the way you deceived our true Queen, Armona. He is not pleased about the council meeting you had with the hired help about me. It is not I that is the Khovahsh."

"Meaning?"

"It is you, Alicia. That's why I keep being drawn to you, for not your beauty but our likeness. You are a fraud, but change is coming for you. So, continue to hunt down vampires living in human guises. Continue to be distracted if you must. You are being hunted. Be careful."

"Why are you warning me?"

"I may think that you are a fraud, but I do respect your drive, your passion, what you stand for, your hustle. It is for those reasons I feel that I must step outside of my normal routine to tell you this. You will be called for a purpose."

"The Queen Mother, called to do what?"

"You have been given much."

"I know."

"Much is now required, Alicia. You have run from your truth for so long that you have no clue who you are."

I rose from the smoke beside him. Like we were long-lost friends, and we knew little about each other. I was still deciding whether to punish him or not for killing Slu'Shu and illegally living in Brenda's body. Now I knew why I was so attracted to Brenda.

"Alicia, you are under a spell cast on you the instant you overthrew Armona. It was a loophole she never brought forth. Your memory swirls into your dreams that serve as visions, visions that may or may not happen."

How does he know about my dreams...?

"How do you..."

"Whom do you think wrote 'I will find you!' on your bedroom mirror?"

"It was you?"

"Yes, it was me, Alicia. I wanted to find you to let you know that you are with...."

A huge bolt of lightning shook the earth, and he vanished. He was nowhere to be seen.

"Khovahsh?"

I looked around and considered that I was standing in my massive rose garden, admiring the geraniums and the sweet lilies that lazily lounge in a small pond off to my right. I went over in my mind every encounter I had with Khovahsh.

Most importantly, why was he staring at my womb?

THIRTY
ALLEGED HOMEBOIS

KHOVAHSH

Ever since I was little, she hath always been there for me—my adoptive mother, Sonjai. My dad affectionately called her "Ginger."

I used to love the bedtime stories she recited to me from the heart via her memory. Also, she told equally powerful horror stories. She used to make my heart beat out of my chest with the blood-curdling tales that made it impossible for me to sleep at night. I used to hate her for it.

I remember she told me about werewolves while we roasted marshmallows around a campfire when we were rich. She set up a huge tent. Enough trees surrounded us. It gave our yard a deep-in-the-forest feel.

It was a family affair; me, my adoptive mom, and my dad. After all the laughs and joking around, we would lie next to each other and look for our Zodiac signs in the stars.

They used to go with me to my minor league baseball games, the whole nine. They put me in piano classes (against my wishes).

When I soared, becoming a very gifted kid, the newspapers came calling. I was in them. I made a lot of money playing at birthday parties, wedding receptions, and bridal showers, years before the Feds and the ATF took it all.

I was popular. A lot of folks loved me. They were there for me, until I began being bullied.

With rising popularity came a slew of envy, greed, and jealousy. People were fabricating tarnished stories about my character. I'd never spoken to half of them in my life. I lost my friends. They thought I was too good for them. As much as it pained me, I never lost any sleep.

I figured they'd still be by my side if they were truly my friends. I looked to the left and the right. Nothing but the air remained. Air and space. Space and opportunity. My fake friends thought they were better than me.

When I turned down their advances, they spat on me. They constantly begged me for money. I simply did not have it. We resorted to bloody fist fights.

The rainbow became my best friend. It consumed my thoughts. I never understood why I was so drawn to God's promise. I thought of it day in and day out, even though I didn't believe in anything at that point in my life.

Then I had plaguing nightmares about being of the rainbow and being every color therein when we moved to the projects in Chicago. I always awakened sweaty and bloody. The blood never belonged to me. I was kidnapped once by a few of my friends I used to play basketball with. My alleged home boys, fellows I knew from the block, were snakes.

Being in the ghetto, after living in the upper echelons of the suburbs, was a tremendous change, but one I had to make. After my own friends kidnapped me at gunpoint, they stuck the barrel of the offending weapon in my mouth. They'd found pictures of my adoptive family when we lived in a rich neighborhood. As a result, we had moved from that housing project —sixty miles away to another one.

KHOVAHSH

I became an unknown face again, forbidden from making friends. I was deeply afraid to speak to anyone. I was forced to wear thick bifocals that made my eyes look like peanuts when I wasn't blind——I had perfect 20/20 vision.

Sadly and unfairly, my adoptive parents received all the glory. Even when I soared in baseball during my seventh-grade year, they took the credit. They didn't give two rectums about me.

They cared more about the glory of my achievements than my comfort. Scouts from major universities heard about me and came to my games.

Unfortunately, my parents changed my name. My dad knew someone that knew someone that had someone create fake documents. My identity was hidden. He then slashed the side of my face with a machete, putting me in the hospital after making me lie to the authorities about it.

We blamed some random druggies that were tried, convicted, and incarcerated. I simply fell off the face of the earth. I wasn't allowed to talk to anyone. I took on a name I hated and detested. I was named after my adoptive father, given the title "Junior," when I wasn't of his seed or derived from his genetic makeup.

My father became controlling. My mother became religiously pushy. They used God as a crutch. They only used Him like a spare donut tire when they caught a flat. Once the flattened tire was replaced, they put up the donut spare and didn't use it again until they caught another flat.

They were always throwing God in my face, making me attend Sunday school and church. They were right there with me, observing—and watching.

They only attended church to keep a close eye on me. I couldn't use the bathroom alone; they were always present. The only time they didn't watch me was when I was in school.

That was when the principal watched me. My parents bought the surveillance tapes from the school, under the table, and watched them at home.

They verified that I went to every class and left school when I was supposed to leave. I was environmentally incarcerated. Why would my parents pay the principal to watch my every move? What had I done to them to warrant that type of social control?

My father and mother worked the hell out of me. They'd require me to do manual labor that felt more like slavery. Every day at dawn, my parents awakened me and beat me out into the huge backyard by the dense forest.

First, I had to run drills to the point I vomited, and my limbs were on fire. Rain or sleet, they overworked me. I practiced throwing the baseball over and over. I was nervously swinging the bat, trying to hit my father's pitches.

My mother's circle, circle, and underhand pitches put fear in my heart. If I didn't do as I was told, I was tied to a tree, douched in baby oil, and beaten with an extension cord by my adoptive grandparents.

The worse kind of people in existence. If I missed even a ball, if they got even a strike, I was sent to my room without a meal. My parents never abused me, I tried to convince myself, to keep from killing them.

They forbade me from having friends. I couldn't have them in school. If my parents saw me talking to anyone on those tapes, they sent me to my room without a meal, so I didn't jeopardize that.

They were feeding me rations. It saddened me to see all my friends in school and watch them go out together and go to football games together. I wished I could be a part of that, or be in the boy scouts, or things of that nature.

After we moved to the ghetto, I never had a birthday party again. My ninth birthday was the last party we had in the suburbs before my parents lost their promising careers, careers that only college degrees could afford.

My friends started to fight me, my very dear friends, when I had to cut them off. They tried to fight me because they thought I was trying to be better than them, and it wasn't that at all. I was banned from interacting with them. That was the gist of it. Even though my adoptive parents turned for the worse, when they saw potential in me, they saw dollar signs as well.

They bought me anything I wanted, after making me work for it. They lent me a friendly ear when I messed up. If it resulted in a spanking from my grandparents, my parents always heard me out, no matter how mad they got.

And then, after my grandma spanked me, she said, "Don't always expect praise for admitting guilt. Take it like a man; you are a man just by acknowledging your faults. Sometimes when you succeed, they will beat you down out of jealousy. Always remember these words..."

I took it to heart.

Unfortunately, Ginger wound up working for the federal prison. She became everything those policy books required. Gone was that soft-hearted woman I once loved, and in her place was a dictator that worshiped God only when her husband was home.

Phony bitch. I hated being a domestic experimenter. I played along with the charade. If I did not, she would make my life a living hell. I couldn't tell Bob. He was so in lust, whipped, he wouldn't believe Jesus over his wife.

When he was with us, she listened to me (for effect). She always looked over her shoulder to see if Dad was paying attention.

She gave me what I wanted (for show). It always turned Daddy on, yet when he left, went to work, to the store, or even outside for a second, the demon came out of my mother.

She made me clean everything under the sun four times over before I could get in bed. She blamed me for the mistakes the inmates made and punished me when they got in trouble inside the prison.

She claimed she was doing some sort of scared straight thing with me, and yes, it scared me. I nearly joined the Vice Lords, but I changed my mind at the last min. I couldn't stomach the number of people getting murdered.

After a while, it got old. I started retaliating. Sometimes it led to brutal fights and blood-curdling cursing matches. I never put my hand on Ginger, but she beat my ass religiously. She shouted Bible scriptures that fell in tune with the extension cord.

She made sure she didn't leave a mark on uncovered parts of my body. I cried myself to sleep studying those markings on my chest, back, butt, and upper thighs until a dark rage was born.

No matter how badly it hurt, I never uttered a sound when she beat me. I had a blank look of pain on my face. I crawled in a ball, a place where I felt nothing. Not even my heartbeat.

Why was I being mistreated?

That was the million-dollar question.

I didn't know those inmates, never met those men, and never laid eyes on them. Moreover, she showed them my picture, praising me.

Saying that I was a good sports player. Bragging about me, putting me before God. Throwing it in their faces. "Look what you all could have been, but you are convicted felons!" she told them in anger, making them uneasy.

I was seventeen when that happened, about to graduate high school. That was the day I told myself I would never tell her anything about me again, nor include her in my success.

When I sought redemption after joining the military, all the lies of this earth was uncovered. I must admit that as a bisexual male with deep, dark sexual desires, I wasn't rooted in the essence of God. I turned my back on religion itself.

Religion places handcuffs on the soul and a dead boulder on the mind. I wasn't smart enough to decipher everything there was to know about God or about my sexuality at the time. I chopped it up to "the game," since it was set up before Adam took his first breath, only after the Lord said, "Let there be light!"

I pushed it to the back of my mind every time I made love to random women as a teenager, women my age (and a few years older, whom my mother introduced me to before I started college). Tasting the sweet, gentle opening of a woman filled me in ways I couldn't describe.

Swallowing nomenclatures, making her shudder as inch after inch of my eager member collided, slid... roamed, and breathed inside her cervix when on my mind was Felix, the thug boy that assaulted me after one of our football games in high school.

I could remember when he locked the gym door.

Four of his dope-fiend goons stood outside, clad in janitorial uniforms, pretending to buff and wax the floor for effect.

I was scared as hell.

THIRTY-ONE
CANDID WORDS

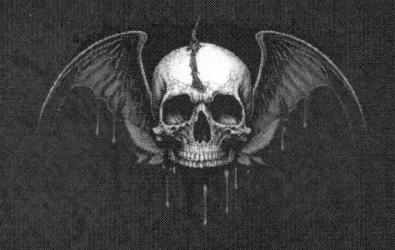

STRYIKES PHARMA

A celebration was taking place within a private clubhouse of a wealthy community in the hidden hills of California. The county commissioner was running for the state senate at the behest of his dying grandmother.

In addition to his cloudy ideals, he was paid top dollar by a crooked government official who was married to the CEO and co-founder of Stryikes Pharma to sabotage farmland around the state so it decreased in value. He also polluted its damns, canals and lakes, with a sub-division that studied ways to destroy the human mind in the name of medical advancement.

Stryikes Pharma was a secret guerilla organization that invested in acquiring barren land to build heavily secured testing sites for developing viruses, abominable breeding and cloning of animals to be used as weapons of mass destruction.

The company was founded by a dark supernatural demigod that loomed in the shadows and hated attention. The company made several attempts to buy the land from Black owners, but they couldn't be bought.

Retaliating, Stryikes Pharma hired a scientist named Kowumba Jah to do their dirty work. Through deadly force, Kowumba acquired acres of land. He was paid to develop a killer virus that could be carried by animals, in addition to fraudulent practices.

Husayn Rogers stood behind the podium, looking over an eager crowd. He stared into news cameras with a prepared statement. Kowumba Jah and his wife stood at his side. He spoke candid words of hope, winning over the hearts of forty million viewers. A bead of sweat trickled down his face. There was an intimidating man with an un-feathered bald head, and immeasurable wealth, using mind control to keep him obedient, unbeknownst to Kowumba Jah. After the telecast, Husayn shook Kowumba Jah's hand. He was whisked to an unmarked vehicle. Once he was inside, he was startled to find his un-feathered bald-headed associate.

"I think we can secure that win, Husayn." he said emphatically.

"I'm pretty sure I'll get the seat. I can feel it." Husayn was eager for power.

"I'm happy for you." He could care less. "You better win, Husayn."

"I appreciate all you've done for me, Jahja."

"I'm glad that you do, but I don't accept appreciation as payment for the use of my political resources for your career advancement."

"What are you talking about, dude? I didn't ask for your help. You approached me about destroying farmland so you can build testing sites. I gave you my rate."

Jahja leaned forward with crazed buzzard eyes, rendering Husayn speechless.

"I'm famished. I haven't eaten a human, a thing I meant, in days..."

Husayn was horrified. "What are you?"

"Clearly not what you preferred. Have I ever told you that my friends once suggested that I become a comedian?"

"I'll give you anything you want! Just don't kill me!"

"What was that? I can't hear you."

"Please!"

"Poor, poor pathetic human. Who said I wanted your meager possessions? I feed from your anxiety with no regard for your fear. This is quite entertaining."

Jahja started pecking away Husayn's face like sunflower seeds, paralyzing him from the neck down. Blood splattered on the car windows.

"Do I have your blessing?" Jahja asked with delight.

"Yes, yes, yes! Please stop!" Husayn screamed.

"You have a peculiar taste." Jahja regained his composure. "I invested fifteen million dollars into your campaign. All I want is for you to destroy the farmland with invisible toxins and fertilize the crops with agents that shut down the human respiratory system in a matter of minutes. I build testing sites for that divine purpose."

"Yes, Jahja."

"As a matter of fact, I'm sitting on an unknown zombie strain. Maybe we can turn humans into brainless ghouls."

"It's whatever you decide."

"I want you to create vegan meat made out of those poisonous crops. I'm going to test it on less fortunate beings no one will miss if this plan doesn't work. Maybe you can run it by your scientist friend, Kowumba."

"I'll get right on it." Jahja pecked his face a few more times, feeding on his skin and blood.

"I'll do it right now, Master Jahja! *Pleeaaseeeee!*"

"Master Jahja. That has a nice ring to it."

With blood on his face, Husayn called Kowumba's phone. He was surprised that he answered. "Husayn. You're interrupting family time."

"I have a proposition for you. If you accept, I'll build you a high-tech lab to use at your leisure to accomplish an agenda set forth by Stryikes Pharma."

"I'll talk to you later, Husayn. My family is waiting for me to join them for brunch. My wife already said that I work too much."

Jahja looked into Husayn's huge black marble eyes. "How does forty million dollars sound?" Husayn said. Kowumba coughed a few times.

"Are you serious, man? That's a lot of money! When can we get started?"

Jahja placed a finger over his lips.

"Its top secret, Kowumba Jah. Shh..." Husayn had black eyes.

"My lips are sealed," said Kowumba.

"I'll be in touch with the specifics."

"Looking forward to it."

"Make sure you tell your cloned wife I send my regards."

Kowumba Jah frowned. "How do you know about..."

Jahja took the phone and hung it up, chuckling.

THIRTY-TWO
ENCOUNTERED

ALICIA CHAY

The Oxford English Dictionary dated the first appearance of the word vampire in English back to 1734, Ah! in a travelogue titled Travels of Three English Gentleman, published in the Harleian Miscellany in 1745.

Yes, I read this document. I existed as well. It was amazing how mortals thought evolution started and stopped with them. Didn't they know that everything hath an opposite, even death?

No, I was not talking about life itself. I was talking about human life polarized into a zombie of its own design, the opposite of one's goodwill and charitable contributions.

Well, as old Jack Nicholson says, "What till they get a load of me!" While the beautiful country of Austria gained control of/over northern Serbia and Oltenia with the Treaty of Passarowitz in 1718, I busied myself killing the very mortals that didn't cherish or honor animal life.

Serbia. Ugh, the country was far from memorable.

Unfortunately, the place was a bore. I wanted to leave an hour after I arrived.

If I was getting frequent flyer miles, I'd be angry if I lost all those miles flying to Serbia expecting worldly entertainment and wound up with nasty-tasting humans on distorted diet plans. Intuitively speaking.

The natural waters tasted of something unnerving to my tongue; my taste buds gagged like drunken sailors. The turf itself was rough on my immaculate toes. I was too purified by the darkness to be tarnished by human soil on the polished marble of my feet.

Siberian human life left little to be desired. I chased a few mortals for fun and for something to do. I was tired of being bored. I wound up regretting the spurt of their blood in my mouth and on my elegant white dress. It was a seductive dress ahead of its time during that era of my life.

The way my Serbian victims screamed annoyed me. By the time I sank my fangs into their necks, I lost interest. Their veins were thick and visibly full. I rolled my eyes, snatched their spines from their bodies, and left their birthday suits an RSVP for cake and ice cream another time. I took a rain check because I was lactose intolerant.

Why I was so attached to animals ran deeper than the roots of rivers run dry, crumbs chiseled into the sands of time. They were scattered on the imposing wind before lying gorgeously about, like a queen lioness in the Sahara.

A desert that once teemed with life, before it became rock, rubble and golden sand, with scorching temperatures circulating all about the atmosphere.

I spent many nights sprawled nakedly on the cool sand, staring at the moon. I was lost in its glow. The sudden rise of African sandstorms threatened to blanket the earth with untold diseases.

Until this very day, just as I say this to you via my thoughts, that mystified me. It was like Africa had eyes, ears and a heart scolded because she was robbed of her riches by corporate greed. She was sick and tired of being sick and tired of precious human life beaten and forced to dig inside mines with startling humidity levels beyond human understanding for blood diamonds an European queen arrogantly put in her crown.

The stripping of Africa's riches and the tomb raiding led by American archaeologists and archaeologists from all over the world left the continent vulnerable, while millions of people were infected with HIV. Millions of black people died every year without treatment or medical care.

They were ignored by the media. That was why the rich wouldn't inherit the Kingdom of Heaven, if such a place truly existed. Those annoying mortals were intruders on the ancient land and on royalty!

How dare they showed their presence? Raiding tombs and slapping price tags on what they stole. Humans were selfish dinner options put here to do what I asked.

Mortals, peasants, walked among centers of past royalty, world government and rule. They smiled, laughed and snapped memorable photographs in front of African infrastructures (The §phinx, the §tep Pyramid, et cetera), causing deceased Pharaohs, their wives and secondary wives —R.I.P.† — to turn in their graves with disgrace.

They were afterthoughts (or no thought at all) when it came to banking off of Egypt.

In hindsight, what did their reign truly mean if it didn't pertain to me?

Foreigners owned and possessed the pyramids. Tourist attractions tarnished the history of it all.

Have they a heart? Maybe I should eat theirs.

Africa was once my home. I was born there.

I was turned into a vampire there.

My heart was broken there.

Africa was the only continent rooted in the earth.

Khovash Burgoos

To use my Free Will was a gift. I encountered supernatural beings that told me otherwise. My Dragonhead Ancient brothers once tried to influence my decisions, but I had my own mind. I got over things on my own accord. Unfortunately, it led me to doom. I survived it. I was a warrior at heart. I came out a lot harder and tougher, with my sanity intact.

My life was an abyss of blackness. As I plummeted, I flung about my arms in a discombobulated state. I wanted to warn Alicia about Muzzle, but when she burst onto the roof of a penthouse owned by Pastor Ford, the Rent-A-Pastor, I stalled when she brought up the Dershakney.

I tried to warn her again via Brenda Seymour, but the sight of her set me on fire. Then she sent Slush'Shu to kill me, which broke my heart. My brothers and I watched her council meeting from Dragonhead Headquarters in the Bermuda Triangle. Once it ended, they glared at me and left the building, but their thoughts found my ears.

Alicia is an Illuminated One. She crossed over to the other side of consciousness. It's a mystical place she rebels against authoritative measures. She can't be systematically controlled. She has read the gospel of Christ via Brenda Seymour. She's changing...

Back in the day, merely saying, "I love Christ!" got you killed without remorse. I was addicted to man made religions. I attended church services all over the world, for centuries. Most of them worshiped other religious figures that didn't have blonde hair and blue eyes, a rumored Leonardo Di Vinci painting of his secret lover goblins and spooks whispered in the shadows. There were millions of people that didn't acknowledge or believe in him at all.

I rolled my eyes at the religious psychobabble that poured into my ears from a stereo on a shelf by a desk. The disgruntled minister was on a roll.

I fed on a random human just as he turned off his office lights a few minutes ago. I was excited for the kill. The short, stocky man trembled under my touch. His main artery continued to coat my tummy with delicious honey. He was paralyzed from the neck down.

He stood like an erect statue by his office door, next to a wall painting of a Mona Lisa hanging upside down.

"You soak it up, hide thy anger and pain by smiling and turning thy cheek because you believed in non-violent movements, as in what Dr. Martin Luther King stood for," said the minister to his audience over the radio.

He was an articulate man, but he was a human being, a mortal. That killed it for me. Movement itself was violent.

The way it slithered through the womb of evolution was the core of disruption, a heat wave of ripples felt throughout the world via energy and vibrations.

We all operated on different frequencies. Some people tapped into our frequency, and others weren't so lucky.

They would never be illuminated.

Violence poured into everything, from the way I hunted and killed to the way I occasionally sniffed out my victims. I loved toying with the ones that tried to hide, the ones that lived in unauthorized human guises, breaking Alicia's laws, laws that couldn't affect me.

"Violence thumped from video games," said the minister. "Minds of repressed, oppressed, and stressed Black people is stripped down to the polarization of the Negro itself!"

I found that interesting.

"And the fact that racist police officers savagely abuse the Black race is appalling and grotesque," according to the minister. I could care less for humans.

They were puny polka dots on my elbow I leaned on for comfort.

"Violence fuels entertainment. It is evident in the most popular cartoons being spoon-fed down the younger generations' throats. Out with Public Enemy, a rap group that taught us to fight the power. Enter NWA and the 2 Live Crew. Gangster rap and sex." He slammed secular influences.

The minister bored me. Once I was done feeding, I tossed my victim's sunken body over my shoulder with little strength, enough for him to fly out of the enormous window of a forty-four-story building into the waters below.

His screams pierced my ears until the sound of the waters below soothed me with silence. The very waters his corporation polluted, making bio-hazard products for hundreds of countries, killing off four species of whales and crocodiles for LonCha Enterprises and Stryikes Pharma.

After bursting into the air from the broken window, I felt numb inside. I thought a lot about Alicia's *Treaty of the Animals*. Initially, she wanted to protect them all from harm, but that was impossible. How could she be the Queen Mother and slaughter humans for killing animals at the same time?

It took centuries to realize that she bit off more than she could chew, but her Treaty stands. So did the policies of the Dershakney.

I gathered all of this by living in human hosts. Some of their lives were more addicting than others when it came to religion and their pets.

I learned how they moved, thought, and desired.

I learned of their fears, skeletons, angels, and demons. From all levels of society.

From the poor to the generational wealthy.

THIRTY-THREE
SLEEPING CHAMBERS

JAHJA GREGORIAN

Life hadn't been good to Jahja Gregorian. Once upon a time, back in the millennium 2 B.C., he had a life, a wife, a daughter, and a loving son he loved more than himself.

He put them on a pedestal and gave them whatever they wanted. His love and adoration for his son would later cost him everything. As a man with dark features, he controlled his home and his family like a dictator.

Over time it put a strain on his marriage. He remembered when he was turned into a vicious creature. It was on the night he was left for dead by his son's hand and his son's ex-lover's hand as well. He was forty-nine years old.

After a long day of labor in the sun, Jahja entered his bungalow of clay and stone. His loving wife was fixing him a delicious meal. His son, Ferdinand, cultivated his field the night before, which helped as he planted seeds to grow fresh crops for his family.

Jahja, long ago, had an affair with a woman he encountered in a forest while hunting for food. Her foot was stuck between two logs, and he used a sharp blade to help set her free.

She would love him, hypnotize him, and seduce him. During their love making, he saw events involving blood and gore at an enchanted fortress, then the images faded.

After his secret lover grew weary of him, she wiped away certain memories and set him free. Ferdinand always helped his father, but for the past few months, he hadn't been around. He suspected that his son had found a woman to occupy his time.

He was surprised Ferdinand cultivated the field the other day. It was only done out of guilt. "You're worn out, old man," said his wife jokingly. She was a tall, dark beauty with gold rings along her neck. Her breasts were oiled and bare.

He took her into his arms and planted his lips on hers. "A man that doesn't work doesn't have the necessities to put food on the table." Covered with sweat, he smelled like the sun. He selfishly mounted her and rode her wetness until he exploded deep inside of her.

Kissing her left shoulder blade, he pulled up his lower garments. "I adore you and our children."

Yes, she was pleased, but in love, she was not. "We love you for that, Jahja…but…."

His eyes clouded over. "No but's, my beauty. We made our family; I can take care of us."

She pulled away and settled on a wooden stool by a smoke pit built in the ground, used to roast pork or cow.

"What troubles you?" he asked, touching her stomach. With haste, she removed his hand.

"You trouble me." She refused to meet his eyes. He fell to his knees and tasted her sweet flesh. She opened her legs to receive his slick offering.

After endless orgasms, she rose to her feet and started to walk off.

"My sweet, why do you turn your back on me? Haven't I pleasured you beyond understanding?"

She paused. "You don't listen to me or my thoughts."

"You're my wife. I think for you, for us, surely you know this."

She looked over her shoulder. "You adore us too much. I had a dream that we were going to be taken from you. It felt so real, like death is on its way to destroy us and leave you shells of what we never were to you. It's still on my mind. I'm terrified!"

He jumped up to his feet and walked over to her. "What nonsense do you speak?"

"Jahja, I decided that I'm going to move back with my father. He's a glassmaker. He could use the help. I need the distraction."

"Your father...he doesn't like me very much."

"Because you're too domineering. I can't breathe around you unless I ask to inhale. I don't have a life. Everything, from the moment our kids were born, kids that are adults and off on their own, has been to your command."

"I provide the means for us to survive."

She faced him with tears looming in her eyes. It broke his heart to see her cry. He lowered his head in shame.

"It's not enough. If anything happens to you, how am I going to go on? How do I survive when you do everything for us? Yes, I love that you are a strong, resilient man of honor that care for us. But let us help you by loosening the grip you have on our lives."

He slowly looked up at her.

"I can do what you ask."

"I'm afraid it's too late."

She retired to the eating area and began cleaning. "This is the last time I'm cleaning behind you. This is the first day of my new beginning. Our children are on their own. Your suffocation ran them away. Ferdinand has become a tyrant. Because of you, he has no love in his heart."

"And you blame all that on me? I never raised my hand to you. I never struck your face. I never misguided or mistreated you. Your body, I continuously pleasure to your requests. I gave you anything you ever wanted."

"Have you ever asked me what I wanted? Hell, I didn't want to marry you. We were two hot and bothered young people sneaking off into the brush for pleasure. We came from royal bloodlines. I was only eighteen when I gave birth to Ferdinand. I didn't even want him."

"Why are you hurting me like this?"

"The pain of my words doesn't compare to the emotional scars you left on my spirit. They hide like chameleons. Your parents controlled our lives, and your dictatorship didn't make things better. I was a disgrace to my family. You were cut off from yours."

"I never knew that I made you feel invisible."

"And now I want nothing to do with you. I already worked it out. I'm moving down with my friend Yu-yummy. She has space in her hut just for me."

"This breaks my heart."

"My heart no longer beats for you. I apologize for the frankness. Had I been this way a long time ago, I would have been free from your control."

She walked past him, taking linen from the clay table. Covering her breasts, she went out to his crops. He retreated to his sleeping quarters and lay in the darkness until he fell asleep.

Meanwhile, Ferdinand met up with Armona in an abandoned castle in Switzerland. As she caressed him, he cupped her hands and brought them to his lips. His eyes glittered. "My sweet. I appreciate the time we've spent together. This has been something of a dream."

Armona agreed. She was scantily clad in red velvet. "You are a dream, an escape from the reality I face every time the sun rises. Here with you, I am not the Queen Mother or ruler of anything!"

He kissed her lips.

"If that reality dispels your passion, then I'd rather keep thinking that you're a dream." Armona shed her clothes, and stood in the nude.

Her nipples swelled. "Let's discuss this later. I need you, Ferdinand."

He grew pensive. "No, we must talk now. I'm afraid that tonight is the last time we'll see one another." Her eyes turned black. He started moving away from her. "Who…what are you?"

"Your bitter end if I can't have you! I'll turn what you love into what you will never experience again!"

Ferdinand looked around wildly, trying to find an escape route. His heart hammered.

"Leave me alone! This is the end of us!"

Hissing, Armona savagely bit into his neck.

She turned him into a vampire. He used to be Armona's human lover until she wanted to possess him. The sun rose on Ferdinand in transition.

He was dying from exposure to the sunlight. The rest of his body was turning to ashes. He escaped, flying to a home he shared with his family. His ghoulish features sent his mother and sister, who'd just arrived to see her mah mah, into a screaming panic. Ferdinand slaughtered his family.

While he drank from his sister's neck, Armona fell on top of her ex-human lover and started tearing through his flesh. She threw chunks of membrane this way and that.

There was a loud crash. A pack of roaring lions leaped at him as he rushed into his father's sleeping chambers. Four lions shifted into strange creatures that also entered Jahja's sleeping chambers. There were four chambers, and they were dark. Ferdinand and the cock-eyed creatures saw Jahja's body in soft red, green and yellow colors through the thick stone and clay walls, a foggy display of images.

Armona attacked one of the creatures and ate him from the inside out.

Jahja was dreaming of making love to a beautiful vampire in the woods. Once he looked into her eyes, visions of death, blood, and humans battling to their deaths sent him into convulsions.

The crowd chanted "THÈ HÔUSE ÖF THÈ HÔUNDS" in complete harmony.

Loud banging sounds filled Jahja's home. Three ghoulish creatures rushed over to Ferdinand and bit into him in the darkness. Abruptly, Jahja was awakened. He screamed in terror as vicious growls and snarls filled his ears, letting him know that something wicked was in his presence.

His wife's dream was happening. He couldn't do a thing in the darkness. There was no light.

His thick linen curtains were closed. From chamber three, Ferdinand's eyes rolled to the back of his head from three creatures sucking his life away. Armona swung her arms and the linen curtains fell from metal hooks.

Sunlight ravaged the creatures. Their bodies became ashes. Ducking the sunlight, Ferdinand smelled his way to his father, but the Queen Mother ran through the stone and clay wall, taking Jahja into her arms. Viciously, she bit into his neck, and Ferdinand bit the opposite side of his dad's neck and drank.

Each burst of warm, sweet-tasting blood gave his eyes a crazed appearance. He attempted to turn Jahja, to take the victory of killing him away from Armona. After slaying Jahja, she ripped a hole in Ferdinand's chest and the sky turned black, erasing the sunlight.

She left Ferdinand for dead.

She jumped through the glass from the back of the dwelling and flew east. As Jahja panted from severe blood loss, Ferdinand set his parents' home on fire. He set his father's crops on fire as well. He destroyed Jahja's land, a land he was forced to maintenance since he was a young lad.

His father never lifted a finger to help him. No longer did he have to suffer beatings if he refused to do what his father commanded.

After Ferdinand fled, a buzzard swooped through the opening in Jahja's ceiling and started eating his face while he was in transition. Jahja fought the winged creature, but the buzzard continued eating him. Wearily, Jahja looked at his dead wife and daughter and hollered at the top of his lungs.

Angrily, he grabbed the buzzard around the neck and mated with her. Once he was drained, violent lightning struck Jahja. A piercing flash of grayish light blinded him.

And then everything was black.

THIRTY-FOUR
BIRDS OF PREY

JAHJA GREGORIAN

I felt the warmth of the unknown. Seconds after I released myself in the buzzard's womb, she gave birth to me in fetus form enshrined inside a glowing egg. When the shell cracked, I stood six feet, seven inches tall as an adult. The home I shared with my family was a glowing inferno. I was surrounded by flames. I extended my wings. I had supernatural human/buzzard eyes and an unfeathered bald head. I was a supernatural bird of prey. I was a carrion eater, cursed with eating death.

Before the fire could burn my dead wife and daughter, I ate the skin from their bones until skeletal forms remained. Devastated, I cried with each bite. I couldn't control what was in my nature.

I was not the man I was before I died and was reborn. Had I listened to my wife about her dream, an omen, we would still be alive. I changed my name to Vultorian.

I didn't care to remember my human life. I raised my body temperature through thermo-genesis. This allowed me to stretch out my neck and engage my wings. I urinated on myself to stay cool. I could fly in the sun, unlike the vampires that left me to rot.

Dead horse arum kept me alive. I was cursed with eating the meat-smelling fruit for all of my days. One of my palaces was in the Andean mountains. I had a committee of birds that helped guard my fortress. Formed in kettles, a group of vultures in flight, we scoured the earth eating the carcasses Armona left behind, hoping to locate her. We also did the same for my son when he became the Emperor King of THÈ HÔUSE ÖF THÈ HÔUNDS.

I refused to kill my son, even though he thought I died. I watched over his kingdom and his livelihood. My family of buzzards was Ferdinand's security. However, they failed my son because Alicia killed him under orders from Armona, a woman that took my family from me.

I didn't like Armona. In fact, I loathed her. The supernatural at large feared her, but I didn't. In the shadows, I became equal to her in power. I wanted to kill her with my bare hands and watch her die. She took everything I ever loved. Her actions came with consequences and sacrifice. She left me for dead, but I survived. That was forty centuries ago.

With that in mind, I spoke to a room filled with half-human buzzards, vultures, and condors. I devised a plan to heighten security around our domain. One of my wives whistled at me. Gazing to the side, I dismissed myself and flapped my wings twice, gliding a few feet above hay and woven tree branches over to her.

"I don't mean to interrupt your meeting, but you are invited to a fundraiser by Kowumba Jah, one the world's most celebrated scientists with immeasurable wealth."

"I'm familiar with who he is. May I see the invite?"

She had already opened it, without my permission.

Giving her the side eye, I looked at the 8x10 gold and black leather envelope. I pulled out a black card. Spiraling gold calligraphy script formed the message once. A four million dollar donation was required.

"He's into bio-weapons, no?"

"Yes, he is. In fact, his fundraiser is for that reason. He's a genius with molecular manipulation. He worked for eleven governments."

I was thinking to myself. If I played the game right, I could use his fundraiser as an opportunity to change my hunting methods and find Armona.

"Send him twenty million dollars and a million shares from my water company. It'll tank in less than a year, so he won't get a dime."

"Will anyone be accompanying you?"

I smiled. "No. Some things a man should do alone."

"Very well. I'll inform your other three wives of your departure."

"No, a code of silence is necessary. Keep quiet, you hear? I will slit your throat and toss your tongue, eyes, and lips to the vultures as a zero-calorie snack. I have two other wives. Surely, you won't be missed. I need to do this under the radar. Get my best suit ready, the one with the enormous gold metal angel wings. I need mingle with like-minded individuals. It's time to change my strategy. I need some new influential pawns, I meant friends."

"You've never revealed yourself before. Why now?"

I glared at her. "Know your place. Do as I instruct."

"Very well."

I studied her for a brief moment. "Thank you."

"No problem."

"And pick your face up off the bird's nest before I give you venomous injections with my beak."

"As you wish…"

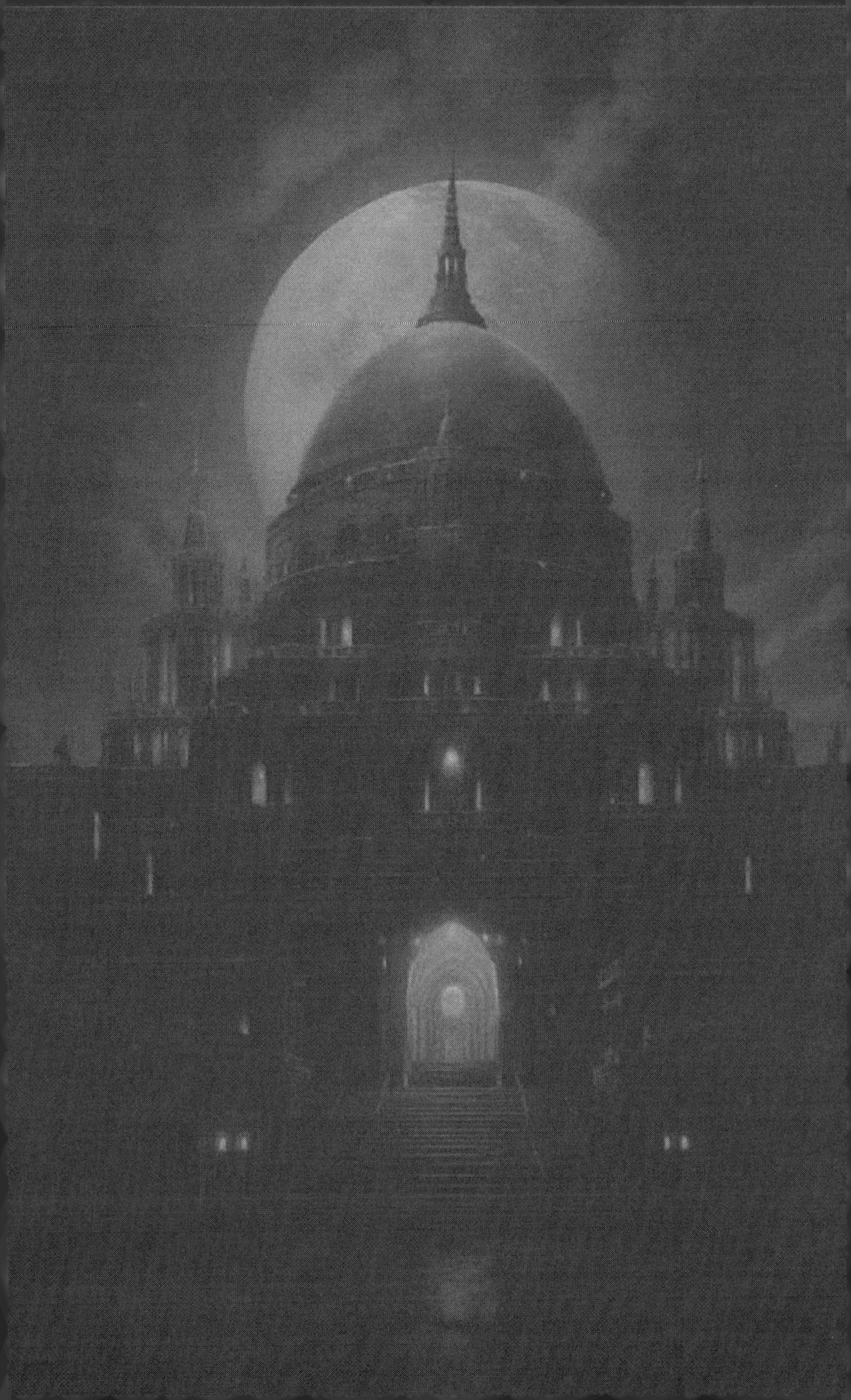

THIRTY-FIVE
MARBLE

JAHJA GREGORIAN

In the heart of Carnival in the Caribbean, thousands of islanders dressed in scantily lavish attire danced in the streets to reggae and percussion.

Alcohol flowed freely like breasts without restraint. Surrounded by towering buildings, it was an unprecedented event. It took a moment for the screams of a voluptuous woman clad in body paint with light blue and yellow feathers to grab anybody's attention.

Inevitably, the music stopped. The curious crowd migrated over to the screaming woman. She was staring at a body that washed ashore chopped to pieces. Once word traveled about the mutilated body, people freaked out and caused a stampede of fear.

The crowd trampled over the screaming woman, stomping her to death.

By the time the authorities arrived, the event was shut down. A few days later, every news channel was interrupted with a Breaking News Report.

Senate hopeful Husayn Rogers was found, mutilated, in the islands of the Caribbean…

Jahja smiled from a couch in his secret nest kingdom, intricately built atop the huge redwoods high above Alicia's estate, on the continent of Vencreashia.

On his lap was a marble plate.

Jahja stroked Husayn's brain with his fingertips while in deep thought.

Next to Husayn's brain was his heart, eyes, larynx, and his crotch region.

"You served your purpose, Husayn," he said, victorious.

EPILOGUE
FIVE OF THEM

JAHJA GREGORIAN

Floating through the break in the wood of the buzzard's nest, I held the plate of goodies as I flapped my wings above the buzzards.

"Plan A was a success, my loyal death-eating subjects." My crazed buzzard eyes were the size of silver dollars.

"Now we indirectly target humanity! The extermination begins! I will not rest until Alicia dies for killing my son, Ferdinand."

The buzzards rose to half-human form, exalting me, their ruler, their leader.

Especially my secret prisoners. Centuries ago, they sold their souls to me after they were bleeding to death in a dungeon at THÈ HÔUSE ÖF THÈ HÔUNDS by the hands of one of their heartbroken brothers. The same way I nearly bled to death before I mated with the buzzard that tried to eat the flesh from my bones.

I dumped Husayn's remains before five special buzzards. You might know them as the beings with skin "as dark as the midnight sky" Alicia Chay turned into vampires against their will centuries ago...

Tresyon, Qu'stah, and Zyath ate Husayn's vital organs together. They looked up at me with contempt. I was flattered by their undivided attention.

Did they have O.C.D or A.D.D.? I couldn't ascertain from a hundred feet in the air. It took Ki'Wah and Crusha a moment to join in on the feast of the Slaughtergus.

I thought back to the day Armona ordered their deaths. I quietly loomed in the shadows. They begged to live forever after their brother brutally attacked them. Once they took their last breath, they awakened in my kingdom as buzzards with a curse put on any of their descendants.

I happened to have one of their descendants in mind. He was a young twenty-something-year-old named Ka'Darius Slaughtergus.

I flew to the defunct House of the Hounds, swooped through the hole in the stained glass dome and dropped before what was once the Glittering Throne. I stared at The Golden Ssstafsss on either side of it, a throne that was active when Alicia was Queen of the Hounds.

Back when I had an affair with Armona behind my wife's back, long before she encountered my son. She put a lapse in memory spell on me. It erased much of our history, leading up to her bursting through the stone wall of my sleeping chambers, trying to kill me before my son could.

She also gave me the gift of slow aging. In the human form, I attended every murderous game, fight, race, and event Alicia and her Slaughtergus family of vampires hosted as Armona's secret eyes and ears.

If I was honest with myself, I'd admit that I'd been a vampire since the day my secret lover cut me loose. Turned me, then wiped my memory away. It was the only way I could live with my family without killing them, long before Ferdinand was born.

And when I find Armona, I was going to kill her for secretly giving birth to our child and refusing to tell me anything about it or that his name would be

KHOVAHSH

Ferdinand...

She hypnotized my wife into thinking she was Ferdinand's biological mother. It was the worst kind of make believe.

Even my daughter was fooled. Armona destroyed my family to hide her affair with our son, which started after he became an adult.

With no memory of their paternal bond.
When I find her, I was going to slowly eat her alive...
Until she stopped breathing.

To be continued...

BOOK 1 Act II
COMING SOON

ABOUT THE AUTHOR

Dapharoah69 is a multi-award-winning, best-selling, independent literary force born in Salinas, California and raised in Goulds, Florida.

For twenty years, he has entertained millions of fans around the globe with his unapologetic writing. He is an LGBTQIA sex symbol, spoken word artist, poet, HIV activist, actor, professional model, dancer, literary icon and a living legend.

His success and killer ink have influenced a sea of writers in numerous countries for two decades. The Law of Beasts, Book 1 - Act 1 of his vampire series, was written in June of 1998 before he became Dapharoah69 at the age of 22. He was known as Ja'Breel Le'Diamond.

He published his first book when he was homeless. He has penned thirteen books and three memoirs and notched ten Amazon.com and Barnes and Noble.com Top 100 bestsellers.

He won Book of the Year and Male Author of the Year via the African-American On the Move Book Club, The Men of Integrity Award from Utopian LLC and a Certificate of Recognition from the New York State Senate for his literary achievements.

JA'BREEL LE'DIAMOND

Meanwhile...

ALICIA CHAY

HIDDEN CHAPTER

THE CONTINENT OF VENCREASHIA

Quietly, I floated along the rows of my vineyard. It was located across the lake from my three-structure-empire. It loomed over the hills. I saw the acid rain barrier and the violent thunderstorm that protected it. Frowning, I thought of Khovahsh. He beheaded Slu'Shu, used Brenda against me, intercepted my plans for Pastor Ford, and forced me to Armona's summons.

Regardless, Slu'Shu was going to die had he returned without Khovahsh. I gave him twenty-four hours to assassinate him. Slu'Shu was dead in twenty. Part of me detested Khovahsh, but another part of me was flattered that he kept crossing my path.

His deep baritone register gave me goosebumps.

He invaded my dreams that ended in orgasmic bliss. I once sprinted across forty miles of ice just to cool down my loins because a cold shower wasn't enough.

I pushed thoughts of him aside. I was in awe of the gorgeous sunset, the tail-end of the day. The dimming rays were too weak to harm me. The air was crisp.

A slight breeze blew across the nape of my neck, and then it was gone. I brushed my fingertips along the Sangiovese and the chasselas grapes posted on high wire cordon trellising.

Swiftly, I rose in the air and smiled at the pink and orange hues splashed across the sky and the clouds as they gradually became gray.

In front of the sun I'd perish, but on the threshold of the darkness I chased the rays until they vanished over the horizon.

A strange noise invaded my peace. No one knew of my vineyard. I was on guard. I looked around. Nothing stirred. I relaxed, closing my eyes.

Something spun around me with unconscionable speed.

Swo

osh

Suo

oosh

The green-faced witch appeared from combustible sparks, taking me by surprise. She rubbed the head of a possum that was sprawled around her neck like a sash. Crawling tarantula legs hung from her scalp like hair.

"Horishia Valiseah..."

"A proper greeting would have sufficed. I'm surprised that you remember my name."

"And the way you smell. Obviously, hygiene isn't your thing."

"Well, I can never run a government smelling like apple cider vinegar with a splash of pineapple."

"Careful, witch. The last time we spoke twelve horseshoe-shaped knives chopped you into chunks of meat. I can still feel the warmth of your blood when it splattered in my face."

"I survived, Alicia."

"Why are you here? We are not friends."

"I come for payment," she said, confusing me.

"*Payment*? The Queen Mother owes no one, and certainly not you."

Her eyes widened. "Ah, but Coffey does!"

I was caught off guard.

"Coffey? The slave woman?"

"Yes, the dark-skinned con-artist that met a devastating fate."

"She was a con-artist?"

"Yes, Queen Armona, I meant Alicia, no disrespect."

"It takes a con-artist to know one."

"I guess we're two peas in a pod."

"How so?"

"You rule from within Armona's biological flesh. You inhabit human bodies, but punish others that do the same thing. You're a con-artist as well as a hypocrite."

"Tell that to your dead mother. Wasn't she a married man's concubine that led to your cursed ugly green face?"

The witch frowned. "Touché. Regardless of your perspective, Coffey was a brilliant painter. Her canvas was backhanded promises she made behind the scenes."

"I'm not proud of sparing humans, but Coffey and I had something in common. We were bound by the darkness against our free will."

Horishia coughed a few times. "Are you sure about that?"

"Yes, I'm sure of it. I freed the slaves and gave them Queen Lufu's wealth. All of it!"

She laughed, patting her knees. "I commend you, but things aren't always what they seem. Sometimes, image isn't everything."

"I've learned not to trust you. Your words mean nothing."

Inwardly, she smiled. "You're going to regret doubting me."

I stretched out my arms in front of me and clapped once. Seven bolts of lightning struck her, knocking that smile from her face.

Retaliating, she threw a string of fire balls at me. While I dodged them, she rose from the ground behind me and grabbed my neck, squeezing it.

I rotated in her embrace, head-butting her crooked nose.

After a screech, she fell to her knees. Brutally, I kicked her in the chin

When the back of her head hit the ground, a sparkling dagger spun from the confines of my hair and pierced her heart.

Her legs thumped on the ground while she choked on purplish blood.

"It is taking everything in me not to chop your head off."

I was annoyed. Ever since she came into my life it hadn't been the same. What kind of games was she playing now?

"If Coffey owes you, take it up with her. Spike is the only slave I didn't emancipate. He starved to death. Queen Lufu's castle is his unmarked grave."

She grabbed the dagger and immediately withdrew her hands when the metal electrically stunned her.

"You can't...bury the truth, Queen..."

"See you on the flip side, witch."

"Armona?" came a familiar voice, distracting me.

I knew that voice.

Reluctantly, I relieved the witch from torture.

"Armona, is that you?"

Who was that?

The witch stood up, gasping for air. The dagger lay behind her feet.

A woman appeared from behind one of my grapevines a few miles away. She sprinted along the row towards us, leaving a long trail of dust.

Dressed in leather and velvet, two young men ran behind her, carrying enchanted machetes. Extensions of their dreadlocks were knotted around their arms like a winter sweater.

The strange woman jumped in the air and landed in front of the witch. I could only see her backside.

Momentarily, they stared into each other's eyes.

Did they know each other?

Ignoring the witch, she floated over to me.

I gasped!

"Coffey? Is it really you?"

"Yes Armona, my Queen!" she gushed with joy. "These are my sons, Red and Face."

They nodded.

Overcome with emotion, blood welled in my eyes. I ran my hands through her mound of mountainous hair. In spiked red bottom heels, she stood six feet tall, adorned with reptilian leggings and cotton earrings.

JA'BREEL LE'DIAMOND

A platinum breast plate covered her upper body. Diamonds sparkled from her lips and her eyebrows.

"I've searched for you over the ages, but I could never find you!"

"Is that so?"

"This feels like a dream."

"How did you find me?" I asked, curious.

The witch cleared her throat.

"I don't know. I was traveling with my grown children through Amsterdam and this location suddenly popped into my head, followed by a voice. It brought me here."

I gazed at the witch. She lured them to my vineyard without my permission.

Nonetheless, I was happy to see that she survived. Spending Queen Lufu's wealth certainly did her some good. Her skin was glowing! We hugged each other and wept. I was the reason she was free, along with her sons and the other slaves. I gave them a better life than the abuse they suffered at the hands of Queen Lufu.

Coffey's blood stained face confused me. I became noticeably silent and reserved. She narrowed her eyes, placing a caring hand on my right shoulder.

"Queen Mother, Armona, what is wrong?"

"Wait a minute. You ran with supernatural speed, floated over to me, and you have fangs. This can't be!"

Horishia said, "Armona...Queen Lufu was immortal in the millennium 3,200 BC."

Coffey's head snapped in her direction at the same time as mine.

"You shouldn't make things up," Coffey said blandly.

"You're lying, witch," I said in disbelief.

"What's done in the dark comes to the light." She looked at Coffey. "Queen Lufu was a vampire. There is something else you should know. Once upon a moon you were a serf, a peasant."

"I was never a peasant," Coffey scoffed. "What lies do you tell? I come from a long line of royalty—"

"You come from a small tribe in Africa," Horishia said. "Queen Lufu and her men abducted you and your family. Her goons threw your immediate family off the ship to the sharks because they were damaged goods."

Coffey sunk to her knees in denial. Red and Face comforted her. They could care less.

The witch gazed into my eyes.

"Queen Lufu's castle was where you held your council meetings, Queen Mother, Armona. The gatherings Queen Lufu hosted were formalities. You were present at every one of them."

I remained silent. I studied Coffey and her sons. "Coffey, rise to your feet," I commanded. She obeyed, wiping blood tears from her face. "Never mind the witch. This is a joyous occasion. We are reunited, after forty centuries."

She gathered herself. "Armona, your plan worked!" She brushed strands of hair from my face.

"But I'm not..." I didn't say it. I wasn't going to tell her that I was truly Alicia. Not yet. I didn't like the feeling in my gut.

The witch smiled at me, knowing why I paused. The breath caught in my throat. It just hit me like a ton of bricks, taking my breath away.

Coffey knew Armona? How was that possible?

Horishia was stunned as well.

"I bet you don't remember what that plan was," I continued, probing for more information.

"Queen Mother Alicia," said the witch with sarcasm. "We have bigger issues to deal with than your family reunion."

"One you initiated without my permission." I gazed at Coffey. "Do you remember..."

Coffey grinned. "Yes, I do! You were fascinated by an unauthorized vampire making the rounds for killing your lover, Reinkarnation."

JA'BREEL LE'DIAMOND

I gasped. I couldn't believe what I was hearing. My maker used to be Armona's lover?

"No vampire had ever defied the natural order of the Dershakney. You approached me in Queen Lufu's courtyard and made me an offer. You said that if I helped lure the unauthorized vampire to your fortress, you'd set me free."

The witch said, "Objects appear closer when you look in the mirror, Coffey."

Coffey ignored her. "I accepted your offer and you vanished. I never saw you again! Before I was pregnant with my first son, I was approached by the green-faced witch."

I wasn't surprised by Coffey's words or the fact that Armona bamboozled her, then laid the groundwork before she encountered the witch.

"Go on," I encouraged. Coffey laughed hysterically. She was going in and out of consciousness. Something wasn't right.

"I was depressed. She told me that she'd make my dreams come true. Since Queen Lufu was sleeping with my husband, I wanted to trade places with her."

"Queen Armona," Horishia said. "Coffey was enraged about Gree Lufu murdering her family. She made a deal with me seeking revenge, and she wanted her future kids to be free if she decided to have them behind Queen Lufu's back."

"I wanted to live as Queen Lufu!" said Coffey. "She took my husband. If he didn't do what she wanted she was going to kill him. He was the only family I had left."

I closed my eyes. I didn't know what to believe.

Horishia cast a revelation spell.

A huge portal formed in front of us, taking us back to that precise moment.

༄

Adorning a magical dark cloak, Horishia paused before Coffey. She was clad in rations. "You want to be Queen Lufu. Interesting! What you're asking for comes at a hefty price."

"I don't have much to give," said Coffey, smelling sour. The bottoms of her feet were as black as her face.

"This isn't a game, Coffey."
"I'll do anything, just make it happen! I'm desperate! I would rather be Queen Lufu. She can be a peasant. That way my husband will really be laying with me!"

"You have spoken." Horishia waved her arms as clouds formed above her open palms. "So, it shall be!"

The instant Queen Gree Lufu stood before her bedroom mirror, it began to tinkle like diamonds, hypnotizing her. She closed her eyes and opened them as Coffey with amnesia, in the courtyard.

With no memory of ever being from a royal bloodline. Panting, she looked over her feet and her hands. It took a moment to collect herself. Meanwhile, Coffey opened her eyes before the enchanted mirror as Queen Lufu, two decades before I wound up on the threshold of the castle.

Coffey was cursed.

She had to admire herself as Queen Lufu in the enchanted mirror for all of her days, or she would die.

༄

15

I'd been tricked! I felt sorry for Coffey when Queen Lufu was stripping away her humanity. Now I found out that the roles were reversed. Queen Lufu was Coffey. She was the one being beaten, violated, and disrespected. She was punished for poisoning her parents, improperly taking the throne, and for destroying Coffey's family

With Coffey's body, Queen Lufu gave birth, twice.

Coffey as Queen Lufu witnessed the births and breastfed her own children in private behind her back.

I was deeply impressed.

The level of thought that went into pulling that off was next level deceit. Even I had to blush.

Sometimes Coffey's sons, Red and Face, laid in bed with Queen Lufu and Spike. They were really laying with their biological mother as the Queen, free from the dungeon while Coffey (Queen Lufu, cursed) was treated poorly and fed rations.

Spike promised to keep his sons hidden, but Coffey was two steps ahead.

Spike played himself. He was only a pawn.

Coffey as Queen Lufu attacked the slave women that threatened to foil her plans. She drank their blood until they stopped breathing.

Queen Lufu was a vampire, and I didn't know it.

When I witnessed Queen Lufu cutting Coffey's hair, she was doing that to herself from Queen Lufu's body. She unleashed the hate she had for her Black skin.

My mind was blown. I held my throat, backing away. The swirling revelation portal disappeared.

"Queen Lufu! You've always wanted to be Coffey. You got your wish," said Horishia, smiling with greenish teeth.

Seeing her as Coffey caused me to look at myself. I started to feel guilty about what I did to Armona.

Queen Lufu poisoned her parents for power. I abandoned the House of the Hounds to ascend another woman's throne and Coffey made a deal for the crown.

"This is absurd."

"I am the witch that granted you your heart's desire! I'm a sorcerer as well. Do you remember the wish you made on the falling star?"

"Yes! I wished to be human again. I made two wishes! Once the star faded, I realized that I was already breathing like someone else."

"And now I want payment for services rendered, Queen Lufu. You've enjoyed Coffey's body for centuries. You built a paradise with your wealth, but Coffey hasn't paid me for granting her request, and her wish. And neither have you."

"I am Coffey, witch! You're speaking as if..."

The witch snapped her fingers, and Queen Lufu grunted from within Coffey. "What is going on?" She rubbed her face, her breasts, and her neck, devastated. "Why do I have Coffey's body? What have you done?"

"Coffey made a pact with me at your expense. She hasn't atoned for it, but I have insurance."

The witch snapped her fingers again.

Red and Face laughed wickedly.

"I swapped out both of your brothers' souls with Coffey's children the moment Coffey's second son was born. When Alicia possessed Coffey, she drained your body, but it had Coffey's soul within it, setting you free to inhabit Coffey's skin forever!"

Queen Lufu frowned.

"Alicia thought she was freeing Coffey and her family, but she was emancipating you and your family. Red and Face are your brethren inhabiting Coffey's sons."

Every time Coffey looked in her sons' eyes as Queen Lufu, she was really looking at Gree's brothers.

Coffey's sons were the two red-faced savages that abused Queen Lufu as Coffey.

I was stunned into silence. Queen Lufu gazed at me with bloody eyes.

"Armona, is this true?"

Before I could respond, Coffey's mouth fell open.

"The witch called you Queen Mother, Alicia. I'm sure she did."

A mirror formed in her greenish hands. "Queen Lufu. The mirror tells all." She tilted it so the moon's glow reflected on me.

Queen Lufu looked at my reflection. She gasped, taking a few steps back.

"Alicia?"

My reflection glittered from the shattered glass of her enchanted bedroom mirror that burned into my skin when I destroyed it. My cover was blown.

I thought about my sadistic side, taunting me from the bedroom mirror so long ago.

She said she'd always be with me. I was marked. Queen Lufu glared at me the way I glared at the Bat King when he revealed that he was my Maker.

Smoke snaked all around us.

"You're the Queen of Queen's, a fraud? You engaged me while pretending to be Armona?"

"I am still your leader and your ruler. I suggest you stand down."

"You are guilty of the same crime as I? You possessed Armona, took her throne and ruled with her body and her face."

I turned my back to her. When the smoke cleared, we were atop of a monstrous mountain, called the Pedra da Gávea, overlooking Rio de Janeiro.

I was teleported to the place I was going to die.

The witch set me up.

"Alicia, if you're the Queen of Queens, face me. You won't do to me what you did to the witch shortly before I arrived."

Overcome with rage, I spun on my heels.

My sparkling dagger appeared in her grasp with the witch's blood dried on the blade. "Die, Alicia!"

She slit my throat.

Grabbing my hair, she kicked me towards the cliff. We were 2,769 feet above the ocean.

She glared at her brothers: Coffey's sons.

"Red and Face, destroy her. She murdered my biological flesh that was pregnant with my unborn child and left my lover, Spike, to rot. Alicia took my wealth and gave it to my slaves. And for that she must die!"

The witch was amused. She glared at me, hoping that I perished.

"It's funny how the tables turn, Alicia."

I held my throat with wide eyes. Red and Face hopped towards me like rabbits. In an instant, the possum uncoiled from around the witch's neck, shifting into Spike.

"Not now, Red and Face," he commanded.

Immediately, they obeyed.

He took Queen Lufu into his arms.

"Spike?" Queen Lufu began to weep. "Is it you? The love of my life?"

"I never dreamed that you were cursed with my wife's body. This is perfect! Now we're a family!"

"How did you make this happen? Alicia thought that you starved to death."

"I was dying, sweetheart. It was slow torture. The moisture in my body dried up and my organs were shutting down. When I was near death the green-faced witch appeared from a burst of sparks. To my amazement, she said that if I helped kill Alicia, she would give me wealth, power, and influence. I just wanted my family back."

"And now you have us! It's because of your sacrifice that allowed us to be."

"I felt guilty about throwing my wife's family to the sharks of the sea, but I had to show you that I'd do whatever it takes to survive."

He was as powerful as ever. He had the body of a god. "Rip out Alicia's heart," he instructed his sons, "and devour it until it is gone!"

"No!" commanded an unknown voice. Suddenly, Spike's lecherous eyes rolled to the back of his head and his body began to levitate forty feet above the turf.

Golden stairs formed from Spike's back, spiraling towards the ground. A vicious vampire swirled from Spike's body, standing atop the glittering gold.

Slowly descending the golden stairs, the turf began to tremble. He wore black tar and gold. Batting brimstone eyes, he glared at me with hate. Two leashes formed in Queen Coffey Lufu's hands, attached to the electrical collars on her brothers' necks. They walked like three-legged dogs towards me. They were possessed.

"I thought you'd never make it," said the witch, kissing his lips. "She nearly killed me."

"You are of no importance," he said, pushing her back. He galloped like a horse over to me.

"Alicia Chay," the vampire began. His crown glittered with volcanic lightning and hot lava. "You can call me the String Puller!"

My mouth vanished from my face, causing me to choke on blood with no air going into my lungs.

"The witch said it best. All the world is a stage, but mine is a chess board I use to play checkers and backgammon."

He wrung his hands and I floated towards him.

"I used Coffey, Queen Lufu, Spike, Armona, Red and Face, as the game pieces to find you. Horishia played everyone against themselves under my orders. I'll make this brief, since your time is limited. I'm taking the throne and re-writing the Dershakney. Your animal treaty is abolished as of now! How can you be the Queen Mother when you never renounced your throne as the Queen of the Hounds or atone for the brothers you turned into vampires against their will?"

"But she wants us to care about her free will," said the witch.

"You can't have both. You won't live past this moment, unfortunately. "

He never took his eyes off of my mid-section.

Shifting into half vampire, half gator, he threw enchanted dust into my eyes, making them disappear.

Holding my belly, I was engulfed with fear. Grunting, he sank sulfuric fangs into my neck and began to drink my blood, and absorb my power. "You taste so sweet, Alicia!" The sky became smoke and flames, taking him aback.

Queen Coffey Lufu pierced my heart with the sparkling dagger. "I am the new King of the supernatural realms!"

"Congratulations, Muzzle," said the witch.

Roaring, he bit off both of my feet and my hands, swallowing them with one gulp.

Picking me up, he threw me over the cliff.

Unbearably weak, I heard the waves. I clung to the last few seconds of my life as I plummeted towards the ocean below.

The last thing I saw before I went blind were four dragons breathing fire and ice, flying towards us from a mile away.

And the mirror the witch cast my reflection began to tinkle, and glow....

To Be Continued

THE LAW OF BEASTS

Excerpt from

<u>The Law of Beasts</u>

<u>Book 1 – Act 2:</u>

<u>**VULTORIAN:**</u>

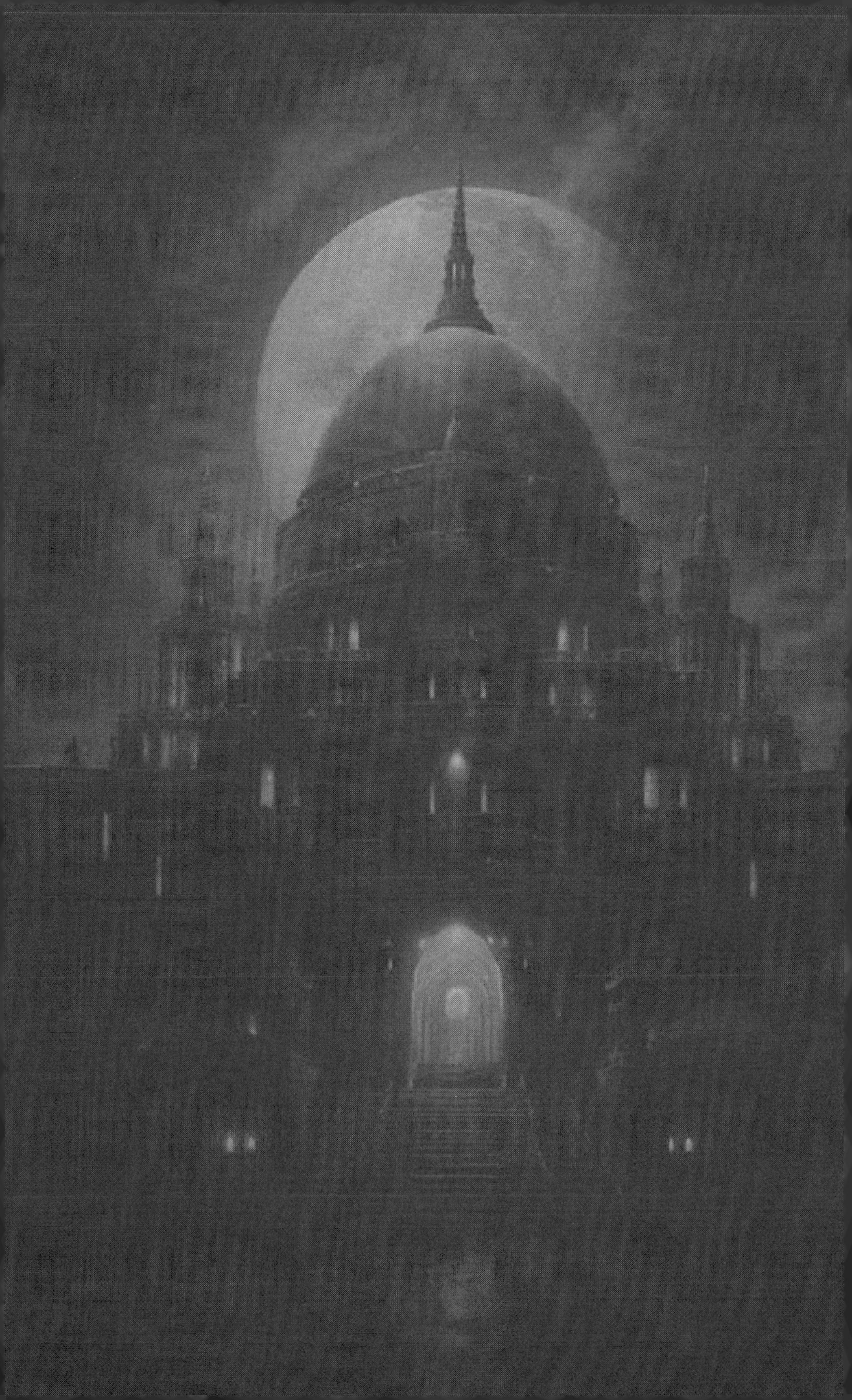

Khovahsh Burgoos

Grey walked up to me, clad in a resilient black suit with a scalped horse mane thrown over his broad shoulders, hanging like a cape.

"It's not every day we meet a vampire as tall as you," said Grey. "I'm intrigued." He shook my hand and I smiled faintly.

Jules was extremely jealous, but we paid him dust as compensation.

"What was your name again?" I asked.

He cupped my hand and planted luscious warm lips on my ring. His mustache tickled my skin and broke me out in goosebumps.

"I don't feel comfortable revealing that a second time, but I do know yours."

I took my hand back.

"Please, have a seat. Stay a while, since you're here uninvited," said Grey.

"Thank you."

I sat on a cushioned recliner across from him. Jules poured a cup of blood, brooding. I looked him in the eyes.

Something vicious stared back at me beyond Jules's eyes. Our recliners began to levitate. We faced each other.

"Khovahsh, are you familiar with the Snake Tribe?" Jules asked.

"Yes, I'm very familiar."

"You are? What do you know?" Grey asked excitedly...a bit too excitedly, but I thought nothing of it.

"I don't volunteer information, unfortunately."

"You don't or you won't?"

"I'm only here because of the claims you have on..."

"I can assure you that's not the purpose of this meeting," Jules interrupted rudely. Grey shot him a knowing look of disappointment that struck me as odd.

"Is that so?" I said, narrowing my eyes.

"You are exactly where you need to be," said Jules.

I stared at him. "I don't follow."

"Are you familiar with the Glittering Throne?" he asked.

I was quiet. "How do you know about that?"

"I know a lot; more than you think I know. I know an entire Tribe of snakes are gold statues because of your choices. You seem to have forgotten your orders…"

I gave him the side eye. The recliner chairs lowered back on the plush carpet by the low table.

"I've overstayed my welcome. I'll be going…"

Jules paused beside Grey. They stared into each other's eyes, bobbing and weaving side to side, in a trance.

Grey and Jules walked into each other, forming a life-sized Viper snake with golden eyes of acid.

"Ssshulkeeyatta!" I said out loud.

I never ran from a battle. Now was not the time, day or place. I bum rushed the snake with two heads and four slithering tongues. Retaliating, he spat venom on my arm that ate it away in its entirety.

"What have you done to my arm?" I shouted.

Frightened, I jumped through the ceiling, dropping to the ground below.

The snake was on my tail, exuding speed and god-like power. My arm grew back in place like new.

I sank into a snake hole that appeared out of thin air.

I tumbled down a smooth path in the darkness before my body hit a dead end. I began digging in the earth with the force of power drills.

The Viper snake slithered behind me, casting its venomous tongue at my ankles.

For miles at a time, I dug with supernatural speed, before I ventured further South…

The Viper Czar bit into my ankle the instant I plummeted into my underground Egyptian lair from an escape portal…infested with snakes.

"Surprise! Welcome to our snake nest! I hope like how we re-decorated your secret place!"

THE LAW OF BEASTS

My wrought body crashed onto the stone floor, sending cracks in all the hieroglyphics as the words filtered into my ears.

Viper Czar landed on his feet, separating as black-headed pythons Jules and Grey with multi-jointed skulls.

Laughing uncontrollably, Grey sat on the floor next to me.

"You didn't plan on things ending this way, that I'm sure of."

Jules grunted. "After we watch you die, Alicia is next."

"Then the golden curse shall be lifted from my people."

Jules spat in my face. "You look thirsty. Maybe I can offer you a drink." He unzipped his black jeans and urinated on my lips, making me gag with disgust.

In grave pain, I screamed from the poisonous venom that slowly ate the skin on my face.

"One of the original founders of the Drägonhead Ancients is finally meeting his undue fate. Any last words before we devour you?" Jules asked rhetorically.

I began to weaken as my body cast a soft green light that began to heal and rejuvenate me.

Ja'Breel Le'Diamond

Prematurely my wings expanded.

"Oh, no, no, no, no, Khovahsh!"

Jules cut both wings from my upper shoulders with his venomous claws, sending me into convulsions.

I'd never experienced this type of excruciating pain, ever.

"Once we kill you, Muzzle will abolish Alicia Chay!"

Jules laughed wickedly, gazing at Grey.

To Be Continued.

The Law of Beasts Book 1 – Act II

Coming Soon.